To Crown A Chimera

V.C. Sanford

341 Enterprise

USA

To Crown A Chimera

Published in the United States of America

By 341 Enterprise

Rossville, Georgia 30741 USA

www.bellbookandclaw.com

Copyright 2019 by V.C.Sanford

ISBN: -978-1735343525

DEDICATED TO ALL THE SURVIVORS OF STROKES
AND THE ONES WE LOVE WHO DIDN'T.

THE ONE WHO WRITES THE STORIES,
RULES THE WORLD

Chapter 1

Raffiel had his plan.

Carefully he worked his way throughout the Inn learning the layout. Going from room to room along the upstairs hallway he tried all the doors. Upon finding a few unlatched, he opened a window in each room in case he needed alternate escape routes. He made a mental note of which rooms were occupied and which ones were empty. Once he was satisfied he had covered all possible exits he made his way back to the Inn's main room, to rejoin his waiting friends for the evening."

During the nightly Pakur game, Raffi had been compelled to offer his mark to the local physician, after finding his cash running low. The possibility of losing his sword or his mare because of a card debt bothered him. Earlier in the week, he had raised a little money by selling a few trinkets he had picked up along the road. The local jeweler had purchased most anything of value, jewels, snuff-boxes, watches, and a pair of diamond shoe-buckles, leaving him with little he could offer in pawn for his debt. Three days earlier, Moth had tossed him a small purse after learning he had lost all his coin, which enabled him to keep up appearances… until today.

"With this, I think I shall call it done," the hulking, bleary-eyed old doctor said as he raked his winnings into his leather purse. "Shall we agree to meet to settle up around noon tomorrow?"

Everyone agreed that noon seemed a fair time and the game ended.

As everyone rose to go up to their rooms for the night, Raffi lagged behind the others. "I need to go to the privy first. I may be a while." He shifted his weight from foot to foot.

"Better there, than losing it into the air while we are trying to sleep," Moth replied as he gathered his winnings from the table.

Brinn Jernigan silently agreed. For such a young man, Raffi produced an inordinate amount of methane gas. There were times he feared to sleep in a room with a fire if the Duaar was inside the room. He stood to follow Moth up the stairs. Keeyun was due to arrive by daybreak and he wanted to be ready to travel soon after the final member of their party arrived.

Raffi waited until the two men had begun making their

way up the stairs before he slipped across the main room and out the door that led to the stable yard. Everything was quiet, even the barn boy had gone to sleep for the night.

He paused for a moment in the dark doorway and then went into the barn. To his enhanced eyes, the light from the moon made the pitch-black barn as easy to maneuver in as during the brightest daylight. He walked directly to the stall where the party's packs were stored next to their horses. Working quietly in the dark, he saddled his horse and then attached his packs to the saddle. Once he was satisfied with his preparations, he took out his knife and cut the girths on all of the other saddles he could find. He also cut the reins on every bridle before he headed for the outhouse.

Less than a candle-mark later he joined his friends in the room they shared upstairs. It was almost midnight, less than three candle notches to wait before he could put his plan into action. Waking would be no problem; he had always been a light sleeper and found he could awaken within moments of the time he set himself to rise.

He could hear the soft rumble of the two sleeping men. Both had enjoyed a beer or three in the pub downstairs while playing Pakur. It was easy for him to slip into his clothes, grab his knife belt and then while still in his stocking feet, slip out the door carrying his boots in hand. Making sure to step near the wall to prevent the loose wooden treads from squeaking, he made his way down the dark staircase. The inn was silent. Everyone was sleeping…or were they?

The sound of pots rattling and voices arguing came through the doorway that led into the inn's kitchen. Raffi managed to duck down behind one of the high-backed chairs before the door opened and the innkeeper made his way over to the main hearth. He laid a spitted loin across the spit-jack and hung a metal cauldron on the hook. A small grey-haired woman watched from the doorway as the innkeeper measured out the grain for the porridge, before returning to the dining area.

Raffi waited until the door closed behind the innkeeper, then swiftly he crossed the main room, keeping to the shadows around the edges as much as possible. He had scouted out the hostel earlier and knew exactly where the innkeeper kept his money. Listening by the kitchen door to ensure he was alone he relaxed when the only sounds he could hear were the innkeeper and his wife discussing the morning menu. He slipped away and moved over to the door leading to the inn's small office. Removing a short length of metal from a pouch around his neck, he manipulated the lock, opening it in seconds. Easing his way in, he closed the door behind him but did not latch it.

He began his search in the chest against the wall, finding it full of ledgers and other paraphernalia necessary to run a business. Next, he moved to the back of the fireplace, searching for loose stones. Finally, he made a meticulous search of the floor, starting beside the fireplace and working his way around the room. Nothing. That left one place.

He sat down, bracing his back against the heavy chest, and used his legs to push back against it. It took two tries, but finally, the chest slid away, uncovering a small hatch set into the floor. The edge of his knife was thin enough to slide between the crack, enabling him to lift the wood out. Inside were three small bags. He placed the first one into his vest and was reaching for the second when he heard the door behind him open.

"What the hell do you think you are doing?" the old man roared as he swung a heavy wooden broom toward his head. Raffi somehow managed to roll out of the way of the heavy oak handle. Seeing no way out of the room except through the angry man, he barreled straight into his ample stomach, ducking the next swipe of the broom. His blow caused the robustly obese innkeeper to collapse, gasping for breath. Raffi took this opportunity to bring the pommel of his dagger down upon the fat man's head. The innkeeper sagged to the ground, his breathing ragged and fading minute by minute.

"By Grall and Mephib, I did not want to do that." He turned back toward the chest he had been going through. The money would be easily carried. There were also a few odd papers and another book that must have been for record-keeping. He poured some of the oil from the lantern hanging over the desk into the chest drenching the contents. Using a straw, he lit the flame and then dropped the lantern inside. In a short time, the fire was burning well. With luck, the fire would completely obliterate any evidence of what he had done before the old man woke up and called the alarm. He crept to the door and listened. There were no signs that anyone had awakened. Unless someone got up to go to the jakes and noticed the smoke, the ancient timbers would burn for a while before anyone discovered the fire. He slipped out the door locking it behind him as he went. Then he turned toward the kitchen.

Balancing her weight carefully upon the narrow wooden ladder, Mekiva Bell wrestled the heavy tome from the top shelf and slowly began her descent. Once her feet were again safely upon the polished wooden floors of the library, she carried it over to the assigned table, dropping it atop a pile of similarly thick books already waiting for her perusal. Somewhere inside one of the massive texts was the answer to her problem. Unfortunately, the only way she was going to find it, was to scour the contents, page by page, until the solution was found.

The library was quiet; a false calm before the impending storm of students that would descend upon the building once the first bell rang for classes to begin. Already, the normal sounds of everyday activity drifted through the thin glass of the windows as the school staff went about their preparations for the awakening students.

Mekiva's face stretched into a wide yawn. The lack of sleep was beginning to catch up with her. Her fisted hands rubbed unconsciously at her eyes, removing the crusty grains of sleep that had formed as she struggled to remain awake during the night. One hand went to her lower back and she rubbed absentmindedly at the muscle that threatened to spasm after candlemarks of bending over the books. With an effort of energy, she didn't have to spare, she stretched her arms high overhead and bent from side to side, before running in place for a moment. The extra candlemarks of study were beginning to take its toll on her body.

She sighed and flipped the cover open, resuming her routine. Somewhere, there had to be an answer to why her spells were so erratic. Someone had to have experienced the same disruption in the flow of magic she continued to be plagued with. After weeks of searching, she had been unable to discover why some of her spells worked normally, while others refused to work at all. And then there were the wild reactions, in which her spells became so powerful they were almost impossible to control. She was already on academic probation after a simple candlelight spell had set fire to the classroom, the flames engulfing more than half the study area before two of the master's arrived to put it out. It had been Tyche's own luck that no one had been injured in the conflagration. Sighing deeply, she moved the glow closer to the page and began to read.

The bell in the tower announcing the beginning of the school activities rang, pulling her from her studies. She quickly gathered up the books she had finished browsing, placing them on the shelf behind the librarian's desk to be examined and returned to their proper locations. The final book she kept with her, slipping it into the leather satchel she carried during the day. The spells inside it were slightly more advanced than the ones the instructor was currently covering, but she was confident she would have no trouble casting any of them. Lately, none of the spells she'd attempted had been beyond her capability. Power wasn't the issue. She had more than enough power. Often too much.

With any luck, there would be no repeat of yesterday's debacle, in which her attempt to create a small glow to light the room, turned in to a spinning vortex of colors that grew and intensified, becoming brighter and brighter until no one in the class was able to see. It was only Master Olagive's quick spell of dismissal that prevented another unfortunate disaster.

A subsequent visit to the headmaster's office and the warning of possible dismissal followed by half a day scrubbing the stairs leading up to the chapel had spurred on her nocturnal visit to the empty library in hope of finding a clue as to her inability to control her power.

If she hurried, she had enough time to grab a quick bite of breakfast before time to begin her first class of the day. She ran.

"I told you that stunted whelp of a drunken camel could not be trusted," Brinn muttered. "I should have shoved my knife into his gut while I had the chance. But no, you had to give him one more chance. See where that chance got us." He leaned over and splashed a little more water on his face, then shrugged in disgust before dunking his entire head into the now dingy grey water; shaking his head like an animal to remove the excess water from his short blonde hair. The muscular hunter wore a long sleeveless tunic made from some type of lizard skin, grey with an unusual pattern of scales, belted at his waist. The leather of his pants and boots, while of good quality, was well worn and showed signs of multiple repairs.

Moth dropped the reins of his mare to the ground, before joining Brinn at the water trough. The strident tones of Brinn's voice caused the dark bay horse to shift her weight nervously, however, she was too well trained to disobey the implied order to stay in place, ground tied, as she had been taught. Rabbit flinched once or twice as the wind blew a few stray embers in her direction, but the experienced mare settled with simply laying her ears back and rolling her eyes. The lingering smoke from the now extinguished fire irritated her nostrils; however, the annoyance was not sufficient to risk Moths' erratic temper.

"Raffi and me, we've been through a lot together," Moth replied, his voice surprisingly soft for such a large man. He pushed his long silver hair back from his face with his free hand, allowing a slight grimace of distaste to cross his almost patrician features at the sight of his soot darkened fingers. "He always had my back. War draws you together, even more, when blood is shared. Raffi and I, we see a lot of fighting--- he saved my life more than once." The two men locked gazes for a moment, then Moth allowed a slight smile to cross his features, the movement softening the hard lines of his face in the moonlight.

"Almost cost you your life this time," Brinn snorted. "If you hadn't needed to use the jakes, we would 'a roasted in our beds. It's bad enough that red-haired skunk broke into the inn-keepers' rooms and stole all his gold. Hells, I could deal with that; I could even understand it. But that scoundrel couldn't be happy with that. No. That drassted Duaar thief had to kill 'um both, old Harpeth and his wife and then set fire to the place to cover his escape---with us all upstairs asleep." He coughed; a series of short hard hacks tinged black from the smoke. "My lungs are burning and no clerics within two days ride… and them being a good half a day's ride back the way we came. I'm gonna skin 'em."

The soft sound of horses' hoofs in the darkness caught his attention and he turned to see Keeyun swinging his leg over the back of his steel grey gelding before sliding to the ground. Not that he had far to slide; the gangly mage, half-fae or not, was taller than any man Brinn knew. At six foot four, Keeyun towered over the muscular ex-ranger. However, their weight, while similar, appeared drastically different when stretched over Keeyun's' too-tall frame. The lanky young druid looked like he had never eaten a good meal, while Brinn, at slightly less than six feet, appeared almost portly in comparison. The druids' emancipated appearance was further highlighted by his choice of attire; both tunic and leggings were woven of some dark greenish grey material that shifted color in the light and blended into almost every shadow. The leather of his boots and cloak were stained a similar color which gave him even more of a spectral appearance. He had shaved his head entirely, leaving only a slender topknot that dangled across one shoulder. Small bits of bone and one or two metal beads were woven into the braid, the only sign of vanity his friends had ever seen him exhibit.

"You two might be tight," Brinn found himself grumbling, "but me; I'm countin' on fate offering me another chance to put my hands on him. Hands, hell, one would do. I would snap his weasel neck like ol' Harpeth snapped that stringy hen's neck for last night's dinner. Five ticks are all I'd need." Frustrated by Moth's less than enthusiastic encouragement, Brinn lifted the back foot of a slightly darker gelding, inspecting the horse's hoof before taking out my knife and removing a small stone from the frog. A stone could cripple a horse in minutes and a man afoot was an easy target. Three feet later, he was finally satisfied that the hoofs were as clean as he could get them. He gathered the reins and swung his leg across the saddle of the now restless gelding. It was such a waste. He found himself studying the shapeless heap of fire-blackened rubble that was all that remained of what was probably the only decent stop-over for at least a hundred miles. "That was a big place for one old man and an old woman to run by themselves. They had to have help. I seem to recall at least one barmaid and a rather large handyman working out in the stables. Couple a half-grown runts too. Someone is sure to remember that Raffi was with us when we arrived. Might be wise for us to put some distance between us and them that's scheduled to show up come daybreak. Save us from too many questions we don't have good answers for."

"I see no reason to remain, there is little chance we can find work around here now." Moth sighed. Even with the heat off the still-smoldering ruins, the mountain air was cold. Raffi had taken away their chance of a comfortable haven in which to wait out the possibly long period between contracts and with winter coming on the chance of them finding another was slim to none. It looked to be a hard winter. Away from the heat, the pines were covered with a slight dusting of frost, a sure sign of worse weather soon to come.

"There will be other work, next town we come to. But not if we are languishing in some flea-infested prison because of Raffi's little bonfire." Brinn sighed. He didn't regret the last few cycles of his life, drifting from town to town, hiring out to whatever merc unit needed an extra hand or two. He could barely remember the last time he had stayed more than a fortnight in one spot. His life had been better since teaming up with Moth's little band of wanderers, even after taking that drassted Duaar thief into consideration. Still, that bed had been warm, the supple female body lying next to him even warmer and the idea of another night in the saddle ticked him off. He missed the convenience of the camp followers. It had been a long stretch between wars and even longer since he had been able to enjoy a willing woman's embrace. Most of the time any decent female disappeared soon after they entered a town. He had grown to ignore the pointed stares and snide remarks that accompanied their unusual group. It had taken him a while to stop staring himself. Moth, though handsome, was unusual enough, with that pale almost ghostly coloring; but put him alongside his lanky half-breed brother and the scarred up thief, it was a combination sure set anyone's nerves on edge.

"You still got that tracer spell on Raffi?" Brinn asked Moth.

The silent mage smiled and nodded.

"Then let's go find him." Brinn kicked Onyx into a slow easy trot. Without being told Rabbit moved to follow the gelding, Keeyun's steel grey mare following close behind. The three horses topped the small rise and then vanished in a flash of light.

Chapter 2

The Bite of the Boar Tavern, a two-story cabin built of crudely felled logs then mortared and chinked with mud from the nearby creek, was the only option for rooms. The trading post rented both closet-sized bedsteads for the ones with coin and floor space for those who couldn't afford a private room. They also offered a decent morning feast, at least until it ran out for the day. From the sounds of activity coming from below the tiny room, it wouldn't be long before that happened.

"I don't know about you, but I could use a good meal before we hit the road," Von said before he opened the wormy wooden shutter over the window. He wasn't thrilled with the limited facilities available in the area. During the previous war, few travelers had used the narrow gap between the mountains, fearing attacks along the winding passageway. After the war ended, the fort had become something of a midway stopover between Ornatar on the Northern coast and Hyperion on the southern peninsula. Midway had grown from the tents of the camp followers and now consisted of about twenty permanent buildings, amongst which the Boar was the largest.

Jaxx winced at the bright sunlight streaming through the open window and did his best to ignore him, pulling the thin pillow over his eyes in hopes of getting another candle-mark of sleep. Von was a stickler for schedules. His plan called for them to be on the road by low sun and nothing short of a freak snowstorm was going to change it. Resigning himself to leaving the warm bed, he stretched and reached for his boots. He could smell the bacon frying and thought a rasher or two, along with a stack of harvest cakes and some spiced potatoes might appease his grumbling stomach. Within minutes he had packed away everything in his travel sack, tying the thin leather trusses tightly around the burlap so that it would fit behind his saddle. Afterward, he grabbed his cape and followed Von down the stairs.

The Tavern's common room was packed with off duty soldiers and the young men were forced to wait on a table to open. Jaxx cursed whoever had built the building for skimping and cutting corners. Despite wearing several layers of cloth-ing, it was cold inside. A couple of the older men had claimed a regular spot near the fireplace, hoping to become warm by sitting by the fire. Von figured he hated the cold much as Jaxx did it wasn't worth dwelling on it. No matter how cold it was in the tavern, it was at least twice as warm inside the building as it was out there on the road. They would simply have to wait their turn.

One man, a craggy ex-mercenary with an awkward limp approached Von.

"I hate to eat alone and look like you are in a hurry." He pointed out the table two of the city watch had vacated. " That's my table she's clearing now, you boys are welcome to share."

Von looked at Jaxx and shrugged. The old warrior had to be six-foot-two and a good two hundred twenty pounds. In spite of his injury, he seemed to get around well. Von figured the man's size often intimidated people. He was probably happy to see Jaxx, who was a couple of inches taller and out-weighed him by at least twenty more.

The young man nodded their thanks, flashing a quick smile at the harried waitress as she rushed past with a loaded tray.

She grinned, indicating with her eyes her intention to return.

As promised, the buxom brunette returned with a heavily laden tray. She set platters heaped with honey cakes, golden eggs, and crisp fried potatoes before the three men. An oversized platter of bacon and sausages and warm brown bread, fresh from the over completed the meal.

"Would any of you like a mug of kafka? Only a quarter bit extra."

All three nodded and she hurried away to fetch the steaming hot beverages. She smiled as the three men added cane sap to the bitter brew and hurried away, hoping her weariness had not diminished her speed to the point that they would not forget to leave a tip. Despite her exhaustion, her step was light and her hips moved sassily, with just the right amount of motion to catch a man's attention.

Von hid his smile behind a discrete cough. Women tended to throw themselves at him, finding one with the talent to flirt with her customers while making it clear there was nothing else implied, was rare. He proceeded to dig into the food, eating heartily before it got cold. They managed to clear most of the food before sitting back with a sigh.

The old man excused himself, needing to find an outhouse, so they were able to speak without constraint.

Finding themselves alone Jaxx wasted no time. "It was

nice of Professor Shalestone to give the girls a lift back to Ornatar. Mekiva wanted to arrive before the session started. Wonder how that's going?"

"I think the idea of her running around without supervision scared him more than having to teleport them back to the city. He turned pale as a ghost when she mentioned being able to cast the spells she used." Von opened a warm biscuit and added a few strips of bacon. He repeated the process three more times before wrapping them all in a napkin and slipping it into his travel pouch. He noticed Jax was doing the same thing with several slices of cheese and the last few harvest cakes.

"And Gwen being able to heal. That's something that is usually handled by an experienced cleric, not a novitiate that hadn't yet taken her vows." Gwen had healed him after a severe back injury that could have left him paralyzed. She had brought Von back from the brink of death. It had made the hunt easier, knowing that she had her deities favor.

"I don't know about you, but I needed a break from female company. Don't get me wrong, I enjoy having them around." He grinned. "It's tiring having to constantly worry about saying or doing the wrong thing. Of course, that doesn't mean I won't miss them. Right now, I want to concentrate on our business. If we leave now we can be in Hyperion tomorrow. With luck, we can get a load going back to Ornatar and possibly even set up a regular customer. It would be a great start to our business."

"Sounds good to me," Jaxx agreed. He cut his eyes toward the old man who was approaching the table once again, alerting Von to his presence.

"Did I hear you say you are heading to Hyperion," he said as he pulled out his chair and sat back down.

"Yes. We hope to establish a regular trade route between Hyperion and Ornatar."

"I travel that way regularly. I can recommend stopping by Muamer's trading post. It's about halfway to Hyperion, at the mouth of the passage through the mountains. Tell him Tellar sent you and he will treat you right." He grinned, showing a ragged gap-tooth smile. "We served together during the war."

"We will keep that in mind," Von said. " Any excuse to sleep in a warm bed instead of a tent is always welcome."

Jaxx nodded agreement. "Von, I'll get the horses while you take care of the bill." He turned back to Tellar, "Much as we enjoy the company, we need to get on the road, or we won't make the trading post before nightfall. Hope to see you on the return trip." Jaxx grabbed his travel sack and headed toward the barn to saddle the horses.

Von signaled for the serving maid as he rose from the table. She nodded, gesturing for him to meet her by the counter. He paid for the meal and then passed her a Ryl for her time. This brought on a huge smile that changed her face from cute to beautiful.

"I saw you eating with Tellar. You must be heading toward Hyperion. You sure you don't want to stay around another day?"

The implied invitation was tempting, especially after spending so many sleepless nights thinking about Mekiva. Von returned her smile. " As great as that sounds, we have to be going. We will stop in on the way back."

"Take care," she said, her eyes darting nervously toward the table where Tellar sat. It was clear she wanted to say more but hesitated.

"We always do," he replied, wondering if they might put off the trip another day. Deciding there was no way he could convince Jaxx to postpone their departure, he headed for the stable.

As the two friends set out for Hyperion, he wondered if he had made a big mistake.

Chapter 3

A loud clap of thunder broke almost directly overhead, making his horse crow hop sideways before taking off at a dead run. Raffiel had always hated riding in the rain and today's storm only reinforced his belief. Pulling his oil greased slicker closer he huddled down into his saddle as the cold rain pounded his head and back. The remorseless storm showed no signs of letting up.

The wind whipped storm was moving fast, unfortunately along the same path that he needed to travel to reach Hyperion. Raffi was far from a horseman, he was huddled beneath his oilskin, one hand clutching the wet leather cantle of the saddle the other hand clamped hard on the waterproof cape, trying to prevent a random gust of wind from removing the hood from his head, or even worse, blowing away the entire slicker.

From out of nowhere an irregular shadow lunged at them. Raffi's bay reacted instantly, veering to the right and off the main path. Hitting a particularly slick clay surface underneath the thick mud the horse's shoes lost traction and she went down, hard. Fearing being caught beneath the thrashing hoofs, he threw himself the opposite way, landing about ten feet away in a patch of cockleburs.

The raw scream of the frightened horse drew his attention from the tiny thorns. Through the twilight murk, he saw dark shadows circling them. Wolves, at least ten of them. One small horse would not last long when shared amongst the ravenous pack. As the meat ran out, a lone Duaar on foot would begin to appeal to the younger members of the group. In between the lightning flashes, he could see that the bay mare was trying to regain her feet. That wasn't happening; even through the rain, he could see that one of her forelegs was shattered. Trudging through the thick mud, he managed to get close enough to her to remove his saddlebag and bedroll from the saddle. His sword was under her body and had no idea how he would get it out. The frightened animals thrashing legs could shatter his bones as easily as the misstep in the mud had broken hers.

She was desperate to get back on her feet before the wolves she could smell grew bold enough to attack. It took Raffi a few tries to catch her on an upward lunge, but he was able to snatch it out of the scabbard before she slid back into the morass. There was no way he was trying for his waterskin. If the wolves were hungry they would eat the leather, if not some lucky scavenger might find the saddle and haul it back to the trading post for the few ryls it might bring on a resale.

Struggling to his feet, he ran, looking for higher ground that he could defend. The hungry pack ignored him. They realized it would be impossible for him to outrun them on foot.

The bay horses' desperate whinnies and terror-stricken screams followed him through the darkness, but all too soon they were silenced. He imagined the shadows converging on her; his sweat-slicked body covered by the hungry wolves snatching mouthfuls of the still quivering flesh. The stronger, older wolves in the pack would eat first, then the young and very old would get their chance if any remained.

As more of the meat was consumed the stronger wolves turned on the weaker. One of the half-grown males yipped and turned away from the hungry horde surrounding the horse and a second soon followed. He vanished into the darkness.

Even though nothing could be heard over the rain, Raffi knew the minute the younger wolves of the pack had begun stalking him. Even with his long legs and slim body, there was no way he could outrun the shadowy group on his trail. Now the rain became his friend, making it harder for the half-grown cubs to track him. With nothing but his sword and side blades, there was little he could do to slow them, but he would be damned if he simply stood there and let it take him down. His only chance was to reach the pile of boulders he had passed and prayed the Gods gave him the time to climb high enough to avoid their teeth and claws. As the pack started towards him, he found himself praying to whatever god might be listening. He wasn't exactly pious and never made it to the temple, but he did occasionally offer up a few coins to Grall and Mephib. They were the only ones he felt deserved his respect, let alone his coins… or prayers. But he prayed now.

"Mephib drag them all to hell," he managed to squeeze out as he reached the first of the oversized boulders. Now that he was closer, he could see that the formation he thought to be natural stones, was the remains of something man-made, possibly an abandoned temple or roadhouse.

He wasn't sure how he felt about it and didn't have much time to consider. He knew his only chance was to get high enough they could not reach him.

Unfortunately, that was not going to be easy. Anywhere

he could reach, a wolf could jump. Unless he found a way to climb atop one rock and reach a higher one, there was no way he could avoid the pack. He drew his sword, determined to make the warrgs pay for their supper. He was once a Duaar warrior, though it had been many cycles since he'd fought with a military unit. The Gods would remember his death, even if no one else would. That's when he noticed the opening, a dark hole beneath two fallen stones that looked big enough for him to squeeze inside.

His sense of self-preservation kicked in and he knew his salvation was only a short climb away. With his eyes set on the narrow opening, he focused on reaching the opening before the pack reached him. It was a race. He could smell the sharp tang of his sweat; hear the erratic beat of his heart and feel the wet leather of his armor rubbing against his skin as he ran. He didn't look back over his shoulder, he knew they were on his trail and they would not stop until there was no chance, they could catch him. With every lightning flash, he could see the opening coming nearer; and he focused all his energy on reaching safety. Once he was inside with the opening safely blocked, he would sit down and think.

Somehow, he managed to reach the narrow opening

before the pack arrived. Blame it on the rain, they had separated into hunting pairs and spread out in all directions. He had never heard of a wolf pack doing this. That meant it wasn't wolves after all. It was warrgs. Damn them all. Warrgs were not descended from wolves as many people thought but are the result of magic. Unlike a wolf or a dog, the hybrids had been created by a mage for a specific purpose and then abandoned after that objective was met. One of them might have been used in the original spell, but it was also possible a large cat of some kind had been used and they had mutated over the cycles since.

The one in front of him had the muscle structure of a large cat, strong and powerful. He doubted a knife would have much of a chance in slowing them down. The head was the most vulnerable spot. He had found the surest way to kill one was to remove the head from the neck. Completely. Neat and clean, like a physic would do. That was not easily done. He had seen a warrg bite a man's arm off as he swung his blade. No, you needed to stay out of reach of those teeth at all times. And its size was deceptive, it was long like a horse but slung lower to the ground like a cat.

Even if you could get a swing at it, chances are the body

wasn't in the spot you were attempting to hit. The same magical spell that made them smarter and larger, had given them an inborn ability to camouflage itself. He knew it was difficult to see them; his eyes seemed to waver in and out of focus as if the animal he was watching was moving in and out of reality. Sometimes it looked solid, at other times as though it was partly here and partly somewhere else…all at the same time. In this weather, the dreary greys of the unusual beasts seemed to be comprised of smoke, always shifting and changing until they clamped their all too solid teeth into you.

As he slipped sideways through the narrow opening, Raffi prayed he would be safe inside the crack. The possibility of the animal being able to shift reality scared the hell out of him. It was hard enough to fight the various carnivorous animals, but how do you fight something that can vanish in seconds? Something not from this plane of existence?

He began piling rubble in front of the entrance, pushing the rocks and dirt with his feet until the opening was closed except for a small section at the top too narrow for a paw to reach through. He could not see any animal bigger than a rat getting through the opening. He jabbed the lone paw that managed to slip inside with his dagger, drawing a yelp and a stream of bright crimson that continues to flow even after he pulled it back outside. The injury should give them cause to hesitate. He intended to locate a more defensible location before they began to dig out the blockage.

As he expected, the rock pile was not natural. Behind him stretched a narrow hallway, with a set of stairs going down into the darkness. He shoved an additional two big rocks in front of the opening, lit the torch from his backpack, and headed down the stairs.

"I could put an arrow through his black heart without him waking. Serves him right to die in his sleep; ironic even." Brinn held the arrow notched and ready, his fingers tensed and white from the pressure of holding the bowstring pulled tight against his ear. It would be so easy to let go of the string. But he knew Moth would never believe it an accident. Even so, it might be worth it. From their position atop the small tor, he could see the outline of the Duaars body clearly defined within the flickering light of the small campfire. All he had to do is let go and the small group would not be bothered by the self-absorbed thief again.

Moth shook his head slightly and pointed upward, drawing his gaze to the shadowy figure wedged into the split of a nearby Aspen, high above the well-lit campsite. He should have known it wouldn't be so easy. He relaxed his arm, frustration evident on his face as he lowered his bow. He still had a slight chance of hitting Raffi, but only a slight chance. Keeyun could have made the shot, but Raffi was smart enough to position himself where his body was shielded from any but the most expert archer.

"I should have taken the shot anyway. Grall and Mephib take him!" Brinn turned to remount and then stopped, allowing a wicked grin to replace his angry frown. Moth might not let him kill the arrogant pain in the ass; however, he would not stop any of them from a bit of innocent revenge. Removing a small hand ax from his saddle he started creeping toward the slender Aspen and the sleeping dwarf.

Moments later the silence was broken by the sound of splintering wood accompanied by Raffi's frenzied shouting and curses and Brinn's nonchalant whistling. Keeyun and Moth struggled to keep their faces from showing how much they were enjoying the spectacle but eventually, they both gave in to their desires and peals of laughter rang out, periodically interrupted by Raffi's indignant threats and Brinn's taunting repartee and finally the crash of a heavy body hitting the forest floor.

Moth topped the rise first; pulling up sharply as the view of the stone-walled city nestled in the valley below excited and surprised him out of his earlier misconceptions. Brinn, arriving astride his big buckskin seconds behind the mage, let out a long slow whistle of appreciation at the sight of the prosperous and completely unexpected metropolis located so far from the more commonly traveled roads and highways.

"Surely that is the home of a very rich man," Raffi agreed, as his eyes took in the high stone walls, neatly laid out streets and well-manicured grounds surrounding the large manor situated in the center of the city. "Must have cost a small fortune to have all that marble quarried, not to mention paying to have it installed; someone with more money than sense, there has to be some way we can profit from that."

"I certainly hope so. We are going to be down to eating the leather in our boots before long." Moth examined the well-maintained keep and the grounds around it a few minutes more before signaling it was time to move on. Distances were deceptive in the mountains and they had several candlemarks of travel ahead of them before they reached the gates of the city. Even then, there was no guarantee they would be admitted through the gates, much less that they would be able to find work once inside. People did not build in secluded areas without reason. Whatever reason had brought the lord of the keep below, lack of funds had not been one of them. Another consideration was always at the front of his mind. Men with money usually brought their own security forces. Moth could see guards patrolling the walls below. From the outward appearance, this lord had prepared for almost any possible situation, choosing not only a highly defensive location and then supplementing it with high stone walls topped with turrets. Even the keep's entrances screamed security, with two double-banded iron doors, designed so that one would open only after the second one closed. Inside the city walls, Moth spotted a large tavern, no less than twenty small businesses, one, possibly two public stables and multiple private homes and outbuildings. The town appeared clean and well maintained as well, unusual for such an enclosed area with such a large population. Someone was maintaining a high level of control, which necessitated there being a highly trained and competent force already on hand, none of which boded well for their employment chances. Still, it was the only city available.

Raffi squinted out from under the floppy wide-brimmed hat that now capped his unruly auburn mop. He still sported the purplish-brown remnants of the bruises gained after his undignified descent from his sleeping perch several nights before. Moth had made it a point to ask Keeyun to act as a kind of unofficial buffer between the two men and he had obliged by keeping his mare between Raffi's new stallion Onyx, and Buck.,

Since Brinn's' buckskin was an ornery brute with a tendency to bite other studs Keeyun didn't complain, it was entirely too entertaining watching the Duaar struggle to stay in the saddle every time the young stallion crow-hopped and twisted in his attempt to avoid the big buckskins teeth. While it didn't make up for the lost shot, it did make the time pass by a bit faster.

Raffi fixed his bloodshot eyes on the distant spires of the city, doing a mental calculation of the distance in his mind. The city was still several clicks away, at least half a day's ride and it was all he could do to stay awake now. From habit, he reached inside his jerkin and checked once again for the small leather pouch nestled against his heart. At least he could afford a room when they did arrive. No more mildewed hay lofts damp from leaking roofs. He might even invite Moth to share. It wouldn't be the first time the two old friends had shared a bed. Keeyun and the arrogant blastard could kiss his golden-brown behind, and he would still lock the door in their faces. He let his hand drop, running his fingers along the top of his left boot, gently caressing the ivory handle of his favorite dirk. He longed for the day to arrive when he would finally be able to drive it into the breast of the boneheaded blonde that had taken his place as Moth's right-hand man. Just because he had made a few minor mistakes of judgment and got into one lousy bar fight, why should that affect their friendship? It wasn't as if it had cost them anything. He was the one who spent three weeks languishing in that hell hole of a prison. So, what if they all were asked to leave town? They were not going to settle down there anyway. No, it was all Brinn's fault. All the merc had to do is back him up, but no, the skeezy jackass had sat there, guzzling beer. Then he had the gall to laugh as the city guard dragged him away in shackles.

Brinn's day was coming. He could be patient…

Chapter 4

Vondal pulled his heavy wool cape tight against his neck, trying to keep as much of the icy rain off his clothes as possible. Of course, it would start raining when they were in the middle of nowhere. There was not a tree in sight, at least nothing large enough to shelter two grown men and their exhausted mounts. Within a matter of moments, the verdant green field more closely resembled the bog near the mouth of the Hogshead river back home. Some people might call it a swamp, but the ground underneath was too porous to hold standing water long enough for the plants to rot or for sinkholes to appear.

The wind-whipped storm was rapidly moving, making it impossible to move fast on the mud slick road that ran between the fort and the pass. It showed no signs of slacking off. If anything, the wrath of the storm was increasing.

Without warning, a dark shape lunged from the shadows. Von's horse shied, stumbling off the main track as she tried to remain on her feet while sliding in the thick mud. He threw himself to the right as she lost her footing and went down hard. From where he was lying he could see her struggling to regain her feet, but even through the misty rain, it was obvious she could get no traction while lying on her side.

Somehow, Jaxx managed to bring his horse safely to a stop. He was waiting some fifteen feet further down the trail for Von to take care of the injured animal. If she could not be saved, Von would need to put her out of her misery. Killing such a noble beast something both men dreaded having to do.

From the corner of his eye, he caught a glimpse of movement amongst the brambles. The sun was setting but the storm had brought about an early twilight. The anxious screams of the unfortunate mare had attracted several hungry predators eager for the anticipated feast. The approaching animals left no time for compassion.

Von got to his feet and ran for Jaxx, shouting ahead to warn him of the incoming pack. Jaxx needed no warning. His gelding had scented the wolves and he had his hands full maintaining some semblance of control. The panic-stricken mare screamed for assistance but her desperate cries were soon silenced as the animals converged on her.

One of the wolves turned away from the group surrounding the dying mare and snarled a challenge, but neither of the men was interested in staying around any longer than neces-sary. They would be riding double and wolves were intelligent enough to realize that would make them vulnerable. If they hoped to live to see another sunrise, they needed to put as much distance as possible between them and the pack. The rain would wash away their scent, but the wily old alpha male had learned as a pup how easy it was to stalk their prey when it stayed on the well-traveled track through the grasslands.

"We could always cut the mule loose, accept our loses, and circle back to the fort." Jaxx was pragmatic about things. Logic said it was better to lose coin than lives.

"No way we are returning to the Fort Gherra. We came for a reason. You knew things could go wrong when we started the business. We planned this trip out in detail. After com-ing all this way, it would be stupid to go back empty-handed." Vondal remembered hearing some talk around the bar back in town at the Fort that claimed the trading post was the best place to stop overnight. "The trading post can't be far. I can see the pass through the mountains." He glanced back over his shoulder but didn't spot any of the wolves. Even though the stars were out the night was a discomforting sheath of shad-ows. The journey before them was difficult enough without thinking too much about what could happen if the wolves managed to cut them off.

Both men knew there was no way they could outrun the pack. With one sword and one ax between them, their only option would be to kill enough of the wolves to show the alpha they were not worth the losses the pack would incur. According to the directions we had received at the fort, the trading post was less than a candlemarks travel further along the main track. The mule was heavily laden. Even if they stopped and unloaded the packs, it was doubtful the stubborn creature would allow Von to ride without a sturdy saddle. Right now, there was nothing to hang on to.

For now, he was running slightly ahead of Jaxx's gelding, but that would not last. There was no way they could keep up this pace long enough to reach the pass. Pushing the animals until they foundered would only put them on foot at the worst possible time.

Gradually the exhausted animals slowed to a shambling walk. It was a race from that point forward. Von turned and studied the path behind them. He flinched when the howl of a wolf came from the darkness to the left of the trail. The pack had split, with several of the younger wolves silently following them. Something must have changed for them to break the silence with their howls.

"The trading post," Jaxx said. "I think I can see faint lights in the distance. The wolves are smart, that's why they stopped worrying about surprise. We are getting too close for them to wait."

As if the wolves could understand his words, they acted. Von swung wildly as the first dark shadow leapt from the heavy underbrush. With their heavy winter coat, unless his blade struck one of his legs, or across the spine, there was little chance he could hurt it. He was determined to try. Wolves this big could bite a man clean in half and even if they missed a killing blow their teeth could easily rip out a man's innards. These were experienced hunters; they knew it was important to take out the horses and leave the humans on foot. Then they could pick us off one at a time. It was only a question of when the time would be right. The night seemed to grow darker as the wolves began to converge on the weary animals. The cocky one who always seemed to be out in front was content to wait for his companions to get into position before he attacked.

As Jaxx grasped the wet leather of his ax's handle, he cursed the wolves, the weather, and every deity he could remember. His father would have been aghast at the sacrilege, but at that moment, he could not see how they deserved his respect, let alone his prayers.

"Grall and Mephib drag them all," he managed to get a few words out as one particularly large male snapped his mouth closed inches from his leg. Any closer and the wolf might have dragged him from the saddle. Stress grew stronger as he realized it was going to be close. His breath came in short pants and his hand began to tremble and sweat.

His instinct for survival kicked in and everything seemed to slow and move into sharp focus. He could smell the wolves' wet fur over the pleasant scent of wet grass; hear the soft growls as they moved through the rain; feel the wet leather of his saddle against his skin. As lightning flashed and thunder rolled overhead the wolves seemed to pull back. He could see the lights of the trading post becoming clearer with every stride and realized there was some chance of survival. The storm was moving closer, he could feel the electrical discharge in the air. He noticed the hairs all over his body was standing on end. What was going on? The air around him felt thicker… heavier with moisture. Then the rain abruptly stopped.

"Drasst. Von! Drop your sword. Now!" Jaxx yelled as

he dropped his ax onto the ground. Von reacted out of habit and did what Jaxx said. Almost instantly after dropping the weapon, a bolt of lightning crashed to earth directly in front of the running horses. The light blinded him, but he had no time to throw an arm up to shield his face. Gradually the glare faded from his eyes and he could see two of the wolves were lying in the mud, evidently dead from the strike. The rest of the pack had vanished.

"Twizzle," Gwen whistled sharply and continued walking through the crowded marketplace, discreetly trying to spot the elusive Mir Cat. Since the two young women had returned to the city without Von and Jaxx, Twizzle had been impossible to control. Letting him loose in a market full of food and shiny objects was probably one of the biggest mistakes of her too-short life.

An image of the impudent animal flashed through her mind. He was somewhere nearby and didn't mind letting Gwen know it. Before she could react, a cold nose nuzzled against her neck causing her to jump and earned her more than a few strange looks from passing shoppers. Twizzle was getting stronger, a few moons earlier, the idea of him turning invisible was beyond comprehension. Now the bold rapscallion did it without thought. Mekiva had no way to discover exactly how strong the Mir-cats' powers would grow as he approached adulthood, and this scared Gwen almost as much as his expanding appetite did.

"Stop doing that!" She lightly scolded the kitten while struggling to regain her composure. She offered a half-hearted smile to the remaining onlookers, a silent plea for understanding. Twizzle sent a mental huff into her mind. The Mir cat had never spoken aloud though she was sure he could if he wanted to. He preferred to use mental pictures to convey his messages. It always left a mental imprint that was difficult to forget that way.

The butcher didn't buy it. The mistrust in his eyes held her fast until she had paid for her order and moved on. Twizzle raided his booth regularly and he knew she was now taking care of the adolescent Mir cat until Mekiva finished her semester. She heaved the sack of fresh sausage links over a shoulder and headed over to the baker's stand. Less than five minutes later she had filled her shopping basket and was ready to pay the baker. Unfortunately, Twizzle had vanished again.

The astute baker stood in the doorway using his apron to wipe loose flour off of his hands. He kept one eye open for Twizzle, who had the habit of turning invisible and then tossing flour at him. He eyed Gwen suspiciously but went about his business, quickly rolling out the fresh dough for his baked goods. She waited as he sprinkled brown sugar and cinnamon on the flat surface and added a generous portion of cracked nuts and raisins before rolling it into a tight tube. That's when she noticed Twizzle was back. He settled down atop the pole outside the door, enjoying a snack of cheese he had filched from some unsuspecting farmer. One more stop she would need to make before heading back home…if she could find the farmer.

As soon as the baker finished slicing the dough into sections, he laid them flat on a pan to bake. His raisin nut cakes were a favorite and there was nothing better than when they came hot from the oven.

"Would you put a dozen aside for me? I need to see if I can find Twizzles' latest victim. It should not take too long."

"I don't know why you put up with that flying lizard. You should sell him to the cobbler and let him make a pair of shoes. Finally, get some value out of the little thief."

She laughed and passed him the coins to cover her purchases.

A soft earnest whine echoed throughout her brain as Twizzle tried to get her attention. Something had happened, it was both a mournful whine and a warning of imminent danger. The door opened and two men walked in. Neither appeared to be interested in the baker's product. Rita, the baker's wife paled. She appeared to be frightened. Behind her was feline trouble, claws out, back arched, and hissing. Whoever the men were, it was evident the Mir cat did not like them.

Gwen decided to stick around until the buns came out of the oven. "How much longer do you think it will be? I don't want to fight the rush of customers when those buns get ready."

Rita took the hint. "Not long, maybe half a candle mark longer." She opened the oven door to check and the scent of fresh sticky nut buns wafted through the air.

The two men didn't like her answer. A store full of hungry customers would make it difficult for them to discuss anything privately with the baker. As the first few shoppers drifted in, they whispered together and then left without making a purchase. Twizzle was right behind them the entire time.

Gwen knew the Mir cat would follow them until he found their headquarters. We would make a stop on the way home and inform the city guard that a new pair of shakedown artists were in town. To ensure they would not remain in the area, she had asked Rheaaz to place a blessing on the bakery to encourage any evil to leave the area. The goddess must have granted her request because they were both scratching heavily as they walked out the door.

She didn't mention it but Rita must have suspected what she had done. She found a few extra sticky buns in her sack when she arrived home. Between the description of the two men and the location of their house provided by the ever-curious Mir-cat, it would not be long before the two men relocated their protection service to another city or landed in the city jail.

"You are home early Gwendolyn," her neighbor greeted her from his porch as she approached the building.

"Twizzle behaved for a change," she replied as she ascended the stairs to the two small bedroom flat she shared with her mother. Twizzle was already sitting atop the newel post at the top of the stairs, taking one of his many daily baths.

Gwen was still agitated after her experience in the bakery but tried to make her voice sound as normal as possible." Mother?" she called out as she normally did. "Hope you are hungry?"

No one answered. The was no light, all the draperies still covered the windows. The room was cold, the hearth fire was out and there was no sign of her mother. Nor was there a note or anything to explain where she had gone.

The downstairs neighbor came storming up the stairs. He could hear the distress in her voice and knew something was wrong. The neighbor crossed the room and threw open the drapery that covered the windows, blinking as the bright light from the sun blinded the distraught young Shi'i. The realization hit her, she had left early that morning to do her shopping and had not checked to see if she was in bed before she left. She had no idea how long her mother had been gone nor if she had been home at all that day. The bed was unmade, and her things were scattered around the room, but that was normal. Nothing else was. Then she noticed the knife. Someone had used it to nail a feather to the wall above the bed. A bright red feather. The hair on the back on her neck stood up. She started trembling and collapsed to the floor.

The night was turning cold. The wet weather the young traders had been doing their best to outrun turned to slush as it caught up with them. Overhead, a few stars were still peeking out between the heavily laden storm clouds but that would not last. Jaxx swung back up onto the tired gelding, sliding into place behind Von. They had made a brief stop a short distance from the trading post. He had located a small hollow, shielded from view by a thicket of bramble and a boulder. Von's sword and Jaxx's knives were wrapped in a blanket and hidden under the edge of a rock in the corner of a small crevice, along with most of the coins they were carrying. One of the hardest lessons learned on board the ship was that you didn't carry anything of value openly into an unknown area. Despite the glowing reviews they had received regarding the owner and operator of the post, the place seemed too perfect. On the surface, there seined to be little to be wary of.

Situated at the gap between the hills, the compound at first glance seemed very remote but was actually in an exceptionally good location. All the caravans going between Hyperion and the fort had to pass right in front of the building if they stayed on the main road. The mountains around the trading post were bleak and inhospitable but offered generous hunting; rabbits, antelope, dear, and occasionally sheep or goats could be found. The cleared area around the trading post was edged by verdant green brush, evidence of a ready supply of water. Even in the driest summer heat, the creek provided a steady trickle of water. It flowed heavily in the early winter moons of the lunar cycle. There was an acre or so of grass growing to either side of the creek but the owner had fenced it and was charging a fee to picket your horse on the grass.

Several outbuildings were scatted around the property, the barn being the largest.

The low rectangle building was old but very well built. Made of sun-dried mud-blocks and straw, it would last cycles longer than any of the owners. With tribes of marauding goblins native to the area and no ready military closer than the fort, a secure building in which to stand off an attack was a high priority. Whoever designed the barn had placed spyholes around the room. Spaced at regular intervals around the outside perimeter, each one was the perfect height for an archer but too small for anyone to squeeze through.

Inside was ten open box stalls, each with a private locker

for storing personal tack and trail items. There were five other horses in the stable and a second mule.

Jaxx smiled, "Looks like the owner might keep a few for remounts. Even better, he may have a horse we can purchase to replace your mare." He tossed hay into the manger for the horse and mule and then went looking for the grain bins. As he expected there were prepacked buckets of grain, weighed out and ready. He chose two and made his way back to the horse-box, poured one into each wooden trough, and then hung the empty pail on nails outside the box. The hostler would make sure the cost of the feed was added to their bill.

The main building wasn't as big as the barn; about three times as long as it was wide, but it had a second story of hewn logs. Jaxx studied the layout from the barn, noticing the backroom windows were only a few feet above the roof of the back part of the house. This would allow someone an easy exit in an emergency; however, it would also allow someone east access to whoever was sleeping in the rooms. He figured the house had been built much later than the barn. With a front face full of windows, it not laid out for defense like the barn.

The weather showed no sign of breaking. With the animals bedded down for the night, they headed to the inn looking to fill their empty stomachs. Inside it would be warm and likely to get warmer as the windows were shuttered against the rising icy onslaught. Like most taverns, it was warmer near the fireplace but that could be considered a tradeoff against the smoke invariably drawn into the room by the chimney shaft. Experienced travelers knew to find a central location, where it was not too cool and the air was fit to breathe.

They had been told the compound belonged to a burly, barrel-chested man about the age of Von's father. The respected veteran of three wars was standing behind the bar as they came through the door. There was something reassuring about him; an air of quiet confidence that made the two young men forget their inner trepidation and relax.

Finding a good table would not be a problem. Other than a trapper in his leathers sitting back as far from the fire as he could get and the bartender, the room was empty. Jaxx had been expecting a few more travelers. He was about to approach the bartender to inquire about a meal and a room when he was distracted by a young woman coming down the stairs, the state of her hair, and the cut of her gown hinting at the location of at least one traveler. Von listened, hearing the faint creak of metal springs, verifying the location of at least two more people.

When the disheveled barmaid approached the table, asking for their orders, Jaxx surprised Von by his order. "Two mugs of the house beer. And a couple of slices off that deer on the spit."

She nodded and hurried away, coming back in minutes with their order.

As she delivered the sour mash beer, she asked, "Will that be all. There are rooms available upstairs if you are interested." She glanced over at the innkeeper before offering them a wistful smile. It was a rare day that a young and handsome man stopped by the trading post. Seeing two at one time was a welcome change from the usual clientele they were forced to service.

Von had been looking forward to the better quality Duaar Ale the mercenary had suggested. He figured there had to be a reason Jaxx had gone with the cheap stuff, not that he was drinking much of the sour mash. Something had his friend on edge and that was enough to set him at attention. Jaxx sometimes noticed things that he missed. It was apparent something wasn't right about the setup here.

The bartender waited until they were sipping on their beer

before sauntering over and pulling out a chair. "Haven't seen you in this area before. You come over from the fort?"

"We passed through, dropped off a load of supplies. Figured since we are so close, we'd try to pick up a load in Hyperion, heading back toward Ornatar."

"So, you'd be needing a room for the night, as well as stabling for your animals?"

"One room, two beds. A horse and a mule. Lost the other horse to wolves coming across the valley. We would be interested in buying one to replace it if you have any for sale."

"A sunrise meal on the morrow?" he asked.

"Yes. And a packed meal for the trail."

"Half a ryl for the room, a quarter for the food and another for the animals. One and a quarter ryls." He seemed to be thinking about something. "May have a gelding I can let go. You can take a look at him in the morning."

"Done and thanks," Von said. The price was high but not unusually steep. There was not a lot of competition in the area to bring the charges down. He pulled out his travel purse, carefully counting out a half steel piece and three of the smaller quarter sections. He left a few quarter sections lying on the table. They acted as both an incentive for the barmaid and a way to keep the bartender from asking too many questions. Few businessmen wanted to risk running his customers up to their rooms while unspent coins were showing on the table.

While they were waiting for their meal, Jaxx went upstairs to pick a room for the night. He returned in minutes. "It's set up like a fortress. Maybe the wolves aren't the only thing we need to avoid while moving freight through the area. It would be really hard for someone to break into one of the rooms. All the windows are shuttered with have heavy metal bars across them." He looked up at the ceiling. "Look at the floors, how they are made. The planks are fitted well with each other. No one is going to get in from below. I bet from a front window upstairs you can look out over the entire compound. Wonder what they are trying to keep out?"

Von looked puzzled but didn't respond as the server was bringing their meal. Being careful not to drink much of the beer, they both dug in, enjoying the tender venison. There were fresh spiced root vegetables and a tasty brown gravy made with thickened drippings from the deer. The bread was hot and fresh from the oven. It was the best meal they had enjoyed since leaving Ornatar.

"With luck, we will get a hunk of that venison between

slices of this bread to take with us in the morning," Von said as he sopped the final dregs of his meal up with another chunk of fresh bread.

"If the dawn feast is half as good as this meal, we will not need the travel pack." Jaxx stretched, already feeling drowsy after enjoying the tasty meal. All I need is pipeweed and a soft bed." His eyes went to the barmaid and he debated calling her back over, then decided against it.

Von was already nodding over his plate. This surprised him, the days travel had not been exceptionally arduous. He reached out to shake him back to attention when his head fell forward, the side of his face planted in the middle of his trencher.

"Von?" he asked as he shook his friend's shoulder. There was no response. The food. It wasn't in the ale. The food was drugged. Jaxx rose from his seat, no longer hungry, his stomach roiling. His balance was off. He felt as if he had spent a night of drinking after a day of too little sleep. A glimpse of movement out of the corner of his eye startled him and he managed to duck enough to avoid the man's fist, but the action threw him further off balance. Mentally cursing the trader, he fought as his limp body fell against the table and slid to the floor. His last thought was how glad he was that they had buried both the money belts and the magic weapons before approaching the trading post.

Chapter 5

Raffi pushed the blonde coin girl from his lap, jumped up upon the table, raised his mug, and then announced, "Drinks are on me."

The relative quiet of the small pub was broken by scattered cheers and calls for fresh mugs in response to his drunken announcement. Moth shook his head and went back to the card game. If the drunken fool wanted to waste his coin on strangers, let him. In fact,...

"Come, my friends, join us, all the drinks are on my friend today." Brinn laughed as jovial shouts roared through the inn. The taverns owner raised an eyebrow to his barmaid, and she nodded, confirming she had seen the bags of coin necessary to cover this unexpected offer. He immediately began passing out pitchers of ale to any that asked, marking a line upon a slate each time. When the initial rush was over, he eagerly tallied up the proceeds from the big man's generous declaration, thinking about how happy his wife would be when he showed her the tavern's take for the night.

As they celebrated their newly found wealth, Raffiel jumped down from the table, half fell into the chair, and began to brag about their adventure. Brinn smirked as he described the mighty beast that guarded the treasure as being taller than the market gate, stronger than a team of bull oxen, with claws that could snap a man in two. "Yet it was of no match to my sword," the drunken Duaar boasted, before he fell backward from his chair, landing in the lap of a red-haired courtesan who was busy coaxing a few coins from a pair of Ventish sailors on shore leave.

"Stop boasting," interrupted Brinn. The burly sellsword was a long-time companion of the inebriated procurer. "Come, join us before Moth tells everyone what really happened." He guffawed as a wave of laughter roared through the inn.

Moth had whispered to the barmaid refilling their empty mugs that the cave was guarded by a single mountain cat. The scrawny feline had run away when the three noisy men ran for the opening to escape the torrential rain that had begun to fall. The treasure was a small sack of coins found beneath the scattered bones of some unlucky traveler who had died in the cave many cycles in the past. Their wealth had come from an unlikely source, two leather-bound books in a moldy burlap bag Raffi had tripped over in the dark cavern. A wizard passing through the fort had seen them sitting on a table while they were eating morning fest. After examining them she had bought them both for the school library, offering a sum of ryls so large, that the three men had been afraid to haggle and risk losing the sale.

"Stop grinding your jaws and drink with me," interrupted the third member of the party as he jerked the red-faced Duaar away from the flustered coin girl and her back into his chair.

Finally, everyone was served their fill, the coin girls were smiling and the final cask of ale was down to its last dregs. Assigning the pot boy to begin to clear away the empty mugs and pitchers, the bartender pulled a chair up beside the big barbarian and carefully brought up the total of the tab.

"Whoa ho," Raffi said, "tis more than I expected, but not so much I would not do it again." He shoved his chair back and reached for his coin purse, only to find two narrow leather strands where once the heavy purse had hung. The tavern keeper frowned at his expression, but relaxed when the big man called out to the older merc. "My brothers, it seems I have been relieved of my purse."

Moth lifted his head off the table and nodded. He began to pull his own, still heavily weighted bag from inside his tunic.

His frown deepened as the sack caught on something inside and refused to come free. After a final fierce tug, the obstruction gave way and he pulled the coin purse free only to realize the coin purse was gone, replaced by a burlap sack of similar size and weight. He immediately pulled the sack open, discovering sand and pebbles inside.

"Son of a flea-bitten warrg! Some scoundrel has taken my purse, too. You girl," he called for the barmaid who had been bringing his drink. "You saw my bag. You can vouch for my word that it was there when I began the night."

The young woman looked to the tavern master and nodded. " He speaks the truth. At the beginning of the night, there was a leather bag of coin. Nor has he left the room. His friends too, remained all night."

Moth frowned. Raffi had carried most of the coin since the wily Duaar was easily the most sensitive of the group to his surroundings. Brinn opened his purse, spilling the contents into his hand. As he suspected, there was not nearly enough coin to cover the bill." Good merchant, I fear the coin I have will not be sufficient to cover the tab."

"Ligarza drag me to the depths," Raffiel said. "I want to know who has my gold. Drasst! The red-haired barmaid! It had to be her! The wench was a pick!”

The red-haired wench? He turned to the barmaid asking, “Did you hire a new girl?”

“No. There was a coin girl who came in with a pair of Vents, she left with them, too. She had copper curls.”

The barman shrugged. “She’s not one of ours. I have never seen her before tonight.”

Brinn frowned, “Perhaps we should take a walk down to the shore and have a talk with these Ventish sailors about the company they keep.”

The tavern master removed his apron and picked up a marlinspike he kept on the counter in case of trouble. “I feel I should go with you and help you recover your funds. There is only one ship in town, we should have no trouble locating the wily pair. We go past the city guardhouse on the way to the dock, mayhap we can invite a few of them to join us.”

The party had increased by four guardsmen by the time they arrived at the dock. As the tavern master had stated, there was only one ship in dock. The captain of the local militia approached the men loading freight and asked where they could find the captain. They talked amongst each other in a dialect no one understood before one finally motioned for the men to wait and ran to get someone who spoke the language. Less than a minute later, he returned, a young man in tow.

Upon observing the young man approaching, Brinn was struck by a feeling of despair as the translator was also Hyranthian. Hyranth was located many weeks of sailing south of Vent. They were very reclusive people. The two tall blue-eyed blondes with fish belly skin would stand out amongst the stocky, dark-skinned, black-haired men.

"I am Xinyang, the ship's purser. How can help you," he asked in the trade tongue. Like many Hyranthians, he was not much taller than a child, but few were as heavily muscled.

"We seek two men of your crew, both Ventish, who may be accompanied by a red-haired wench."

The purser appeared confused. "I fear you must be misinformed. My entire crew is of Hyranth. I am the only member of the crew that speaks the trade tongue. My captain will return on the morrow and perhaps he might be of assistance. I am afraid I am not familiar with the men you inquire of."

The captain sent two of his men to check out the ship while they waited. The men returned in a noticeably short time, reported to the captain, and then waited as he approached the tavern master. They spoke for a few moments and then the captain approached Brinn. Two of his men had moved to stand to either side of Moth, as the feeling that something bad was about to happen grew stronger. Raffi was leaned up against a barrel waiting calmly, but a guard was standing nearby to assist if necessary. The fourth man was missing. Brinn had no doubt he would return shortly, along with enough men to guarantee their compliance with the commander's demands.

His suspicion was confirmed as a group of heavily armed swordsmen came trotting around the corner of the building, moving rapidly to assist their commander. Brinn sighed and held out his hands to be bound, as the new men surrounded Moth, weapons held ready in case he attempted to flee. Raffi cooperated until he was bundled into the wagon with Moth and then immediately went to sleep.

"You will be held at the jail until you arrange for the bill to be paid. The Lord magistrate will be called to hear your plea and make a decision about the case."

Brinn turned to the tavern master, "We have horses in the stables, will you accept them to make up the difference in the coin"

"Unfortunately, the horses will have to remain in the stable until the judge makes his decision. At that time, if you have not made arrangements to cover the tavern's claim, they will be sold to cover the stable bill. Anything remaining will go to the tavern owner."

Keeyun was expecting them to return within a few days. When they didn't come back, he would come looking for them. Once he arrived he would cover the stable bill and take care of the Tavern owner. That may not get them out of prison, but at least when they did get out, their gear and horses would be waiting.

Callisto looked up as the trembling young woman was escorted into his office by his aide. Taking her mother and leaving a message pegged to a wall or door with a knife was always the quickest way to get someone to respond to his request. It usually prompted an immediate response. Today was no different. The young healer had no way of knowing he had no intention of hurting the old woman. It was simply a means to an end; leverage to ensure the inquisitive Shi'i-Lakka would show up.

At least he thought it was the same young woman; for all he knew, it was her mother's mother or even her brother. It was really difficult to tell underneath all those layers. He would have to take her word for it anyway. During her previous visit, he had not bothered to look at her face, so he had nothing to compare. "Please be seated. I will be a moment."

"Where is my mother?" She remained standing, feet apart, arms crossed against her chest.

Callisto continued to ignore her presence until he had completed his calculations. Once he was satisfied with his figures he added a notation to the bottom of the scroll, scribbled his signature, and rolled it up. Before sliding it into the case, he added a dollop of hot wax and then he pressed his ring into the wax to seal it. The case itself was spell locked, adding a second layer of security. Then he passed the case to his aide, saying only, "Make sure to place it in his hands." He shifted his weight and stretched his back, then he turned to address Gwen. "My employer wants to know his nephew's location."

"And I want to know my mothers," she snapped. "So, we are both waiting on answers."

"Don't try me, girl. You would not like me when I am angry."

"I do not like you now, so that will not be an issue. Where is my mother?"

"This is not the time for you to be difficult. Your mother is with one of my men. Once you answer my questions, she will be returned to her home. Whether she is unharmed, or not, depends on you. Now…where is Vondal?"

"I do not know. We left him at the fort with Jaxx. They were waiting for a trader to arrive."

"A trader?"

"Yes. There is a Zarni trader who makes a monthly delivery to the fort. His regular agent did not show up on his last trip and he had to make the delivery himself. The trader lost money on the delivery. The meager profits did not cover the expense of sending the entire pack train. Jaxx and Von hoped to convince him to let them make the delivery as his agents. They could be anywhere between the Fort and Hyperion." She crossed her arms and glared at him.

Castillo somehow managed to stop himself from laughing at her obstinate display of defiance. It was a shame she was pledging herself to Rheaaz; she would make an interesting conquest, at least until he finally got a glimpse of the face hidden beneath the burka. "Then it seems our time together is at an end. Sage will ensure your mother will be waiting at home when you arrive." He picked up the next missive in the stack and began reading.

Gwen turned and followed the aide from the room.

The sound at the door at the top of the stairs opening and heavy footsteps stumbling down the stone corridor awakened Vondal. The chain of new prisoners in leg shackles was escorted by two of the regular guards. They were taken father down the hall where they were placed in cells. In the weeks since he and Jaxx had arrived at least fifty additional men had been brought in. He had no idea why they were being kept separate from the others.

Ignoring the crick in his neck, Vondal stretched his arms as wide as the chains would allow. Once his circulation improved, he pressed his shoulders against the wall and slowly raised himself to his feet, wincing at the prickling and tingling pains shooting through them.

Jaxx woke up next to him and finding himself equally shackled, decided it was easier to remain where he was. He looked around, unsurprised to find himself in the same prison cell. At least this one didn't stink. And while the hay wasn't freshly cut, at least it wasn't full of lice and fleas. After they were arrested, they had been taken to the main guard tower and thrown into a standard military cell. A few days later a man had come by and made some notations on a ledger. Within a few candlemarks, they had been transferred to a ship. There must have been something in the water because he vaguely remembered the voyage. He did not remember the trip to his new location at all. That was two weeks earlier.

He soon realized they weren't in a regular prison. For one thing, they were given two meals a day. If the food were bland and monotonous, it was far better than anything he'd been served in other jails. Another difference was the blankets they received to cover them as they slept.

For the first week or so Jaxx had railed against his warders. He would punch the walls and concoct wild plans to escape. Every day Vondal would explain how his plan would fail and he would calm down. Now, after being jailed for two weeks, Jaxx had resigned himself to the possibility of remaining in the cell until the magistrate made his rounds. Finally, that day was almost upon them.

"It may not matter in a few days, once we go before the magistrate, we will be off to the mines to serve our sentence. Wonder if the girls will come and visit us?"

Jaxx grinned. Being sent to the mines did not bother him. He'd spent most of his life below the surface in his family's delves. With a pickaxe in hand, the possibility of finding a way to escape increased tenfold. He intended to escape as soon as possible and then return to the trading post. There were a few things he wanted to discuss with the owner. "The girls have no idea where we are. They were probably in bed in Ornatar when we were taken. They would have no way of knowing we were heading toward Hyperion. We had no idea where we were, so how can they know?"

"True. There is no way they can help us. Caldra. Of all the hell holes to end up in." They would be able to start over. Most of their money had been left with Addie and Tula. No one would suspect the two old women had so much coin hidden inside the inn. Not that they were without funds. They had lost their winter capes and coin pouches but the specially made belts had been overlooked and they had buried his sword and Jaxx's knives, along with most of their coin near the trading post.

His eyes went across the cell to the three men who'd been brought in late the previous night. The appeared reasonably clean and well dressed, other than one or two splatters of dried blood. Despite the overwhelming aroma of soured beer, they seemed affable men. Admittedly, he was surprised to see one of the men was a Duaar since Jaxx had made it clear it was unusual to see them so far from their homeland.

When asked, Jaxx confirmed he did not recognize him. The unknown Duaar was still sleeping, his deep snores easily drowning out their whispered conversation. Von was curious about how the three men had come to be there but decided to wait and see if either man spoke. The sound of a key turning in the lock on the cell door made him look away before he had an answer.

A brow-beaten servant entered the cell with two buckets; his head down as if he feared looking into the eyes of the prisoners. He shuffled over to a battered wooden bowl and dumped the contents of his bucket inside, dropping two chunks, of course, brown bread atop the congealed gravy. Without looking up, he edged around to the three new men, repeating the process in a similar bowl, then sliding it within their reach. Once he was done, he shuffled back to the door, waiting quietly in front of the bars until the jailor remembered to let him back out.

Von frowned at the stew, as he did every time the servant

delivered the evening meal. Invariably, it was the same thing, a tasteless mash of whatever remained of the food after the jailers finished their meal. The bread wasn't much better, but it was not the worst he had eaten either. At least it wasn't full of warbles and maggots.

Jaxx ignored his frown, unconcerned with the lack of variety in their meal as long as he had something to eat. Every day that passed brought him one day closer to the mines. He would eat rats if it kept him alive and of sufficient strength to escape the hell hole they found themselves in. They had one chance one slim possibility of getting out of there with their heads attached and he wasn't about to screw it up by being picky about the pig swill they were fed each day.

He stretched out on the ground and began a series of push and sit-ups to keep his muscles in some semblance of tone. The heavy manacles around his legs chafed his skin, but he fought through the pain. A few more days… he could handle it. He prayed Von could do the same.

Brinn watched the big man exercise without comment. Like the outspoken young man, he was sick of the lentil and root end stew but considered this a big improvement over what they had at the previous prison. The bland, unsalted gruel they had received there each morning was no better. But it had kept them alive. Every day they remained alive was one day closer to freedom. He had been surprised when they were removed from the general population and brought to the small cell in which they were now held. There had to be a reason. He was afraid once he found that reason out, he would wish had did not know it.

Raffi must have been awake because as soon as the servant was released, he sat up and inched closer to the food bowl. He sniffed the contents, then inserted a finger-tip and tasted it before smiling and picking up a chunk of bread.

Moth watched as the dour procurer gave in to his baser instincts and began eating, using his bread to scoop up a small serving before popping it into his mouth. Realizing he needed to act fast or face the possibility of no dinner, he joined him. He carefully divided the stew into three portions, leaving equal portions for Raffi and Brinn. Then he portioned out the bread.

Raffi immediately began eating again. Even with the surprisingly palatable prison food, it was doubtful he would not go to sleep hungry. During the previous week, he had lost some weight, not that it was that evident on his lanky frame. Cycles of living on the street had taught him to eat while he could, there was no guarantee more was coming.

As he ate Moth's eyes kept going to the young Duaar across the cell. There was something about him that struck a chord deep with the recesses of his memory. The young man was tall, taller than Brinn or Raffi. Even on his toes, Moth knew he would still be unable to look him in the eyes. Big too. He could tell by the difference in coloration that the jailor had to use extra links to fit the manacle around his massive ankle. He was also the only one to retain his footwear. There was no one at the prison with feet large enough to covet the heavy hobnailed boots. The boots gave him hope. From the glint in his eye, Raffi had noticed them and came up with the same idea.

Raffi began his nightly pacing as the jailor greeted his shift relief, a thin, stoop-shouldered, middle-aged man who had lost in arm in battle. Granting the crippled warrior, the position of night watchman was probably considered a boon by the elected leaders of the village.

The one-armed man had found few opportunities for employment, eagerly taking on the disgusting job of guarding the five miscreants until the high lord arrived to hold court and decide their fate. It offered him a rare opportunity to lord it over the prisoners, with little chance of repercussion. Not that the position had provided him much power.

The two young men never said a word when he was around. The blonde man and the one with skin and hair like the belly of a fish simply ignored him. And the other Duaar dwelled on every taunt, considering him a walking dead man and made no secret of his contempt…or of his intent to speed along his death if the opportunity arrived. Now he was sitting with his back to the wall, staring at the door as if it would open if he looked hard enough.

Moth had other things on his mind. Ever since he woke up next to his comrades he'd been thinking about what had happened. He accepted the fact that they were still in prison, however, it was doubtful they were still in the same city. He was certain they weren't in a regular prison at all. For one thing, he was certain he could smell brine and fish. That meant they were at least forty leagues from where they were incarcerated. For another thing, he had begun to grow a beard. For that to have happened, at least three or four days had to pass. They had been drugged and transported. Where he did not know. Perhaps the two young men did.

"Do you know where we are?"

Jaxx was surprised that Moth had asked. He had not said a word since waking up.

"Caldra."

Caldra. That meant the mines. Someone wanted to make sure they disappeared. "How long have we been here?"

"At least three weeks. A mage kept you asleep during the trip from the Trading Post to the coast. Once we were loaded on the ship, the mage ensured we would cause no problems. You managed to knock out one of the guards before he was able to cast their spell. They separated us when we arrived. Until today no one else has been in this cell."

Moth nodded. He looked at Brinn, but no words were spoken. Regardless, both young men were certain some decision was made. "We were in with about twenty other men. Then last night they moved us. We have no idea why."

"The magistrate is due to arrive any day. We have not been sentenced, though I get the impression that it is simply a matter of paperwork. No doubt we will be sent to the mine… if we are not there already."

"Close, I think. But not at the mine. Most likely within a day's travel. That explains the food. They would not want to risk the judge releasing you for unfair treatment before you are sentenced. Someone must have realized we have not been before the judge and moved us here."

Moth looked at Jaxx. "I like your boots. Have you had them long?"

His question caught Raffi's attention. "I would say he's had them since well before he left his hold. Custom made too. Some of Kelvor's best, I reckon."

Jaxx nodded but didn't say anything.

Vondal had no idea why they were discussing his boots.

Moth nodded. "If what you say is true, then we only have one, maybe two days before the magistrate arrives to hold the hearing. We all know what the verdict will be. There's no way they will allow us to go free."

"We've stayed here for too long already. Any ideas on how to get out of these chains?" Raffi was tired of playing the word game. He wanted answers.

"One. I think I can get us out of the chains, but I need to wait until everyone is sleeping."

Jaxx's answer puzzled Vondal. He had never mentioned the possibility of escape to him. His eyes went to Jaxx but Jaxx wasn't paying attention to him, his eyes were on the pale man across the cell.

Moth's eyes sparked fire. "Get us out of these chains and I can get us out of this prison."

"How do you expect to do that without weapons?"

"Take care of your end. Leave that to me."

"Von, I need you to do something. It's gonna hurt me worse than the time you got skewered by that tridex in Muu. But it's something only you can do."

Von was puzzled but he didn't ask questions. " All right. What would you have me do?"

"You know the mithril ring I wear in my ear?"

"The one the guards threatened to cut out. No. I've never seen it. Why?"

"I need you to rip it out," Jaxx said.

"Yaaga blast you to the Nine Realms. If you wanted the drassted thing out, why didn't you let the guard cut it out with his knife?"

"I didn't want it out then. I want it out now," Jaxx snapped. "It doesn't have to make sense."

"Good. Because no sensible person would ask someone to rip their ear apart," Von replied.

"Shut up and yank the blasted ring out," he growled.

"Well, don't blame me when it swells up and stinks to high heaven. Not that anyone will notice if they don't change the piz pot soon." He shifted his weight to his back leg, slid his finger under the silvery band, and jerked downward.

Jaxx let out a high pitched grunt as the flesh in his ear tore. Then he began cursing. "You rotter! You were supposed to rip it out. It's still in my drassted ear."

"How is it my fault you have fat ear lobes? It's gonna take another tug to tear it free. You had better have a drassted good reason to justify why I am now covered in your blood with no way to wash it off."

"Just get it out!" He clenched his teeth and prepared for the pain to come.

Von rolled his eyes and jerked the ring again, only to watch as it slipped from his bloody fingers and rolled across the floor, stopping beyond his reach.

"Please tell me that wasn't some kind of magic ring. Something that could help us get out."

"Can't do that," Jaxx snarled. "The ring is magic alright. But the ring won't help us get out of these chains."

"Then why am I covered in your blood? Is it some kind

of Duaar pain fetish you failed to mention during the five cycles I have known you?"

Raffi laughed. "Boy needs to learn patience. I figure it's at least six candle marks until the second moon appears. Someone wake me when it's time to leave." He lay his head back against the wall and closed his eyes. Soon after the soft sound of a snore could be heard in the dark cell.

"Make sure you are ready at moonrise," Jaxx said. "We will only get one chance."

Moth surprised them all by answering, "We only need one."

Chapter 6

Silver streams of pale light from the second of Ardin's twin moons caressed Jaxx's hand, the only part of his body he was able to place in the moonbeams path. For a few seconds, the glow around his hand increased, then it faded away.

Von strained to see what was happening but the lack of light made it impossible to see more than faint shadows. He could hear the faint sounds of movement, then the weight on his feet vanished as Jaxx sat up. He waited, expecting to hear his partner snarl out some obscure remark, a few words to let him know what was up, but Jaxx did not speak. The inside of the cell was too dark to make out the three figures lounged against the opposite wall. There was a brief scratching sound, then a faint click followed by a change in the darkness nearby as Jaxx moved closer. He could hear the same scratching sound and a second click before the shackle on his ankle opened.

Von winced as blood rushed back into his foot, bringing on an intense prickling sensation as the tissue woke up. He started to make a snarky comment but overcame the urge as

Jaxx placed a warning hand against his mouth. This surprised him, as he had never realized how soft Jaxx's hands were before. No one was talking, the only noise in the darkness was the faint rattle of chains and the sound of five men breathing.

Jaxx stood and worked at the manacle holding Von's wrist above his head. In seconds, the offending metal released its grip, allowing him to lower his arm completely for the first time in several weeks. It was still too dark to see anything in the cell, but his mind could distinguish a slight degree of change in the shadows as Jaxx made his way over to the three men bound to the far wall and released them from their chains. In a matter of minutes, all five men were free. But they were still locked inside the cell.

Jaxx had done as promised and freed them from the chains. Now it was up to the other man to get them out. He could hear two voices whispering in the darkness, talking in a language he didn't understand. One he thought was the man they called Moth, the other appeared to be shorter and slimmer than he had looked against the wall.

After a brief conversation Moth moved over to the cell door, looked out the narrow slot at the hall outside the cell. He muttered a few words. Then he vanished.

No one appeared to be bothered by his disappearance, so Von waited. Jaxx was still on the far side of the cell. He was surprised that he had not rejoined him, but not to the point of asking what he was thinking.

Several minutes passed in silence, then the sound of keys rattling in the lock of the cell door and the slide bolt being thrown drew his attention back to the exit. He braced himself, holding the heavy wooden water bowl as a makeshift weapon, as the door opened.

Moth stood at the opening, gesturing for them to follow.

Still clutching the only weapon available Von followed Moth, knowing without being told that Jaxx and the others would be right behind him. The five men slipped down the darkened hallway. Moth appeared to know where he was going. Approaching the cross-hall where the guard had been stationed when they were brought in, he was surprised to see the chair empty. Nor was there a guard in sight.

Moth grinned, picked up the lantern on the desk, and opened a door to a room beyond the cross hall. Inside the room were two men, both bound and gagged. The glare from their eyes was a silent threat of reprisal once they got out of their bonds.

" My boots!" whispered the unknow Duaar. He immediately began tugging them off the feet of the angry guard.

The pale mage measured his feet against the remaining pair of boots. "Too small for me. Brinn's feet are bigger than mine, so unless one of you can wear them, they can stay where they are."

He reached down and picked up a narrow-bladed stiletto and passed it to the man pulling on boots. "Raffi, this yours?"

"Yes. There should be three more."

"Not here." The pale mage slid a larger hunting knife into its sheath before tossing it to Von, indicating he should take it. He gestured to several smaller knives lying a short distance away from the two guards.

Brinn, the apparent leader of the trio, examined the blades, choosing the one he liked before passing the others to someone behind him.

Von could make out the dim outline of a large person standing outside the glow of the lantern. He could not tell if it was Jaxx or the other Duaar, both men being similar in size.

His hand resting on the knife's pommel made him feel better, but it would not be much protection against a sword or an arrow. He was about to mention it when one of the other men said, "There's got to be a room nearby where they store the items taken from the prisoners. Or maybe a weapons cache." He began walking down the hall, opening each door as he went.

Von turned to follow him, surprised that Jaxx remained standing in the shadows outside the lantern's light.

Per your orders, my agent traveled to the fort at Gherra to search for your nephew. He had no idea why you wanted him found. At first, I thought it was only coincidence, albeit a fortuitous one, that he was traveling toward the trading post when I contacted him. Now I find out he was supposed to meet a trio of men there. I ordered him to arrange a meeting, perhaps even find a way to join your nephew's party. Having a man traveling with them would have made it easier to keep an eye on him.

Unfortunately, the group he was traveling to join up with ended up being arrested and sent to Caldra less than a week after the records show the first Duaar was obtained. My belief one of the three men was the second Duaar in the record book. I have arranged for them to be moved to the same cell as your nephew and his friend. It would have been better if my agent had been with them. He seems to think there is no problem, that they will find a way to escape on their own. Necessity will bind them together; there is safety in numbers. They will head back to the trading post. My agent was supposed to meet them there and they expect him to be waiting.

"So, you suggest we stay away from Caldra and let them escape?"

"In his opinion, they will escape with or without your assistance. Then they will be looking for a way off the island. I can have a boat moored in a convenient location. We cannot stop the local navy from chasing them, but we can put a man or two among their crew to slow them down. Once they are back in Hyperion we should have no trouble following them.

"See to it. I expect updates they are delivered to you." He waved his hand in a derogatory manner that did little to irritate Castillo. Lord Botherton's opinion was only important in that his commander had ordered him to show a pretense of respect. As long as his coin held out, he would live. After that...

"How many drasted rooms are in this place. It feels like

we have been searching for several candle marks." The strange Duaar made Jaxx seem almost pleasant.

"Stop bitchin' and keep opening 'em," The older man, the one that seemed to be in charge, snapped.

Eight doors later they found the armory.

Von began digging through equipment, testing each choice for weight, fit in hand, and sharpness by swinging and stabbing at the wood of the boxes. There were only two bows, so both Von and Brinn took one and the matching quiver of arrows as well as a sword.

They moved toward the end of the hall to keep watch while the other three searched through the arsenal.

Moth added a stout cudgel to his belt. Then grinned when he spotted the piled up leather armor in the corner. "Raffi. Think I found your leathers." He began passing the leather pieces to the tall Duaar who fitted the pieces to his body. In the end, he was only missing one vambrace.

The older Duaar began to hide knives around his clothes, then he moved to join the others at the end of the hall.

Unable to locate an ax, Jaxx settled for a sword and a set of throwing knives on a bandolier. They had lost their armor at the trading post and doubted anything inside the cache would fit.

Von watched as Raffiel picked the lock on a door near the end of the hall. The corridor opened up to a formal foyer, complete with ornate leaded glass windows. Across the vestibule was a set of heavy wooden doors. They assumed there was a courtyard on the other side, but it was impossible to know. Brinn hoped he would be able to see outside from the room once he got the locked door open. It had taken longer than he expected to reach this point. It was only a matter of time before someone discovered they were no longer in the cell and sounded the alarm. Finally, he heard the faint click and the lock opened.

The room was set up as an office, complete with a large window. The light from the twin orbs made the small space as bright as a cloudy day. Brinn moved straight to the opening, looking out across the prison yard. "I can see over the prison walls from here. Once we get past the gate we can follow the main road all of the way to the coastline. It is easily half a day's hard ride from the prison to the coast. There's only one problem. You used your teleport to get out of the cell. How do we get out of the gate?"

"I guess we bluff our way out."

"What do you mean?" Brinn asked.

Moth whispered a few words to the weathered mercenary, making sure no one else overheard his plan. Brinn shook his head, but he didn't argue. It was a long shot but it might work. Then they only have to find a way off the island. "They will expect us to follow the road."

"Then we will head another direction. If we stay hidden, stick to the shadows, and only move after dark, we stand a chance of avoiding the pursuit."

Brinn frowned. "We will need a distraction. Something to surprise the gate guards long enough for us to overwhelm them."

"What do you suggest? There are not many things that would shock a seasoned guard."

"No. But I can think of one." He turned and looked toward the figure leaning against the mull post.

Von's eyes followed his, pausing at the tall, slender, blonde-haired woman standing in the doorway holding a rag to her torn ear. The naked woman wearing Jaxx's boots and a leather bandolier.

Chapter 7

Lord Botherton grabbed a heavy bag of coins from his desk, sending it hurtling through the air at the startled messenger. He missed and the bag struck a table, spilling most of its contents across the carpet. The messenger hastened to gather the coins that spilled on the floor, shoving them back into the bag as he inched his way toward the room's exit. It was only after he had reached the tentative safety of the hallway outside the office, that he was overcome by trembling limbs and wheezing. He stood quietly allowing his pounding heart to return to its normal rhythm and then he made his way to the door.

Calisto watched the messenger leave without making his presence known. He pushed a few stray locks of his silvery blonde hair behind his ears, silently chastising himself for not braiding it back that morning. Instead, he knocked lightly on the door and then entered without waiting for a reply.

Lord Botherton looked up as he entered the room but did not comment on his arrival. His eyes continued to scan the pile of documents on his desk. Every so often he would scribble a notation on a sheet of paper, before continuing his perusal.

After pouring a cup of kafka from a silver pot set over a candle flame, Calisto helped himself to one of the fruit pastries and a large slice of cheese. His immediate needs satisfied, he sat down in one of the two oversized leather chairs in front of the desk and waited. The chairs were not particularly comfortable. They had been designed to place the user in a subservient position to the Lord Mayor. But he had long since passed the point of being affected by such trivial matters and was well aware that Lord Botherton knew it. Still, he was surprised when his lordship slammed his hand down on the desk in frustration.

"My agents tell me that the redhaired mageling and the Shi'i Lakka maiden have returned to the city with the headmaster of the academy. My nephew and his partner are not with them. Neither of the young women is distraught, so I assume this means my nephew and his friend are still among the living. Apparently, they were not been able to decipher the medallion."

Neither Calisto's expression nor his opinion changed upon hearing his words. "Perhaps they were unable to locate the next clue. Nothing we found in the hidden laboratory provided us with sufficient information to continue with the search."

"We can't assume anything. Perhaps we made a mistake by removing the medallion before they had an opportunity to evaluate it. None of our historians have been able to deduce the meaning."

"Perhaps a financial need brought about this decision. I have noticed it is difficult to carry out an extensive search without sufficient coin to pay for the supplies."

"True. It could be something as simple as a lack of coin. That is easily rectified." He sighed and removed a key on a chain from around his neck. Crossing his office, he knelt before an ornate chest and pressed his thumbs against two of the carved flowers. A hidden door located near the bottom of the chest popped open. He fit the key into the lock and waited. Once sufficient time to diffuse the trap had passed, he opened the top of the chest. Inside was a plain wooden box.

He carried the wooden box back to his desk before opening it. Lying atop a bed of velvet was the mithril medallion. Holding it in his hand, he held it before the light streaming through the window, studying the building with the four towers. There had to be something he was missing. Originally, he had been certain the etching had referred to the burnt-out keep and the towers. He had spent several days examining the blocked up room, as well as the passage that emptied high above the road between the two cities. He could find nothing to connect the etching and the family secret. Izabal had been delighted by the discovery of the wizards' final resting place, however, the spellbook she had been looking for was not among the books and scrolls recovered from the room. This had not surprised him; it would be a foolish person who would bury a mage alive with his spellbooks. Despite all his idiosyncrasies, Ammaonth had not been a fool. Convincing his nephew to reveal the location of the family treasure was turning out to be more of a challenge than he expected. Somehow he needed to find a way to get his nephew's mind off the shipping business and back onto the hunt for the treasure. Now he had been presented with yet another obstacle to the quest, one that could be manipulated, if not removed.

"It's too late to contact my man inside the fort, by the time the messenger arrived they would have already reached Hyperion. That means you will have to go. Have Privier open a portal to the trading post. You can ride from there. Once you arrive in Hyperion, arrange for the young entrepreneurs to receive a contract to deliver some freight to Ornatar. Make it something light, but of high value. Saffron. Or Myrrh, the scent makers are always looking for that. That way they can travel quickly. That should be of sufficient value to ensure they can afford to continue the search. Maybe you should have a talk with the girls?"

Calisto shrugged, feeling that was a sufficient response to a redundant question. Once again, they had underestimated young Vondal and his brusk companion. In his opinion, all his manipulations were a waste of time and money. It would be simpler to wait until the two men located the treasure and then steal it. He debated telling him he had already spoken to the Shi'i girl but decided it would not change anything.

The lines around Lord Botherton's mouth tightened but he held his tongue. Calisto's insubordinate attitude was a minor irritation. How he was going to explain another delay to Izabal required a more delicate touch.

"I doubt the two women would know anything of value," said a sultry voice that sent chilled ripples of tension up his spine.

Lord Brotherton winced but refrained from replying. The last time he had snapped at her, it had taken weeks for all the blisters to heal. It was amazing that something so beautiful could be so ugly inside.

Castillo looked up at the sound of Izabal's voice but other than a slight lift of one eyebrow did nothing to acknowledge her presence. Instead of her usual scarlet gown, she was robed in a shimmering black fabric over set with pale silver runes. The dress followed the lines of her frame, emphasizing every soft curve of her slender well-toned body while revealing only a glimpse of the treasures hidden beneath the silken material. It was a body that begged the touch of a lover's hand, not that he was foolish enough to try. No doubt, she had a collection of mummified hands and other more personal body parts strewn around her bed chambers.

He was surprised to hear her footsteps moving near and then her hand upon his shoulder as she bent to whisper in his ear, "It would be worth it." He trembled as the warmth of her breath caressed his cheek and her finger stroked the outline of his tightly clenched lips. Castillo sighed. Serious business awaited his return, he had no time to waste playing cat and mouse with a gorgeous enchantress, no matter how tempting the woman. And she was tempting, with her dark blue eyes twinkling mischievously and the slightest flush of red highlighting the height of her cheeks. And those lips…

She smiled, showing perfect pearl white teeth and four razor-sharp incisors.

All thoughts of bedding the sorceress fled. Castillo suddenly realized he was needed elsewhere. "My Lord, if we are finished, I have business to attend to before I leave on your errand. My lady… if you will excuse me."

"Yes, yes, of course. It is imperative that you arrive before my nephew. I will explain the situation to Izabal. You are dismissed."

Heaving a sigh of relief, Castillo walked out to the sound of her laughter and the eerie conviction that he had barely escaped with his life.

Chapter 8

"Wha?" Von felt his mouth fall open as his eyes gaped wide. "Something you forget to mention your best friend and brother during the last five turns? Like how you can turn into a woman."

Jaxx sighed. Her first impulse was to lie. Several possible answers crossed her mind, not real good ones, but they were close to the truth. Well, as close to the truth as she was going to admit. She wiped away the sheen of sweat on her forehead and swallowed the first words that sprang to her mind. "No time," she snapped. "It's going to have to wait until we get out of here. Now shut your mouth before something flies into it. It's not like you haven't seen breasts before."

Von shrugged and walked back to the front of the group. Jaxx was right. Until they got out of prison, his little omission of facts could wait. But he better have a drassted good explanation."

"Well," Brinn said as Von joined him, "you did want

a distraction. If this does not distract them, nothing will."
He shifted the heavy crossbow from his shoulder to a firing position against his arm. His sweat-stained outfit caused his skin to itch. He would love to have something clean to wear but the tunic and trews were similar in color to the dark grey shades of the rough stone blocks, from which the prison had been constructed. When he was standing still it was difficult to see him. He walked a few feet behind Jaxx. Occasionally he muttered a comment that made Raffi chuckle but Von and Moth were too far behind to hear it. They had made their way through the stone building toward the main exit without challenge. It seemed that the prison was staffed with a skeleton crew; enough men to keep control until the detainees were transported to the mines. For some reason, the five men had been designated for special treatment. It could be because they had not been convicted of a crime. They were waiting for a judge to arrive.

Now Jaxx stood with his ear against the far wall, trying to get an idea of how many guards were stationed at the next cross hall junction. He grinned as one of the guards mentioned needing the privy, waiting until his footsteps faded into the distance before nodding to Brinn. Brinn cocked the crossbow and made ready to shoot.

Jaxx laid a finger across her mouth in a silent admonition, put on the biggest fake smile she could manage, and stepped out into the hall.

The remaining guard noticed the tall naked woman walking his way and rose from behind the heavy wooden table, eager to find out why she was there. He took two steps toward Jaxx, then stopped, a shocked expression on his face. His hand reached for the bolt sticking out from the middle of his chest before his mouth gaped open, blood dribbling down his chin. Seconds later he collapsed to the stone floor.

"Quick, get him out of sight."

Brinn and Raffi quickly lifted the body and carried him down the hall to an empty cell. In the meanwhile, Jaxx made herself comfortable, sitting at the table with her long legs draped across the top.

As they hoped, after what felt like an eternity to Jaxx who was sitting in a draft at the table, the returning guard reacted exactly as they thought he would. The absurdity of a naked woman lounging at the guard station wearing nothing but heavy leather boots that were at least four sizes too big for her feet made him careless. Instead of drawing his sword, he walked closer to get a better look. Brinn's crossbow took him out as soon as he walked into the light of the final torch.

"That was easy," Moth said. "Don't expect everyone to be quite as excited about the sight of an unknown woman, naked or not. No one needs to get cocky. We are still locked inside a prison and we have no idea how many guards there are."

"At least we know there is no one behind us, so all we have to do is look out for someone coming our way. Let's get moving." Brinn laid the heavy crossbow across his shoulder and pulled a short sword from his belt. He preferred the much longer reach of his usual blade but the only choices available had been three short swords and an unusual curved weapon Jaxx claimed that must have belonged to one of the prisoners. Since Jaxx was normally the biggest Von was carrying it for him, or was that her, to use if the ruse failed. Raffi had gathered most of the knives and had them stuck in various locations around his belt. The wily procurer was one of the best knife men he knew. One time he had driven five blades into an oak tree, within a hand's width of space, from across a paddock. In less time than it took him to walk across the paddock the tree.

Moth had a couple of spells handy for emergency use

but carried a short sword. He had never been one to ignore a sharp blade simply because someone said mages did not use them. Those mages did not live long. Without his spellbook he was limited to the easier spells and cantrips he had memorized cycles before, however, he intended to return to the officer who had arrested them and reclaim it at his first opportunity. He had a backup copy in Ornatar, hidden in the house they shared, but that was hundreds of leagues away from the mines. As soon as he could get another copy made it would go into his bag of holding, just in case.

The sound of approaching footsteps on the stone floor drew their attention but there was nowhere to hide so they spread out along the sides of the hall, hoping the guards would not notice them until it was too late to call for backup. Once again Jaxx stood waiting, hoping to distract whoever was drawing near.

The two guards did not seem concerned that a naked woman was inside the prison. Ignoring her presence, they immediately drew their swords and moved to confront the four-armed prisoners. Jaxx waited until they moved to engage Vondal and Brinn, then used the unstrung bow to trip them as they rushed past. One man stumbled and fell sideways, slamming his shoulder on the stone wall. Von wasted no time, driving the curved saber into his stomach and out one side. The stunned man dropped his sword, grasping his torn stomach with both hands in a futile attempt to stop the flow of blood. He took two hesitant steps and fell.

Von turned, seeking to help Brinn with the other assailant, only to find the second guard with a knife sunk to the hilt in his right eye. His eyes widened but he didn't comment as Raffi pulled the blade out and wiped the blood on the dead man's tunic. Noting the dark-haired Duaars prowess with a knife he vowed to keep one eye on him at all times. For now, they needed to work together. Something about Raffiel that made him uncomfortable. Not as uncomfortable as looking at Jaxx, only uneasy. He felt like he was hiding something. Of course, that could be a Duaar trait. Jaxx had been hiding something for five turns. What was it is mother used to say: the wisest man can be fooled by his own mind. He seriously doubted anything he was facing now related to what she had in mind.

They worked their way down the hall, checking each open door for a possible exit. One of the group always made a point of checking every window, but so far there was no possible exit. The only windows that opened had heavy metal bars spaced close enough that no one could squeeze through. Nothing short of a pickaxe was going to remove the stone surrounding them.

Raffi signaled for quiet.

Brinn gestured for them to move against the wall as Raffi edged around the corner, slipping across the open floor to the closed door. He laid his ear upon the wood, listening. Nothing. He eased down to his knees and then to his stomach, as he looked through the narrow gap between the stone floor and the bottom of the door. After peering underneath a few moments, he reversed his path, returning to the waiting men.

"There's a courtyard beyond but no one guarding the door. The only exit seems to be through a portico and a metal gate. The only way to raise it is inside the gatehouse. We are going to need another distraction."

"Anyone have any ideas?"

"All the guards have been wearing the same green capes. We have three of them, so three of us can walk across the yard. Since its cold outside, no one will question out presence, at least from a distance."

"That gets us across the courtyard, how are we going to get inside the gatehouse?"

"We let Jaxx knock on the door. Unless they are two souled, at least one of them will open the door to see why a naked woman is knocking."

Von interrupted, "That's going to put Jaxx in-between the guards and you. Without a weapon, he, I mean she won't stand a chance against a sharp blade."

"Have you got a better idea?" Jaxx asked. "If we don't get out of here before the judge arrives, we will probably be hung for attempted escape. There's a trail of dead guards, remember?"

Moth finally spoke. "I can't guarantee your safety, but I might be able to help." He muttered a few words. Jaxx felt a brief moment of warmth.

"It's only good for one blow. So, make sure you get out of the way and let the others fight. Nothing will stop the second strike and I don't have a healing spell."

Jaxx nodded. Head held high, she walked across the empty courtyard and stopped before the door. Brinn, Vondal, and Raffi walked behind him, draped in the green capes. Despite knowing the spell would keep her from immediate harm, she was nervous. She was not familiar with this body and wasn't sure how it would respond in a battle. It had been many cycles since the last time she'd been affected by the curse and her muscle memory was weak, if not completely gone. At one time she had been able to fight as well in this form as she did in her natural state. That had been at least ten cycles ago. Now she would need to rely on feminine wiles and hope the guards would be lax in their duties.

Taking a few deep breaths to steady her nerves, she knocked on the door.

A viewing slot opened and a man's voice asked, "what do you want?"

"Well, that depends on you. I have been released from my duties inside and unless you can think of a reason for me to remain, I would like to leave."

She could hear several voices talking and then she heard the sound of a bolt being thrown. The door opened inward, revealing a skinny, red-haired guard with a face, not even a mother could love. His eyes widened as he took in the naked woman standing before the door. " Sent you out without any clothes, huh. Who did you piss off?"

Standing behind him was a burly middle-aged guard with a calculated leer on his face. He leaned out to ensure there was no one else around, then ordered her inside. "Well, we can't have you standing out here in the cold. Come on inside and have a drink, we can discuss what you can do for us." He reached for Jaxx, clamping a ham-like hand around her wrist.

Jaxx had no intention of entering the gatehouse. With one guard standing beside her and the other pulling her toward the door, she did the only thing she could think of. She pasted a come hither grin on her face, looked right into the big man's eyes, and kicked him squarely in the groin with the heavy metal lined boots.

The big man's eyes rolled up into his head and he dropped to the floor, wrapped his arms around his legs, and moaned. Seeing his partner down, the skinny man pulled his sword and swung at Jaxx. The razor-sharp blade slid off her shoulder, doing no damage, but Jaxx knew that would not last. Nor could she let him get inside the room. The older guard was blocking the door from closing but he was already trying to rise to his knees. She needed to get inside now and raise the gate. She dove over the corpulent guard, rolling forward onto her feet inside the room, surprising a third guard entering the room from an adjutant doorway. He reacted instantly, reaching for his sword as he ran towards her.

Jaxx whirled, snatched a potted plant from the table next

to the door, and threw it at the started guard, throwing off his swing. Knowing she would not get a second chance, she dove at the startled man, tackling him around his knees; causing him to fall forward into the big man who was trying to get back to his feet. All three hit the ground in a tangle.

Brinn's first blow blocked the swing of the skinny guard's sword. He kicked him in the shin and then ducked inside the room, as the unfortunate guard dropped to one knee.

Von stepped forward, blocking the next attack with the hilt of his sword, his blow preventing him from rising back to two feet. The curved saber crashed against the shorter blade which slid downward along its length, gouging a narrow gash in his wrist. He shifted his grip as the warm blood made it harder to keep a firm hold on the smooth metal handle.

The lanky soldier wasted no time, moving into a rapid series of short snaps that did little damage but kept Von off balance. As the slender guard circled him, Von swiveled to keep him off balance, being careful to keep one eye on the door. Lack of experience made him reckless. Instead of protecting his injured hand, he brought the sword in tight and slashed across and up. The blades path brought it underneath the shorter sword and into the guards' side below his ribs. With an upward Twizzle, Vondal tore a deep gash across his stomach, pushing through the last layer of muscle into his liver and out the other side. Mortally wounded, he dropped his sword, grasping his stomach with both hands, before he slipped to the floor.

Von immediately looked around for Jaxx, spotting her on the ground, struggling beneath the weight of the fat man's body. Then he saw the blood.

Chapter-9

A blind man could follow the trail of our footprints through the snow. Von pulled the heavy green cloak tight against his body, hoping to ease the chill sinking into his bones as the temperature fell. Omissions' second sun was high overhead as they tramped up the long hill at the back of the stone fortress where they had been confined but it wasn't helping. The weather was changing fast and until the storm broke there was no way to know if it would be rain, snow, or ice. In the distance, a stand of woods thick with evergreens and leafless birch and maples offered some cover. The field they were crossing was white with snow, but its depth, except in shaded drifts, was only an inch or so thick. The ground was cold, it was easy to hear the ice crunch under their boots as they walked along. Unless the storm reached them soon, dogs would not be needed to track them; the footprints pointed out their path for all to see.

Von was walking point, avoiding the conversation with Jaxx that he knew was coming. He was having trouble wrapping his mind around the idea that the surly, foul-mouthed Duaar he'd roomed with for the last five cycles was now a slender, full-breasted beauty with a smile that could light up a room.

Moth had tried to explain it to him as they walked along. "It's rare; even amongst the Duaar. Once a generation a child is born that is said to be of two souls. The Duaar call such a child a Chimera and claim it's both blessed and cursed by the gods. Within a few days of its birth, the child will choose a dominant form, either male or female, and remain in that form until puberty. That's when everything changes. Once it reaches adulthood, it will continue to swap sexes, randomly shifting back and forth along with the stages of the lunar giant."

"But Jaxx didn't change…" he argued.

"That's true. That the earring he wore in his ear prevented the change. allowing him to maintain his male body. I have never heard of a spell with this ability. Once we reach safety, I intend to ask your friend about the artificer who cast the spell."

That made one of us looking forward to a conversation. There were very few things Vondal avoided, poison oak, beehives, sour milk, angry fathers. Normal things. He had never imagined his best friend being at the head of the list. Much as he dreaded it, once they stopped for the night, he would need to ensure they had a chance to talk. Their friendship depended on it.

It had shaken him when he first saw her. It wasn't because she was naked. His mind still considered Jaxx male despite his outward appearance. Everyone else had easily made to switch to her instead of him, as though changing sexes was an everyday occurrence. It wasn't going to be that easy for him to adjust.

He smiled to himself. Raffiel had discovered it irritated Jaxx when he made lewd comments and he had pushed the younger Duaar to the edge several times during the afternoon. Brinn had stepped in to separate them before it came to blows, sending Jaxx to the rear while he walked behind Raffi to ensure the peace. No one argued, they had better things to do than stand around trading barbs.

They had been walking for several candle marks hoping to find somewhere secluded where they could stop and rest. Earlier it was cold, now it felt as if the air was growing warmer as time passed. The last afternoon sun was melting most of the snow and removing all trace of their passage. Finally, Brinn had signaled a brief rest.

Von had dropped to the ground where he was, using a

broken limb as a backrest as he dug for dry socks in the make-shift pack he'd filled before leaving the gatehouse. Having dry socks helped. While they rested, he hung his wet ones on the back of his pack to dry while they walked. Everyone was wearing decent, if not perfect fitting boots. The heavy woolen cape he wore was another lucky find. There had been several extra hanging on hooks inside the gatehouse door. By layering the scavenged clothing and the addition of the heavy cloak, he'd managed to stay reasonably warm. There had been one pair of gloves found and by reason of elimination, Raffi had claimed them.

Jaxx had added her custom made lizard skin boots to the military pack she'd found while rifling through the gatehouse, happy that the boots worn by the older guard were small enough to fit her feet. The blisters she'd developed wearing the larger pair during the escape had burst and were now a constant reminder of how much she missed her normal body.

Jaxx winced and shifted her pack. She carried her new longbow unstrung, with a quiver of carefully fletched arrows slung low on her back to keep it from irritating the cut on her side. Moth had bound it with strips cut from the bedding they found in the gatehouse after closing the wound with a few stitches. It would scar but unless it became infected, it should soon heal. Brinn had been surprised when she grabbed the bow since most of her people preferred handheld weapons. Von had taught her the secret of bracing the bow along the back of her leg when stringing it and now she could get the loop around the notch in the free end almost as quickly as he could. Like most men, she had a knife at her belt, but she preferred the matched pair of throwing knives now strapped along her upper thighs. Her hand often went to the tail of the ax carried across her back, shifting it so that it would not get caught on the low hanging vines and moss. While in female form it was too heavy for her to handle easily, but she refused to leave it behind. As soon as they reached civilization, she intended to have a priest repair the damage caused when Von tore the earring from her ear and then restore the earring to its normal place, hopefully putting her back into her normal body.

She winced when Raffi and Brinn rose to their feet. The brief rest had done little to ease the cramps and sore muscles in places she had never hurt before. The second sun was slipping behind the southern mountains, leaving the murky grey overcast sky their only source of light. Brinn had allowed them nearly a candlemark of rest, but it could have been all night and it would not have been enough.

"Mephib's bloody bones! It starting to rain." Raffi shifted his pack from his back to his head, hoping to keep the water out of his face. They walked in silence, Jaxx staying well ahead of the others. For two leagues the path led through open, level, wiregrass-carpeted pine woods; then it wove its way along a downward slope. Soon the straggling pines vanished, replaced by a dense growth of scrub, thick with underbrush, reeds, and brambles. Instead of icy slush, the ground was damp and spongy, with open spaces that could easily be described as sloppy bogs instead of meadows.

Raffi began counting out loud as he walked, naming all the ways he was going to kill the owner of the trading post. Von wondered if he intended to hire a priest to bring the dead man back to life each time but decided it was better to keep his comments to himself.

As they walked along the edge of the wetlands they tried to erase the trail behind them. Once the escape was discovered, there would be a pursuit. They would come on horseback, following what remained of the trail of footprints through the fields. The rain would remove most signs of their passage, but a good tracker only needed a partial sign to follow.

Moth sighed as Brinn began to study the wetlands as they walked. Everyone realized their only chance to avoid their pursuers would be to venture into the swamp itself. This was going to make Raffi impossible to deal with.

"It's going to be dark soon. If we have any hope of finding a decent place to camp for the night we have to go in now. They won't be able to track us after dark, even with a dog. With any luck at all, we can lose them in the swamp." Brinn didn't look any happier about entering the dank morass than Raffi.

"I want to get through the drassted thing as fast as possible," Raffi growled.

Moth looked pensive. "Once we enter there will be no hurry. We will have to pick our way through the maze of' channels until we come to the end of it."

"And avoid becoming somethings dinner." Raffi would never let them forget he had almost been eaten by an anaconda. If Keeyun had not awakened to relieve a full bladder the snake would have suffocated the drunken procurer. Moth secretly believed if he hadn't drunk the entire skin of wine by himself after everyone else fell asleep it would never have been an issue. He had passed out in the grass near the edge of the campsite and been too soused to feel the snake before it had him in his coils.

"The guards may not follow us but that doesn't mean we don't need to keep our eyes and ears open at all times."

Von fell back, allowing Brinn to lead the party along the edge of the wetlands while searching for a likely point in which to enter. He trudged along behind him--always a little to the right--carrying a small but sharp hatchet.

Brinn surprised them all as he passed up a likely looking trail a short distance from where they stopped to rest, instead choosing to enter in an area about a furlough east, that was thickly grown over with twisted cypress and covered in considerable part with shallow water.

"To throw off the scent," Moth explained after noticing Vandal's cocked eyebrow.

They waded across two large spans of shallows before crossing a narrow game trail that ran in the direction he had chosen. The path would be difficult to follow but it was not likely their pursuit would stumble across the trail. A mile or so later they were walking down a narrow deer run. Overhead, heavy boughs of grey-moss hung low to the ground, forcing the group to lean far forward and use their arms to avoid being brushed off into the stagnant water. Spiders abounded, not

the big furry kind that was common in the drylands west of
Hyperion, these were small, red, and unafraid. Their bite wasn't
poisonous, but it stung and then itched for days, especially in
the tender spots on the back of the neck or the skin of the
wrist.

Vondal had never been in, much less thought about having to spend a night in a swamp; and the prospect of it now,
under the existing circumstances, was little less than comforting. Even with the torches, they had fashioned out of limbs
and strips of cloth, it was difficult to see more than a few feet
away. Shortly after sunset, they reached a tract of sandy land
dotted with clumps of palmettos, where the ground was firm
and thickly covered with wiregrass that he thought a likely
place to camp but the others insisted they keep walking.

Moth tried to explain. "No use grumbling boy. Once the
moons go down every grass eater in the swamp will head to the
clearing. And right behind them will be everything that eats the
grass eaters. If we are in the grass, we are on the menu."

When Brinn looked around a small clearing at the top of
a small hummock a short time later and declared it was about
as good as it was going to get, he eagerly dropped his pack and
collapsed against a handy stone.

Jaxx rolled her eyes and dropped her pack beside his, then looked around hoping to find some wood that was dry enough to burn. Spotting a termite-infested tree that had fallen against the vee of a stunted oak, she waded out to it and chopped a large limb free. After tossing it to Raffi, she removed two more pieces before slogging back to dry land.

Brinn had a small fire going and was heating some water to make kafka. While she was gathering wood, Moth had gone hunting and had somehow managed to shoot a plump chumuck. Now he was smearing a thick coat of mud over the fur. Once he had the rodent coated, he lay it on the fire atop the coals to bake. It would take a while to cook, but the fire-hardened mud would keep it from burning.

Dry wood appeared to be very scarce and the prospect of keeping the small fire burning throughout the night was more than doubtful.

"Looks like we are going to need more wood. I'm going to walk back along the trail and see if I can find another dead tree." Jaxx wanted an excuse to get away from the others, if only for a few moments. She was having trouble adjusting to her new body. The change had done more than altar her outward appearance, her emotional swings were running wild and she didn't want to break into tears in front of Vondal.

"Don't go far, it will be dark soon and most of the denizens of the swamp would consider you a tender delicacy." Brinn's lips quirked at the annoyed expression on her face. It had to be hard on the young man. He had no idea how he would handle the idea of being a female, but he didn't think it would go well. But it could be worse, he could be an ugly woman. Of course, saying that to the distraught young man would probably earn him a kick to the cods.

Backtracking along the trail they had followed to reach the campsite didn't take long. Jaxx walked back toward the dry area filled with salt grass. She remembered spotting a dead tree beyond the trail leaving the main meadow. She was walking faster than she should have been, trying to make it back to camp before dark, comforted by Moths earlier comments about it being too cold and too early in spring for cottonmouths and bull gators to be out of hibernation. Using her free hand to push a low handing bough out of the way, she stepped into the clearing, coming face to face with a large black bear who was enjoying a snack of the sweet and tender shoots growing from the taproot of a young palmetto plant. She screamed and the half-grown bear, who seemed as surprised as she was, bolted and ran, crashing loudly through the tangle of underbrush. She took a few deep breaths to calm her jangled nerves, then began chopping at the dead tree.

Back at the camp, Raffi suddenly sat up very straight, listening intently. Without a word of explanation, he grabbed his sword and walked off into the swamp, following the same trail Jaxx had followed. He was gone before Von and Brinn realized he was missing.

"You see Raffi leave," Brinn asked Moth.

"Yes. He heard a scream, went to check on Jaxx. Sounded like a big cat to me. Nothing to worry about."

"Nothing?" Von asked.

"If the lynx were after her, he would not have made a sound. If it was her scream, its already too late to do anything. We wait. Raffi will be back soon. He doesn't like being away from camp after dark. Claims he can't see the snakes."

Jaxx took one final chop at the dead tree and sat down on the remaining stump. She figured she had enough wood to keep the fire going for most of the night. There had been a few larger pieces of wood near the campsite that could be placed on the fire while still damp, the wood would dry from the heat and keep burning. She strapped up the bundle of dry wood with a short piece of rope, making it easier to carry, then reached for her hand ax and began to rise.

"Don't move." Raffi's hissed warning caught her by surprise.

Of course, she immediately began to turn to see what was wrong, thinking the bear might have come back. It wasn't a bear. Three wild pigs stood less than ten feet away and unlike the bear, they did not appear inclined to run away. The boar gnashed his tusks and shook his head before digging his front hoofs into the damp soil. He rocked his body toward her, then backed a few inches and started the head shake again. His sharply curved tusks looked to be longer than her hand and as big around as her thumb. She was holding her body completely still about halfway to her feet, an uncomfortable position. But she knew if she moved the boar would attack.

"I told you to stay still." Raffi's voice came from a few feet behind her.

"I'm not sure how long I can stay in this position."

"Well, if he charges, I'm not sure I can kill it before it gets to you. Those tusks can gut a man before he has time to scream."

"I don't think screaming will be a problem. I've already tested it on a bear."

"That explains the yelp earlier. You got a good grip on that ax?"

"Yeah. Why?"

"Because he's about through with the foreplay and ready to bring this standoff to a climax."

About then the young boar decided he had worked himself up to a fierce rage in front of his sows'. He did one final rock back on his heels and charged directly at Jaxx. Jaxx swung the hand ax overhead, slamming the blade down between the eyes of the wild pig. He stumbled, going to his knees, hurt, but no means close to death. Jaxx jerked on the ax free, but the boar slashed her arm as she pulled away. Her foot was up against the bundle of wood and the boar was up against her, his weight preventing her from rising to her feet. He rocked back on his rear hoofs, preparing to drive his tusks into her again. That's when Raffi drove his sword into his spine directly behind his head.

Jaxx collapsed back to the ground, fighting to get the heavy animal off so she could stand again. The two sows went back to foraging as though the boar had never existed. After watching her struggle a few minutes Raffi lent a hand; he was after all, still a gentleman.

While Raffi butchered the hog, Jaxx chopped up the center of a pine stump and made a bundle of fat lighter wood splinters to go in her pack for kindling. The oil in the pith caught quickly, even in damp weather. She wrapped it in a scrap of burlap she'd found in the pocket of the tunic she was wearing and slid it into the pocket. Carrying the hatchet in her right hand and the bundle of firewood under her left arm she followed Raffi who carried the fresh pork hindquarters. He didn't bother cleaning up the mess, knowing the scavengers would make short work of the remains. By morning there would be nothing but bones left to show where the pig had died.

The sun was completely down and the swamp was dark and full of hidden watchers by the time they spotted the campfire.

Von had resorted to staring into the darkness as though Jaxx would return faster if she knew was watching for her. He finally relaxed when he heard their voices approaching the camp.

Raffiel was carrying something heavy on each shoulder, panting from the weight as he walked. Instead of talking, he went straight to the fire and cast his burden down, turning again without a word and going back to his bedroll.

"Roast pork," Brinn said with a grin. The duck would not be ready for candlemarks.

He took one of the leg quarters Raffi had carried, rinsed it off with some of the water, and carried it over to the fire. Earlier he had cut the y's out of two branches, using them to hold the duck above the hot coals. He replaced the duck with one of the thigh bones; the second leg was cut into narrow strips. Everyone jostled for places near the quarter Brinn was cutting up, taking the slices from the fat swine, suspending them from the points of long sticks and holding them close to the coals until done. This frantic behavior lasted until their immediate hunger was satisfied. They were glad enough to feast upon the flesh of the boar, although it was greasy and could have used a little salt. The meat of the leg would provide them with morning feast and they could carry the rest along for an afternoon meal. Fresh meat was never served in the prison.

Now that their stomachs were full, Vondal decided it was

the perfect time to have that conversation with Jaxx they had both been avoiding. Jaxx had found a reasonably dry spot close to the fire and had stretched out, holding her booted feet in the warmth in hopes of drying the damp leather.

Von dropped down beside her. " How's your arm."

Jaxx shrugged. "It's sore. Not as sore as my side but I know it's there."

"You do seem to be taking a lot of damage."

"Everything is different. Nothing in my body works the way I'm used to. Even my balance is off."

"Yeah…your body is …." Von struggled for the words, unsure how he should bring the subject up.

Jaxx seemed to know what was coming. Her eyes darkened and she appeared to be considering her words before she answered. She debated over continuing his punishment, but in truth, all her irritation had faded candlemarks before. Still, it would not be smart to give in so easily. Finally, she took a deep breath and began speaking.

"My body? That's all you are concerned with," she replied frostily. Jaxx's words and the crisp businesslike way she uttered them, cut through Von's confidence like a knife.

"Ugh…" He suddenly felt the urge to watch a hawk flying

overhead.

"So, it's going to be like that, is it? Since when have we started avoiding a straight answer? I thought we were better friends than that."

"A straight answer? All right. The truth is, I don't know how I feel about my brother being my drassted sister!"

"I'm not your sister. I'm still the same person, just look a little different right now," she blurted out. " I wasn't exactly given a lot of choice in the matter."

"Harrumph," he replied. Five cycles on a ship remember? It's not as if you didn't have plenty of opportunities to mention it. It's not exactly something that slips your mind."

Jaxx sighed. "I know you are angry. I can't blame you. It's something I should never have kept from you. To be honest, I had no intention of removing the earring. It has been almost thirty turns since the one time I changed." She held her hand out and looked at it, noticing the soft skin and long slender fingers, so different from his usual thick calloused hands and swollen knuckles.

"Thirty turns. That's a long time."

"Not long enough, in my opinion. I am perfectly happy to remain a man. Not that I'm going to have any choice in the matter now."

Von's eyes went to Raffiel who was sitting across the fire sharpening his sword with the whetstone he had taken from one of the dead guards. "Do all Duaar change like that?"

Jaxx laughed. "No. Only the cursed ones. It started a long time ago. No one is sure who was the first. My father tried to explain it. Once every generation a child is born that has both male and female aspects. It is called the Chimera Curse. It shows up at birth when the newborn randomly shifts back and forth until it decides what sex it wants to be. Once it decides, it remains in its dominant form until puberty. From that point onward, the change is stimulated by different things."

Different things?"

"Stress, fear, the lunar cycle. My father didn't know a lot about it. His older brother was a Chimera. When he died without an heir everyone thought the curse died with him, guess they were wrong."

"So, tell me more about this. Will you stay a woman?"

That was a question I hadn't given much thought. Since I was a child, I had worn the earring. What if my natural form was a woman? Could I handle that?

"No. I will change back to my normal self in a few days.

However, from this point forward, I have no way of knowing when the change will come upon me. My father says it is random, often happening in moments of stress or anger." His face twisted sourly as his eyes darkened. "He also mentioned the possibility of it happening during moments of passion. He stressed the possibility of embarrassing confrontations if it happens at the wrong moment."

"You mean you could start as a woman and finish as a man?" Von's face looked like he had eaten something rotten as he tried to wrap his mind around the image Jaxx's words had put into his mind.

Jaxx rolled her eyes. " No. At least I don't think so. I might go to sleep a woman and wake up in my normal body. It is random. It could happen the same night I changed or a fortnight from now. I guess it could last until the next owl moons, no one has ever mentioned it to me."

"So how did you keep it a secret on the ship? I think I would have noticed something like that during the last five turns."

"It didn't happen. My father saw how upset I was when I changed for the first time. He brought an artificer to my room. The artificer attached the earring, using magic to seal the metal so it could not be removed. Since then the ring has always prevented the change. I do not know if it will work again, even if I can figure out a way to have my ear healed around it. But I need you to understand, from this point forward, I have no way of knowing when the change will come upon me." She paused, gathering her thoughts. "I don't know if the spell was broken when the earring was torn from my ear. Until I find another mage capable of replacing it, I have no control over what might happen."

"Its gonna take me a while to get used to having a sister and brother at the same time, but no one said family life was easy."

Jaxx nodded but did not say anything, choosing to let the matter drop for the time being. Omission's owl moon only happened once every three lunar circuits. He looked up at the twin orbs overhead. One moon waned faster than the other one, so they no longer looked like two eyes in the middle of the night. They should be back in Hyperion long before the next pair appear. With any luck at all, this will be the only time either man had to deal with the curse.

Von continued to clean his sword as Jaxx talked. There was no way he was going to throw away five cycles of friendship over a stupid curse. He would need to learn how to think before he spoke. Maybe Brinn had some tips to share. One thing kept nagging at him since the night they escaped. How had Raffiel known that Jaxx would change if the earring was removed?

"Do you ever think it's a bit fortuitous that they show up in the same cell?" Jaxx asked as she dropped the leafy scrub she'd pulled to sleep on. All five men had a makeshift bedroll, pieced together from the blankets they had found in the barracks, but the ground was cold and wet. Brinn, Moth, and the surly Duaar Raffi had camped a few feet ahead of Von and Jaxx; far enough for them to be unheard while they were talking.

Von shook his head. "I think you are feeling overly emotional because your body is still adapting to being female. Not everyone is out to stab you in the back. This group is our best chance of getting home; it's not as if we have many options to choose from."

"Well, I am still going to keep an eye on them. My father always said; if it stinks, then you had better start looking for the dead rat. Those three smell wrong; they are hiding something and I for one intend to be prepared." Jaxx snatched her ax with one hand and her mug with the other. She finished her kafka with one long gulp and then said in disgust, "This skeptical female intends to sleep with one eye open." Jaxx's scowl did little to hide her feelings; indicating that if she had her way, the two friends would be traveling alone.

"Let it go Jaxx," Von replied with a laugh. " We need to concentrate on getting off this island." He stood watching his friend until the darkness swallowed her up; before returning to his bed. He lay there for a while, thinking about what Jaxx had said. He had mentioned his father more while they were talking than during the five cycles he had known him. Now that he thought about it, he realized he didn't know much about Jaxx's family at all. He wondered what other unimportant details his friend had forgotten to mention. When Jaxx finally returned and stretched out on his bedroll, he relaxed and fell asleep.

From the shadows nearby Raffi rose up and silently made his way back to where Brinn and Moth were waiting.

"Anything we need to be concerned with?" Brinn asked.

"Jaxx thinks we are hiding something but he's unsure what it may be. He thinks you might be working for Von's uncle, someone called Lord Botherton."

"Von is Lord Botherton's nephew! That is something

unexpected. And potentially dangerous if the sorceress is involved. I don't want to make Izabal mad."

"I think you would make a handsome housecat," Moth said, then ducked as Brinn tossed a stick his way.

"I'll leave it up to you to decide what happens next," Raffi said. "I think the boys are as suspicious of us, as we are of them. Von is still trying to come to grips with what his partner is. He still has no idea who she is."

"Let's leave it that way for now," Brinn answered. "Once we leave the island it won't be an issue. For now, we concentrate on getting home to Ornatar."

"As long as we pass through Hyperion. I intend to make a stop on the way home to visit a certain trader."

Moth had cast a spell to ward the area. The ward would alert them to anyone approaching their hidden campsite while they were sleeping. This would not prevent them from being found, however, it would awaken them in time for them to be prepared for the visitor, be it man or beast.

Jaxx was sick of talking about it. Everyone wanted to discuss what had happened with no concern about how it made her feel. It took all her concentration to stay calm since the change; if they kept digging and digging into her past life she could snap. She had forgotten how much she hated the way people acted around her; the magical earring had been in her ear since she'd left the hold thirty-three turns ago.

Changing for the first time after so many cycles had been painful. Physically she was feeling much better. Her father had explained the necessity of the change to him as a child before he matured into an adult. Puberty stimulated the change and it could be extremely painful, depending on the amount of testosterone in the body. Jaxx had been one of the early changers. The timing of the change could not have been worse. It had not been easy to explain to the girl's father why she had run screaming from the barn. She grinned, thinking back. Her father had instructed his mage to attach the earring the next day. He had been warned that the earring should not be worn over a long period of time; that there were certain hormones his body needed that were only produced in his female form. Until Von removed the earring, she had no idea what her father had meant. Now her mind was being flooded by emotional responses; something the normally stoic Duaar rarely experienced. On the other hand, she no longer experienced the horrific headaches that always followed the owl moons. The hardest thing was accepting the idea of being she, instead of he, in her mind. She had been trying to think of herself as a woman but occasionally she slipped. As difficult as it was on her, she was certain it had to be much harder for Vondal to deal with all the changes.

She pulled her cape tightly around her and tried to get some sleep.

Chapter 10

The small group was up and moving as the first red rays of the smaller of Omissions twin suns were breaking through the hazy fog that was everywhere in the swamp. After a quick morning fest of cold pork and thin corncakes Brinn baked on a flat stone, the set out in the direction of the coast.

For about a league they made good time following the game path that led them through open, level, wiregrass-carpeted hardwoods. Gradually the ground began to grow wet and spongy. Straggling pines were succeeded by a dense growth of thick underbrush, reeds, and brambles. Open spaces were often little more than sloppy bogs. The larger sycamore and elms near the outskirts were replaced by scrub pinelands and stunted water oaks with long exposed roots that gave them an eerie look.

Brinn had been leading the way. The path was often mired with mud or shallow water but by high sun it opened out into a higher stretch of sandy ground encircled by fallen trees and stumps rising above the water level. They found themselves on the shore of a wide-open area of wetlands about the size of a small lake. It didn't seem to be very deep but most of the surface was hidden by clumps of some kind of green grass and waterlilies. Wild birds, duck, geese, and other waterfowl were occupied with dining on the vegetation and the smaller inhabitants of the lowlands, minnows and tadpoles could be seen swimming below the surface of the crystal clear water.

Vondal immediately strung his bow, eager to claim a duck or two for their dinner. He skirted more than half the way around the lake, creeping forward stealthily before he sighted a flock of ducks within range. In his excitement he fired too quickly, shooting three times before he finally killed one as the rest of the ducks fluttered away unharmed. To make matters worse, he had to wade up to his waist in the watery sedge to retrieve it. Struggling out of the water with his prize, he retrieved his equipment and returned to where the others waited.

Moth took a look at the solitary duck and sadly shook his head. With five hungry mouths to feed, one duck would not go far. The one he had shot the morning before had barely made a dent in their hunger. Raffi's pig was almost gone. In the gatehouse, they had found a small supply of meal, dried beans, and a few apples but there had been little on hand to scavenge.

The only meat had been a dried out piece of a roasted deer and they had immediately shared it out between them.

Beyond this last dry sanctuary, the land grew wetter and the shallow mirk we walked through branched into a maze of confusing channels, leading deep into the heart of the swamp.

"Looks like we are going to get wet," Brinn stated as he dropped his pack against a tree stump.

Raffi threw a large limb toward the center of the clearing and dropped his pack beside it. "Never thought I would miss Keeyun, but its times like this, that it would be handy having a druid around."

"Don't think we need a druid to tell us we need to keep moving west until the water stops. We will get to the end of the swamp in a day or two."

Vondal was so sure. The vegetation was at some points so dense it was penetrable only by walking where wild animals had made their trails. The trail they had been following wound through a patch of thorny brambles. Some of the briars were an inch thick with sharp thorns adding to the discomfort and difficulty of forcing a passage. Everywhere they stepped the ground was wet. Most of it was boggy, but today they had noticed an increase in the amount of land covered with water.

Most of the water was dark and murky and when you stepped you never knew if the depth was two inches or two feet. Once Raffi had stepped into a quagmire, dropping half his length in the runny mud. It had taken all four to pull his body from the mire. Several times today the hand hatchet Jaxx had claimed in the storage room had been put to use clearing a pathway before they could move forward a step. All five men began to bitterly regret their decision to force their way through the rotting morass.

The short rest did little to improve their outlook. As the shadows deepened the nearby marsh became cold and unfriendly, with the trees adding an eerily menacing appearance. Heavy dew lay on the ground and a thick mist was rising from among the trees. A pale globe was rising over the treetops, providing faint illumination to the group sitting around the fire. From behind a shadowy bush, two amber eyes gleamed a steady unblinking gaze that drew the attention of the friends.

"Probably something looking for food," Brinn chuckled as Von shifted his back to the fire. "This is probably one of the better places to look for grazing animals."

"Then keep that torch away from me, I don't want to be night blind if it decides to add one of us to the menu."

Three days later Vondal lay on his pallet talking to Jaxx, trying to still his overactive imagination and sleep, but he would jump at every sound made in the brush. He was certain it was simply some hungry restless forest dweller, bird, or beast looking for its dinner. But his mind insisted on filling the gloom about them with nameless and sometimes fearful shapes from stories heard in his childhood. At the slightest rustle of leaves in the night breeze in the leaves, he would wake up and listen.

"Thought I heard something!" Von muttered. He heard a stealthy footfall, then another and another, suggesting that an animal of some size was guardedly encircling the camp. The sounds appeared to come from points little more than thirty feet away.

"Bullfrogs croaking," Jaxx answered. "Go back to sleep. You're getting jumpy."

"That's not bullfrogs, that's gators calling out to one another. It sounds like they are encircling the camp."

Jaxx laughed. "I have never heard of gators working together. What you probably heard was the animals that normally graze in this meadow trying to find a place they can eat without us seeing them."

"I don't think its …" The sound of a twig snapping made Von turn to look, in time to see the arrow hit him in the left arm. "Attack! I don't know what the hells it is, but the slitches are shooting at me," he screamed as he dove for his sword. His unexpected movement made the second arrow miss him completely. Instead, the sharp arrowhead embedded into the stump Moth was sitting on. He grabbed the shaft of the arrow in his arm and jerked it out, wincing at the pain as the head was withdrawn. That was a mistake. Blood sprayed on his hand, making it difficult to grip the sword. He wiped his palm on his shirt and turned to see if the archer was still within range. The thing with the bow had moved his position in the darkness and he needed to figure out where it was. Their skin color blended into the shadowy underbrush, making it even harder to spot them.

Jaxx was facing a second attacker, short sword in hand. The bizarre creature began to move slowly around her, waving its chipped obsidian blade in a complicated pattern designed to distract her from the matching blade it carried in its other hand. One minute they were warily eyeing each other, the next they were engaged. Blades clashed, once, then twice, and then

Jaxx lunged forward, shifting her weight into a roll that brought her blade up and over the attackers' head. Instinctively the oversized lizard reacted, throwing both its knives up to block her downward stroke. Jaxx wasted no time slamming the punch blade she'd been hiding in her off-hand into its throat. She ripped the short blade across and out, stepping back to avoid the fountain of blood as it slipped to the ground at her feet.

Raffi was pulling one of his blades from the eye of a dead lizard. He used the dead creatures' loin wrap to wipe the blood off his blade and turned to seek another target. Over by the fire, Brinn was still fighting with his assailant, but the scaled humanoid was tiring under the old warrior's onslaught. When Brinn slammed the hilt of his sword against the glassy stone knife, the blade shattered, cutting the hand of the beast. First shock and then panic, filled its amber-yellow eyes.

"Cover your eyes," Moth yelled before a brilliant flash lit the small clearing brighter than the sunniest summer day. The disarmed lizard Brinn was fighting squealed like a dying pig as the flare blinded him. Brinn wasted no time thrusting his sword deep into the stomach and out the other side. The dying brute sank to its knees, holding his stomach as its life fluids leaked out onto the ground. In seconds he was face-down in the mud.

Raffi spotted the archer Vondal had lost sight of trying to clear his vision as he notched another arrow. He called out "Von! Drop!" before he tossed two razor-sharp knives, one right after the other. Both blades sank deep into their target. The dying archer released the arrow, missing Von by seconds. It flew to the right of Moth, who had cast the only defensive spell he had studied that day, startling him into the muck beyond the stump. In minutes, the attack was over and if any of the unusual lizards remained, they had decided it was not worth a second assault.

"Anyone hurt?" Jaxx asked as she studied the swamp surrounding the sandy hummock they were camped atop. She had seen the arrow Von took in the shoulder, but the bleeding was under control.

Brinn held up his forearm, showing the shallow slice he had received above his wrist. "It's shallow but hurts. Hope he didn't have anything on his blade."

"I might have sprained my ankle," Moth said. "I slipped in the mud." He removed a recalcitrant weed that refused to untangle from his long blonde hair. The muddy sludge had stained his pale silver hair a muddy reddish-brown. Moth hated to be dirty. Being covered from head to toe with the rotting muck floating below the surface of the stagnant water was un-acceptable torture. He cursed whoever had his spellbook and made a mental promise to add a cleanup spell to his traveling chest when he got home. Getting his spellbook copied wasn't cheap but being without one had shown him how important a backup was.

"Didn't think it was some kind of fashion statement," Raffi replied. He tossed Moth a scrap of cloth leftover from the tunic they had used to make a bandage for Jaxx earlier. At the rate they were going through bandages, they were going to be naked before they got off the island.

Everyone was gathered around the dead assailant, trying to decide what it was that had attacked them. Like a gator, it had thick skin and was scaled, with a mouthful of razor-sharp teeth. But it walked upright. And it had webbed feet and hands like a frog.

"So, what are these things?" Jaxx asked. "Some kind of Gyth?"

"No, the Gyth are skinny. And they never go anywhere without their armor. Besides, I have never seen a Gyth with a tail. These things are more reptilian and primitive; see, no metal, only chipped stone blades." Brinn was puzzled too.

"Well they are too tall to be Trogs," Raffi added, "and they don't stink. If you ever smelled one, you will never forget the odor. All it takes is one whiff. I ain't never felt that sick before."

"Whatever the drassted lizards are, they can't be that many of them. This swamp's not big enough for more than one tribe and we killed five of them. We are probably camped near their village, or nest, or whatever they call where they live. They will regroup and be back. We need to pack up now and be ready to move on as soon as its light enough to see where we are walking."

But no one was looking forward to wading through the waist-deep water knowing, besides the snakes and gators there might be another hungry mouth waiting below the surface. This one was intelligent.

Chapter 11

Raffi spotted the smoke before the second sun began its descent beyond the distant mountains. He pointed it out to Moth who brought it to Brinn's attention. Smoke could mean two things, a campfire, or a farmstead. Before the Lizard men's attack, they would have automatically assumed it was humans. Now they were not so sure.

Jaxx sighed. She wanted a bath. Until she had experienced the filth in the swamp, she had considered Moth's penchant for cleanliness something of a joke. In his normal body, he would not have given the dirt second thought. Now he skin itched, her clothes stank and she could not get comfortable. The idea of being forced to remain like this haunted her dreams. There had to be a way to get clean.

"What should we do," Von asked.

"I don't know about you, but I don't want to spend another night in a tree. There's got to be dry land nearby. I'm willing to fight for it." Raffiel began trudging through the muck.

Brinn grinned. " I heard lizard tastes like chicken. I'm

hungry enough to try it out."

Jaxx rolled her eyes but she did not succeed in hiding the smile on her face.

Everyone broke out laughing. This helped release some of the tension that had been building. The hummock was barely large enough for them all to have a dry spot to rest. There was no place to stretch out so stopping for the night wasn't a choice. They had to keep moving.

Von shrugged and followed Raffi, sinking first to the knee, then to the waist, in slimy moss, mud, and stagnant water. The others followed.

Moth tried not to let any trace of the disgust he felt show as he trudged along behind the others. His homeland was farther west and much colder than the island. Snow fell and did not melt until the planting season. There was occasionally mud after rainfall but he had never experienced a swamp until he hooked up with Brinn. If he had his way in the future they would never have to enter one again.

The ground gradually firmed up until there was an easily followed path less than an inch below the surface of the water. More than likely this land was dry most of the cycle. They could tell by the roots; the trees were not normally underwater.

Felling exuberant they pushed forward, wading through the shallow water, for about a hundred yards, before they reached the firmer soil and tufts of saw grass they had spotted from the other side of the thicket. The exhausted group collapsed to the ground, ready to stretch out for the first time in three days. It had taken five days to cross the swamp, double what they had estimated. They could see the smoke through the trees, but they were far enough away that no one could see them through the bushes and groundcover. Their initial impulse was to rush over and check out the smoke, but Brinn decided they were too tired to risk an unnecessary fight. They would spend the night where they were and check it out in the morning.

Chapter 12

Raffiel crouched in the knee-high grass at the edge of the woods and studied the old man and his wife as they went about their morning activities. Beyond the edge of the woods rose a dilapidated old barn, its roof shingles badly curled by the weather. The man was hitching a swaybacked mule to a cart in which he had loaded several baskets of eggs. He went into the barn and came out carrying a small cage filled with chickens. Since there were about twenty hens in the yard and most had chicks following them as they foraged, he figured they were cockerels or older hens past their laying prime. He edged the mule around the hens, stopping long enough to have a short conversation with the old woman. Something she said must have upset him because he began whipping her; striking her across the back and shoulders with the long supple stick he used on the mule. Raffiel watched in horror as he laid it on heavily, ignoring his victim's piteous cries. She curled up into a ball, protecting her face. With a final curse, he kicked her twice before he climbed back in the cart and set off down the road in the direction they hoped led to a port city.

After he was out of sight she rose from the ground, dusted herself off, and returned to her laundry. Raffi watched the old woman as she built a fire and set a heavy cauldron of water on it to heat. Then she went into the house, returning with her arms full of linen faded by cycles of use like the dress she wore. There was a small hound curled up on the porch, more a companion than a guard. Once he was satisfied that there was no one else around that might threaten the five escapees, he slipped back into the heavier undergrowth and made his way back to where others waited.

"Seems to be exactly as it looks, farmers. Mostly chickens though I did see a couple of turkeys and a few goats. The old man left in his cart with a load, heading to market is my guess. He's something of a brute, beat his wife while I was watching. Won't no one miss him." Raffi did not attempt to hide the disgust as he spoke. His eyes darkened and his hand dropped to the pommel of the knife he wore at his side.

Brinn shook his head. "No killing. I will go talk to her. We need to know if they are still looking for us." He turned to

Von, "You come with me."

"Why Von? Moth usually goes with you," Raffi was puzzled. Brinn had been spending a lot of time talking with the boy and that was unusual. Not that he thought Von was seeking Moths position. Moth had been second in command for almost ten cycles. Brinn never did anything without an ulterior motive. Usually, that motive was clear. This time he wasn't sure what Brinn had in mind. Before he could ask, Brinn answered his unspoken question.

"Von can pass for a native. Sides' you said it is an old woman. Women like a pretty face. Anyone seeing Moth will know he's either be from the mines or the prison."

Raffi's eyes went directly to Jaxx who was sitting quietly, a strange expression on her face.

Jaxx was thinking about what Brinn had said. Jaxx had heard women describe Vondal as ruggedly attractive instead of handsome, especially after Nikkia's fathers' paid assassins scarred his eye. Now, with his face graced by a week's growth of whiskers, wind savaged hair and rain-slicked clothing, he looked like something fresh from a doting mother's worst nightmare. That she did not find him attractive confirmed her belief that her natural form was male.

She didn't look any better. Between the guards torn tunic, the oversized boots, and her hair full of mud and twigs, her appearance was even shoddier. To make matters worse, her slender and shorter stature had forced her to trudge through the bulk of the wet overgrowth with the vast majority of the limbs being head high. Her face was a mass of purple striped bruises, but at least they would fade in a day or two. It had been almost a full week since the escape, and she was still uncomfortable in certain situations. Like sitting down to void her bladder.

"No one knows about Jaxx. I intend to keep it that way. When we get to the barn, I want her to stay out of sight." Brinn looked at Moth but he was not paying attention to their conversation.

Moth decided to stay out of the conversation. He knew feared Raffi might be forced to shave his highly prized beard if he hoped to clear up the tangled mess. It was possible a bath might help, but doubtful. Brinn did not look much better. He wielded a clever tongue. It was unlikely he would find a situation he couldn't talk his way out of.

Raffi shot Brinn a puzzled look and muttered a few words under his breath, but he settled back down as he walked toward the tree line with Vondal following him.

Crossing the field, the pair approached the tumbledown building from the barn side away from where the others waited. At the back of the house, the middle-aged woman vigorously scrubbed her laundry against a washboard in an old tin washtub. Every so often she would dunk it in a tub of fresh water to rinse and then either return it to the washtub or add it to a pile to be wrung and hung on a line. She dipped a pan of hot water out of the cauldron and poured in the washtub then began scrubbing again.

She watched as we approached, appearing neither surprised nor afraid to see two strange men come out of the swamp.

"You be strangers hereabouts," the woman observed.

"Yes, we come from Hyperion," Brinn replied. He signaled Von to put his knife away while she was talking with him. Von slipped it into his belt under the cape.

"You hain't been in the swamp?" She used a board to pick up the end of a quilt and began rinsing it in the cooler water as if she saw it happen every day.

"Well, yes, we took a wrong turn and ended up there."

"I am thinking you might be the reason so many horses be riding up and down the road the last few days." She smiled, revealing a mouth full of broken teeth. "You best be coming inside now; it's coming on midday. The men from the mines should be passing by soon."

"You aren't afraid they will stop in and check?"

"I was born in this house. Hain`t no one ever come out of the swamp before you. They hain't no reason for them to think anyone will today."

She hung the last of her laundry on the line before motioning for them to follow her into the house. Before entering she turned and asked, "do you want to invite the rest of your party inside?"

"No, thank you. I think they are fine where they are for now."

She nodded and then added, "well, you might want to send the young one out to warn them away from the barn. Sometimes the men stop and let their horses drink from the water trough. If they got dogs with 'em, you don't want them gittin' hep up."

Brinn silently agreed to her words. "Von, go warn them to pull back to the edge of the swamp, just in case. I will be fine here." He followed her into the cabin and settled into a comfortable lounging position in a chair in the kitchen.

The old woman put a clean apron on over the loose-fitting cotton dress. Opening a small cupboard, she took down two mugs and poured kafka for them. The scent of the steaming hot beverage made Brinn's mouth water after a week without it. She set a small pitcher of cream on the table next to a jar of honey, then added a loaf of fresh bread and some cheese. "I am thinking you might be a bit peckish. You boys like eggs? That's one thing we have plenty of." Without waiting for his reply, she set an enormous frying pan on the fire to heat. There was a basket full of eggs on the floor, she took about half, breaking them into the pan once it was warm enough and began stirring the eggs as they cooked.

"Won't your husband notice the eggs missing?"

She laughed. "That ignorant fool wouldn't notice a snake in his lap until it bit him. He has no idea how many eggs come through this kitchen. Sides, he ain't my husband. My husband died in the mines, cycles ago. Olford showed up one day, saying he was moving in. He worked at the prison until he got where he couldn't do his job." Her eyes grew dark and filled with unshed tears. "After a while, I gave up fighting him."

Brinn's hand clenched under the table. It was easy to understand what she was leaving out of her words. She filled a bowl up with the eggs, added a loaf of bread and a hunk of cheese. "When you finish your meal, take this out to the ones waiting. I heard Olford talking to one of the searchers. Said there were five of you, this should be enough for them all."

She stopped talking as the dog on the porch began barking. As she said, he could see several men watering their horses out by the barn. "I best be talking to them. Might think somethings wrong if I don't come out." She picked up a basket full of clothing and walked back out to her scrub board. After dumping the dirty clothes in the tub, she used the big stick to stir them around, before pulling the first wet item into the soap water. As she began scrubbing it against the washboard, two men came over and spoke for a moment before returning to their horses. Brinn counted eight horses and three dogs as they rode away. She continued with her wash for almost a candle mark before hanging up the last item and returning to the house.

"They are still looking for you. Something got the Wastaii upset. They attacked one of the search parties in the swamp even though they had a Wastaii tracker with them. You wouldn't know anything about that, would you?"

"These Wastaii, they would not be lizard men, would

they?" he shifted uncomfortably when she nodded. "We had a run-in with a group of them. Killed about eight."

She nodded. "That would do it. Eight scouts is a lot to lose at one time. The remaining men will have to take the windows as second wives. They reproduce quickly but it will be a few cycles before the tribe is back to full strength. They will be looking for whoever killed their men."

"I hope it won't cause you a problem."

Her eye lost focus as she gazed into the distance, obviously thinking seriously about what he said. "Can't say as it would not be worse to die quickly instead of day by day," she said sadly. Her eyes widened and she appeared nervous for a moment. "I thought I saw a ghost for a moment." A knock on the door of the cabin made her jump. Then a soft voice called out, "Is it alright for me to come in?"

The old woman paled and began shaking.

Brinn stood and walked toward the door. "Fear not, he means you no harm. That's Moth, one of my men. He was born in a country far from here, a very cold land, that stays covered in snow and ice cycle round. All the people there have pale skin and white hair. I assure you he is very much alive."

He opened the door and spoke with Moth, then passed

him the basket with the food she had prepared.

Moth bowed. "Thank you, good mother, this is much appreciated. Raffiel has begun eyeing your hens. I was unsure how much longer I could keep him away." He nodded to Brinn and made his way back to the thicket where the others waited.

"You might want to be joining him. The old buzzard will be returning from the market soon. He might not be alone. His friends often stop by for a meal and a game of Pakur. Wait until dark and follow the road. You should see the city lit by the twin moons." She paused, thinking. "The guard will be watching for strangers. Stick to the south as you approach and make for the fishing shacks. You might find some there that are willing to help you. Most of the women have lost husbands or sons to the mines."

"Are you sure you won't come with us," he said, then wondered what impulse had driven him to offer.

A winsome smile softened her wizened features, "Tempting as the offer is, my place is here. Knowing I helped you evade Taggard's blackguards is reward enough. One night soon I will find Olford indisposed from too much ale and take my vengeance. Then I will sit on my porch and wait for the reaper to arrive. My time nears."

She stood on the porch and watched as he walked away, a whetstone in one hand and a butcher knife in the other. Once he disappeared from sight, she sat down and began sharpening her blade.

Chapter 13

Trattoria was a coastal city nestled in a hollow on the plains, beneath the shadow of the Misty Blue Mountains and was rarely remarked upon except by those who lived or visited there. Once it was a thriving settlement enjoying bountiful prosperity. Prosperity based on the supply of iron and copper mined in the nearby mountain range. Thanks to a steady onslaught of raids by Tabruk bandits, it was now home to a widely scattered and sparse population of small farm homesteads. And of course, one of the most widely condemned prisons in the kingdom.

It was late the following afternoon when the weary travelers stood on a rise outside of town looking down on the cities market-place.

"One of us needs to go into town and find out if anyone is looking for us." Vondal turned and looked at Jaxx as he spoke, making it evident he wanted her to volunteer.

"By one of us, I take it you mean me," she said.

"You are the only the best choice. No one will be looking

for a woman," Moth added. "It would be foolish to believe the city guards have not received orders for our arrest."

"Can't Moth cast some kind of spell and make one of you look like a woman? I would prefer to have a backup."

"Sorry. Moth doesn't have his spellbook. So that's out of the question. Jaxx is our best bet."

Von hated to admit it but Brinn was correct. They would have Jaxx's description as a six-foot-three man, not a five-foot-ten woman. They might think it unusual to see a woman carrying a sword but not so unusual that it would attract the city guard's attention. "Try not to get arrested."

Raffi laughed. "Don't worry about getting arrested, try not to kill anyone foolish enough to grab that fine arse." Brinn joined him in a brief chuckle, while Von did his best to keep a blank expression. If he hadn't known Jaxx was a man, he might have made a pass himself.

Moth did his best to ignore their comments. "Go down to the shore and look for a likely ship. It will help if we know where the ship we are trying to steal is moored before we try to slip into town. Since its market day, there should be enough people in town to allow you to blend in." He pulled a few coins from the coin pouch he'd taken from the dead guards' body.

"Don't use them unless you have to."

Jaxx scowled at his words. "Best place to find out anything is from a drunk. I'll look for a tavern. Of course, it will be my luck to find out they have some strict religious edicts baring women from drinking." No one disputed her statement. Most everyone heard stories about the prison, but no one knew much about the island. All they could do is hope a strange woman would not attract too much attention.

While the others found a hidden bower beneath a spread of low growing evergreens to wait out the coming darkness, Jaxx continued down the trail into town.

Von was thinking more and more about the idea that Jaxx was both male and female. He had heard tales of shapeshifters, but he had attributed them to the same category as demons, something he never expected to deal with. Now, he was second-guessing almost every concept that formed the foundation of their friendship. He decided to talk to Moth. The quiet mage was easy to talk to and reminded Vondal of his brother Gestor, who had been killed in a market riot shortly before Von had left home for the first time.

Moth knew little more than he did. "Not much difference. I think a bane is a kind of curse. For it to continue through so many generations, it must have been the dying curse of a powerful mage. That's why it can't be lifted."

"I am not sure how to act around him...her...that's what I mean. I am mixed up."

"If you are feeling that way, you can imagine how difficult this had been for Jaxx."

"Jaxx has made difficult decisions before this. She seems to have handled those choices. Give her a chance to adjust to her new reality."

"If that's your advice, I will take it. He always said nothing could damage our friendship. I would hate to think something I did, destroyed it."

Von sat looking at the fire long after Moth walked away.

The unpredictable weather was cooperating for a change, the evening sky was clear and scattered with sparkly stars and the temperature, while not exactly balmy, was much warmer than it had been in weeks. There was a coolness in the air that hinted at a touch of rain before morning. From where she stood on the ridge west of the gates she could see most of the city's business district. It also offered her a clear view of the bay.

The sleepy little town reminded her of home, even though it had been twenty-five turns since she last laid his eyes on her fathers' domain. New construction was everywhere, the sign of emergent prosperity. Even the older buildings were reflecting the prosperity, new paint glistened on walls and the smell of fresh thatch was everywhere.

The gate was unguarded and open when she approached it. She walked in without challenge and began exploring the town. No one was paying her much attention, so she looked around for someone to give her information. The marketplace was quite busy, even that late in the day and an unknown face didn't appear out of place. She wandered in the direction of the shoreline, using the top spars of the ships to get a general idea of the area.

The sun was high in the sky and the sunshine was un-shaded by a single cloud. It was a cool day, but not so cold that everyone stayed indoors. As she approached the residential district near the port she noticed that more people were paying attention to her. One particularly seedy-looking man sat on the porch of a dilapidated shotgun house and glared at her through sullen eyes. making her wonder if an unescorted woman was that unusual to see. After passing a group of shoppers, two of whom were women, she relaxed. There were plenty of women around, though only a couple were carrying a weapon. Whatever his issue, it had nothing to do with her sex. Did she stink? She had done her best to wash her clothes while Brinn was visiting the old woman, using a piece of soap Raffi had taken from her laundry area, but they were far from spotless. Her hair was chopped off short, so she had washed it too, but the swamp water wasn't exactly clean, to begin with. The sight of a public house offering steam rooms and baths was tempting, but she needed to look for a way off the island more than she needed to lounge in a hot tub.

Spotting a similarly dressed woman with a group of sailors heading back toward the ship, she fell in behind them and hoped anyone that noticed her would assume she was part of the crew. Unfortunately, they climbed the gangplank of the first ship in the line, leaving her alone to walk past a trio of guardsmen talking to a coin girl on the corner.

Jaxx was certain she was about to get arrested again. The guardsmen were looking her way and there was nowhere in the immediate area she could use for cover. To make matters worse, she was swaying like a drunk at sea. Her feet were raw and blistered; being unused to the long candlemarks of walking in oversized boots, first through the boggy swamp and then up and over the mountain gap to the spot where the others waited. Hopefully, they would assume she was drunk and heading back to her room. As soon as she could find a tavern, she intended to down several shots of rotgut. She figured after three or four stiff drinks no one would question her story. She had made a conscious effort to move more like a man after Raffi began his aggravating tirade about the way her hips swayed as she walked. His harangue had only gotten worse while walking across the endless grasslands on this side of the mountain. Once he realized his comments were falling on deaf ears he gave up and let her have some peace.

Thinking about the arrogant thief helped keep her mind off the three guards watching her walk away. She was certain Raffi suspected who she was. For some unknown reason, he decided to keep that information to himself, at least for the time being. She had already learned he never did anything without it somehow benefiting him. Keeping that information quiet would end up costing her at some time in the future. Sometime soon she was going to have a serious discussion with Vondal. She only hoped their friendship was strong enough to survive what she had to tell him.

The larger ships in the harbor had given way to smaller schooners and fishing trawlers. She continued to walk along the road bordering the shoreline, blending in with whoever she spotted walking in the right direction. The guards had turned off at the last intersection, so she relaxed and began looking around for a ship they could easily steal.

West of the main harbor was a line of smaller craft, mostly clipper type sailboats used by the community fishermen. She spotted a likely vessel, a clean looking dinghy set up for fishing that was anchored a few feet from the shoreline. It was moving sluggishly in the calm waves, its canvas flapping in the light breeze. Unlike most of the other boats, this one was silent.

Jaxx moved closer, listening, but heard none of the sounds of the active fishing industry about the craft. Despite its well-kept appearance, no one was aboard. She turned to walk away when a flash of movement onboard the trawler caught her attention. A man crawled out of the small cabin, stood, and stretched. He checked a line he had dropped off the stern of the boat, removed a crab from the attached trap, rebaited it, and dropped it back into the water. The crab went into a bucket.

This new development brought a smile to her face. Overcoming one sleepy old man was much easier than fighting off an entire crew. Satisfied that she had found what they needed, she decided to work on the second, more enjoyable aspect of her quest.

She found herself walking along a street lined with weathered wooden buildings. None of them suggested luxury, but they showed all the signs of a healthy economy. She surveyed each building in turn, searching for a sign that would indicate an inn or tavern. No luck. Was alcohol illegal in the city? She had heard of places that allowed no drinking.

A young boy, about twelve turns or so, stood coiling rope next to a pile of crates. He moved toward the edge of a gangway, gazing at her as she walked toward the ship. Tall for his age, he set a queer figure, with arms and legs too long for his adolescent body. He wore his long hair braided back into a rat's tail instead of loose and flowing like most of the men in Hyperion. Like the clothes she had taken from the prison, his outfit was simple; loose sailcloth trousers, a faded blue serge tunic, and a worn and patched black jacket that was at least two sizes too big. The lad was not particularly handsome but possessed a strong, reliant face, though chestnut brown and heavily pockmarked. He would never be good looking, but once he reached his full growth, he would not lack for companionship. Since walking had not led her to find a place to get a drink, she decided he looked a likely candidate to get information from.

"Would you direct me to the nearest tavern," she asked, offering him an ingratiating smile.

"Ur-hum," he murmured blankly. He appeared puzzled, so she tried again.

"Ale or Beer? Will you point me to somewhere I can purchase a drink?" She smiled and pantomimed holding a mug and drinking.

His eyes widened and scanned the area nearby before they finally settled themselves on the magnificent pair of breasts barely concealed by the voluminous folds of the oversized tunic Jaxx was wearing. He made no audible reply, seemingly engrossed with the vision of beauty before him. A backward jerk of the head was the only sign he had heard anything she had said.

Maybe he can't speak. She sighed and made her way back to the side street the three guards had taken. Sure enough, less than a block from the intersection was the common sign for a tavern, a faded mug of beer.

Jaxx looked at the saloon, wondering if it might be better to continue the search for a public house. The place was a ramshackle two-storied shanty that looked like it might collapse in a strong wind. The outside looked like it had already fallen several times and been pieced back together with little regard to the safety of its clientele. At least she wouldn't feel out of place. She doubted any of the clientele worried about dirty clothes…or body odor.

The door of the tavern opened and two men came out, eyeing the newcomer critically. They propped themselves leisurely against the door-casing and gazed silently at Jaxx as she approached. She kept walking, unsure of what to expect. The two men stepped aside without comment to let her pass through the door, though one doused the dirt at his feet with tobacco juice.

Stopping inside the door to let her eyes adjust to the dim interior, she glanced back and realized neither man had moved. It must be a favored place for them to stand and talk.

The bartender looked up as she approached the bar. A twinkle of amusement shone beneath his heavy brows, while a broad grin parted the copper-hued beard on his face. Then shaking his head thoughtfully, a look of solemn wonder replaced the grin. "Well lass, you don't look like no sailor and ya ain't dressed like a doxie, so I'm guessin' ya can handle that sword ya wearing. Seems ah waste of ah beautiful woman. What ya havin'?"

Jaxx was about to reply when an audible snigger came from the doorway behind her. The tone changed her mind. She swung round to face one of the three guardsmen she had spotted earlier.

"I was about to have a drink. I spent way too much time looking for this place and I'm not in the best of mood. So, you can either join me, arrest me, or walk away. Your choice."

The portly guard surprised her." Seems like I decided I needed a drink at the perfect time. Set me up Jeorg. The lady is paying."

Jaxx relaxed; only flinching a bit as she paid for the whiskey at what seemed an exorbitant price. It was not necessary to delve too deeply into the workings of the city. In minutes she learned that here was a constant stream of ocean-going vessels in and out of the harbor. The governing officials had made it clear that the guard was not supposed to interfere with anyone passing in and out of the area. It was not necessary to avoid answering questions since no one asked any. The assumption was if you were not in shackles, you had a reason to be there.

Jeorg purveyed liquor. A big man with quick, cunning eyes and a wide mouth under a reddish-gray mustache that could snap shut in seconds if you asked the wrong question, he looked as gentle as a half-starved wolf. His burly body was as uncouth as his manners and as unwieldy as his slow-moving tongue, yet Jaxx liked him immediately.

Hael, the guardsman, was a genial rubicund fellow that drank more in five minutes than Jaxx could in a candlemark. He took the keenest delight in the little benefits of his job, one being that perfect strangers often felt the need to buy him a round or two when he walked in. He took inordinate delight in making them happy. After quaffing the first two mugs, he lounged in his seat at the bar, nibbling on the dry salty crackers the bar set out to entice their patrons to drink more.

"You gonna be needing a bed for the night," questioned Jeorg, as he broke out a fresh jug. "I'm guessing you aren't staying on one of the ships."

Jaxx swung a leg over the back of a chair and sat down with her arms folded across it and rested her chin upon them.

"No. That won't be necessary. If I don't get back soon, I'm sure they will send someone to find me." She did not explain who they were and no one asked. By listening to the conversations around her, she was able to find out the answers to most of her questions. Most of the fishing boats came into shore around dusk and they left out before sunrise. The larger ships preferred to wait till the tide turned at midday. The guards changed shifts about the same time and within a couple of candlemarks after dusk, most of the day shift was three sheets to the wind or home with their family.

Hael had already passed his credit limit and was ready to head back to the large barracks-like building she had passed on the way into town. Since she was heading back that way, he offered to walk along with her, at least as far as the garrison building.

"Comforting for me," observed Jaxx with a laugh.

The inebriated patrol leader chewed the end of a twig as she paid the for the last round, while Jeorg's twinkling eyes exchanged meaningful glances with her. She gave him a negligible shake of her head and he laughed loudly, noting she was not as tipsy as he had believed. It was more she was escorting Hael home than him escorting her.

"You take care. Next time you are in town, drop by and visit." He had his arms stretched forward to either side of him, as he gripped the edge of the bar with his beefy hands. There was more to the blonde mercenary than she was telling, but experience had shown him it was often better that he did not pry too deep. Even forewarned, he wasn't expecting what happened.

Jaxx surprised him as she turned to leave.

Hael stumbled toward the door and she walked behind. When she passed by one of the tables, a sailor drinking with a fellow crewman tried to stop her from leaving.

"Hold lass, forget him, how about a real man---." The waft of stale beer breath made her shudder. He reached out like he was going to grab her arm.

In an instant, a razor-sharp blade was inches from his hand. "Unless you want to lose that hand, you will sit back down and drink your ale." Her eyes blazed in the flickering candlelight.

His eyes blinked in disbelief before he dropped back into his seat without a word. His partner snarled a curse as his hand went to the dagger at his waist. He opened his mouth to call out a challenge but stopped as she put a finger to her lips and made the gesture for silence. Then she leaned in close and whispered, "Don't tempt me," her sweet voice at odds with the implied threat of her words. The third man found a sudden urgent need to visit the jakes.

Jaxx grunted, moving to put some distance between her and the two much bigger, much stronger men – but fighting the urge to stay close and save the next woman from having to deal with the obnoxious oafs.

Jeorg looked on in amazement. It was all so quick, so sudden. There had hardly been a breathing space between the comment and her reply. As she followed Hael to the door, there was a pause in the conversation followed a few dry twitters of laughter. Jeorg dried some glasses and looked uninterested. He was digesting and sifting through what little he had heard Jaxx say.

What a woman! Drasst it all, he wished he were thirty cycles younger. Whoever she was, she could handle herself in most situations. Yet three against one in a sneak attack would test even the best-trained swordsman. He was certain she was as good nay better than the best in town. He remembered the young woman's heavily calloused hands. You didn't get callouses like those without lots of hard work. She was fast and better with that sword than anyone he knew and that included all six of the guardsmen who liked to boast of their prowess while in their cups.

The briefest twitch parted his lips. He'd met women like her during the last war, quiet and easy-going so that you wouldn't know they were around. One, in particular, stuck in his mind, soft-spoken as a woman and about as vicious as a vole in heat. Killed by a random arrow fired from across a field.

One day, he'd like to hear her story. It was probably a good one. He called out as they passed through the door, "Be careful out there. A woman like you is one in a million."

If only you knew…

The smile she gave him before walking out the door sent a chill down his spine.

Chapter 14

Despite being exhausted, Jaxx was so keyed up sleep would not come. The sky to the north was no longer clear. An angry line of thunder clouds had appeared atop the mountain ridge, forming a thick grey wall though which no sunlight could pass.

Brinn was standing in the wind when she joined him. "There goes any chance of good weather tonight."

"Good or bad, we will have to make it work. We may not get another chance." As the sunset over the southern mountains, they prepared to make their way into the city under the cover of darkness. Jaxx would go first and make sure there was no one actively searching for them inside the city. The rest would follow and meet up near the section of the harbor where most of the fishing boats were moored. Her directions would make it simple to traverse the city without being spotted.

The return trip to town took less time than the previous time Jaxx had approached the seaside community. Unlike her first visit the roads into town were busy, with large crowds heading into town. She fell in behind a couple with several children heading in the same general direction she wanted to travel and easily passed by the checkpoints. Something was happening, there was an atmosphere of excitement flowing through the crowds, a sense of eagerness resting slightly below the surface of their conversations. She moved closer, hoping to get some idea of what was going on, with little results. All she heard was the woman chastising the young boys for running back and forth. The father looked almost as exhausted as she did, yet he was cheerfully carrying his daughter on his shoulders.

After passing through the gates she decided to move away from unsuspecting shields and see what she could discover.

She recognized the steeple of the building next to the barracks in the distance and decided to head that way, hoping to spot Hael. Though he was drunk at the time, there was a good possibility Hael would remember her. If so, she might have better luck getting info out of him. Of course, there was always the chance that he would not remember her, or even worse, would want to arrest her, but at this point, it seemed to be the best option she had.

Four men wearing the gray and blue uniform of the city

guard were winding their way purposely through the crowd. The men continued toward the middle of town. She decided to fall in behind them and hope they did not ask any questions.

The public square in the center of the city had changed since she was there the night before. There was a large platform erected in the center of the field and several tall poles had been driven into the ground nearby. A man was standing on a ladder near one of the posts, installing one of the enormous hooks the fishermen used to bring in the giant grouper fish. At first, she was puzzled, but a man nearby was explaining to his son what the huge hooks what the sharp hooks were used for. She looked around, noticing that similar hooks in several conspicuous places nearby were garnished with the heads of men who had been recently executed. One of the men looked familiar and she identified him as the drudge who had brought in the meals to the prisoners. Sure enough, the two gate guards' heads were gracing a similar cypress pole beyond the platform. Their escape had not been taken lightly. A crowd of inebriated revelers had gathered together in a noisy pack to watch as the town magistrate passed judgment on the convicted criminals. No one was sure exactly what crimes the men had been convicted of and they were too drunk to care.

Jaxx mingled with the crowd and looked on as a portly, richly dressed man stepped onto a raised dais at the front of the platform. He stood waiting as a young man came forward and blew a battered brass horn. Almost instantly the crowd grew quiet, all eyes on the enormous man.

"Come forward and bear witness, I the High Justice do declare."

No one made a sound. Everyone waited for him to speak.

Jaxx watched as four guardsmen came up the stairs at the back of the platform, dragging the bruised and battered body of a man between them. He was wearing what looked to be the pants from the same uniform all the guards at the mine wore. She studied him for a moment and realized she had never seen him before. Before she had more than a minute to wonder what he had done, the speaker began addressing the crowd once more. " This man, Rojer Mormon, formerly commander of the garrison at Wyse Prison, has been charged and convicted of 'Negligence of Duty'. These charges were brought; Rojer Mormon allowed five dangerous criminals to escape from a heavily guarded cell while he was wiling away his time with a coin girl down on at a shoreline tavern. That he left the prison despite direct orders to remain and keep a close watch on the prisoners. Because of his neglect, six guards lost their lives." The High Justice paused to ensure every eye remained on him. Once he had their attention, he declared, "The sentence is death." He nodded to a guard standing to his right and back, who immediately raised a hand and signaled someone out of her sight.

A few voices muttered softly nearby as the man was drug forward and laid on the ground with his face downwards. Both officers knelt by his shoulders to ensure he remained where he had been placed. The face of the High Justice remained expressionless as the men worked. Then the officer sent away the other two guards, who speedily returned with a small blacksmith's anvil and a hooded man carrying a heavy hammer.

The crowd grew quiet as they placed the closest ankle of the prisoner atop the anvil. The two guards held it in place as a large man wearing a black hood approached and raised a heavy hammer overhead.

Jaxx saw, with a sickening heart, that they were about to strike the unlucky man's ankle with the ponderous hammer.

A loud groan was loosed by the watching crowd as the hammer fell. It easily crushed the bones into pieces as the prisoner shrieked in agony. Repositioning his leg farther up on the anvil, the executioner broke it with a similar blow to the shin. After another adjustment, a third blow was delivered to the knee while the guards held the screaming victim down. His third shriek was suddenly cut short as the man fainted from the pain. Unperturbed by his victim's lack of consciousness, the callous executioner went on with his horrible task, breaking the thigh bone.

When he stepped back, Jaxx thought the gruesome exhibition was complete. Instead, the two guards simply moved the man to the other side of the anvil. The executioner stepped forward and proceeded to go through the same process with the other leg… and both arms.

When twelve blows had thus been delivered, the writhing of the wretched victim proved that he still lived, though his laboring chest was incapable of producing enough air to vent his agony in shrieks. When she thought she could not stand seeing anymore, the executioner, wielding an oversized scimitar, removed his head.

The crowd roared.

The Chief Justice held the dripping orb of flesh high overhead, as the witnesses shouted approval. Then he passed the head to the guard officer who waited nearby and immediately left the platform. The officer passed the gory object to one of the waiting guards, who climbed up and impaled it on the waiting hook. As if a signal had been given the watching crowd began to disburse.

Jaxx needed a drink. A strong one. Something to take away the image in her mind of the scene which she had witnessed. She began walking toward the shoreline, then stopped suddenly to recover her breath and to wipe the perspiration from her brow. The executioner had removed his mask. It was a face she recognized…Hael.

Fighting back the surge of bile that threatened the back of her mouth, she began walking toward the shoreline. The sight of the ocean with its fresh breezes cooled her brow and tended to turn her mind away from the horrible thoughts that now filled it. How could she have thought he was like her? She had killed men, in battle, when her life was threatened. But never tortured one. Never without it being a case of his life or hers. She thought about going in the same tavern she had visited the night before but did not want to risk running into Hael again. Instead, she continued down past the fishing boats, into a rougher, working-class neighborhood filled with dock laborers and fishermen.

She spotted the foaming mug sign she now knew meant a tavern and went inside. She had some time to kill before it was time to meet the others. Now she needed to make sure she was drunk enough to go through with the plan.

Brinn took the officers' uniform for himself then tossed the other to Von. They removed their prison garb, quickly donned the uniforms, then stuffed their clothes under a nearby bucket to hide them. The two city guards had stumbled into the alley where they waited to relieve a full bladder. Unfortunately, they had recognized Moth. It was over in seconds.

The wind was picking up, stirring the water into a swirling gray froth. The five escapees trudged through the shallows toward the faded white schooner anchored exactly where Jaxx had expected it to be. This was good since Jaxx was sloshed and probably wouldn't be much help. Von did his best to keep her on her feet as they made their way closer to the waiting boat.

"Mephib drag them all to hell," she mumbled as a particularly strong wave threatened to take her feet out from under her.

"Shhhh", Von whispered.

She cut her eyes at him but did not reply.

Moth shook his head sadly. Jaxx had offered a rambling tale of what she had seen earlier that day. He wondered if he could have witnessed the execution without feeling a similar need to get drunk. Doubtful. He also wondered if her male persona would have felt the same emotions. Jaxx was the first Chimera he had ever met and it was an exceptional opportunity to learn. He realized he may never have another opportunity to get firsthand knowledge of both male and female aspects.

Even Raffi, who had the attitude of a durrrat, was quiet after hearing her story. What Brinn was thinking he kept to himself, only commenting on how easy it was to follow her directions to the meeting point. Raffi had spotted a broken section of the city wall. This had allowed then to enter without anyone seeing them. Now he was concentrating on the task ahead, preferring to keep his opinion private until Jaxx was in shape to remember what he had to say.

He tightened his grip on his blade and inched closer to the quiet ship.

There was a coolness in the air that hinted at rain before morning. Heavy clouds kept the starlight from reaching the ground. There was a brief burst of wind and the schooner swept around in a swift arc, the black shape of the low riding fishing boat almost invisible without the light of the twin moons. As they moved closer the location of the small fishing boat began to prick at his mind. Why was it anchored away from the other boats? A distant rumbling of thunder succeeded a faint flash as lighting ripped across the cloudy western sky. For a moment it was as if the world held its breath, then the wind and rain came with manic fury as if to balance the defection of the electric element. As the sudden darkness fell upon the surging vessel, the desperate men groped at the slime-covered rails in a last-ditch effort to board the bouncing sloop before the weather made it an impossible goal.

There had been no sign of the old man as they walked through the inky water. Perhaps the imminent storm had driven him ashore? He doubted that had happened, a fisherman would sooner leave his wife and family than his ship. He was probably inside where it was dry waiting out the rain.

Brinn's eyes glittered at the prospect of the imminent fight. Earlier the man had joked about getting the chance to use their swords before they rusted. He could not see the faces of his friends, but he could hear Raffi's angry snipes beside him and his mumbled words indicated he had little faith in the makeshift takeover scheme. They had one chance and only one to get off this island. If this failed, it would alert the guards. Once they realized the escapees were still alive and inside the city limits, it was only a matter of time before they were located.

It was too bad the ship would not cooperate. The waves kept it moving, not allowing it to stay still long enough for them to crawl on board. As the next wave passed he sighed and jumped, somehow managing to throw a leg over the rail. It took all his strength to shimmy his weight on board. Von was right behind him. He had no idea where Raffi was, but he was certain the sly thief had already made it on board. The others were coming but he no intention of waiting for them. He began inching his way toward the small sleeping cabin.

Using Moth for a ladder, Jaxx shimmied up and over the slimy rail to the schooner's streaming deck, landing flat on her back and thus avoiding a whistling stroke of an unexpected assailant's saber. Realizing she had only avoided the blow through blind luck, she continued to roll, only coming to a stop when she struck the opening to the small cabin. She moved immediately to her feet, expecting him to follow but he was now trading blows with a much larger, more experienced swords-man. Brinn easily dispatched him and Raffi helped him pitch his bloody body over the rail.

Her sudden appearance startled the second man climbing out of the tiny sleeping berth. He yelled something to some-one behind him and rushed toward her, waving a short sword overhead. As he reached Jaxx, he swung, hoping to take her out before help arrived.

Jaxx was having trouble getting her balance. Somehow she managed to duck beneath the swing. She darted close before he could reset his stance. Realizing she might not get a second chance, she grabbed for her boot knife and slashed downward, ripping his sword-arm from wrist to elbow. Mouthing vicious threats at the crazy woman, the man pushed backward, his movement stopping when his shoulders struck the rigging. He shifted his oversized sword to his left hand, holding it by the blade for a desperate javelin like cast. Wracked by pain, his face twisted into a satanic leer. Uttering a low growl of laughter, he drew back his arm for the cast.

Jaxx knew she was too close to avoid a hit and braced herself for the pain to come.

Seeing her peril, Raffi came storming across the pitching sloop's decks to save her from the pain crazed man, all the while knowing there was no way he would make it in time.

Instead, as the man's wrist flexed to cast his javelin, Von's hand gripped his wrist from behind and twisted, using his weight to swing him bodily off his feet. He fell into the turbulent swell, cursing them all until with a sharp gasp, he suddenly disappeared. Traces of pink and red foam showed his final ending.

Von found himself shaking. He realized he had been in that same bloody water less than a moment earlier. As the shock of the last few moments eased, he burst into a torrent of futile, raving blasphemy, that brought snide grins to the face of Moth and Raffiel.

Brinn cocked one eyebrow and frowned. Jaxx had often been the brunt of his tongue, so the flurry of curses did not surprise him at all.

"I thought there was only supposed to be one man on the boat," Brinn commented as he moved to check out the tiny sleeping cabin.

"It's not as if I had an opportunity to look inside," she replied. "They must have been asleep."

Moth smiled and began to raise the heavy iron anchor.

They had a bit more freedom to move around because of the storm, but that would not last long. The area was prone to short heavy outbursts. He could tell the deluge was easing off already.

Raffi must have been thinking along the same lines as he moved to help with the anchor. There was no way to raise sail in this wind. The tide was going out and they should easily be carried out to open water by the ocean's movement. Unless someone spotted the small ship drifting out to sea and came to investigate, they should be able to gain sufficient breathing room by the time the storm ended.

The was enough room inside the cabin area for all five to get away from the storm and dry out. Inside the small schooner's cabin, the atmosphere was peaceful by contrast with the raucous weather outside. Thunder rumbled in the distance and the wind railed against the rolled-up sails. A sudden burst of wind threw the ship into a sideways roll. Everyone grabbed ahold of anything attached within reach to help keep their balance as the roll of the sea increased dramatically. Slowly it righted itself and everyone relaxed until the next big swell. Below the steep slant of the deck, the shrill, protesting squeal of working frames and beams could be heard. The sullen thud and swish of the wooden vessel's skin racing along the choppy swells kept the storm ever in the forefront of everyone's mind.

Von and Jaxx were sailors, though they had never been at sea in such a small vessel. The dizzy plunge of the bow into the greenish-gray water was followed by its accompanying rise of the stern. Every few seconds they could hear the hollow jar and thump of the rudder-post in its port side mount as it struck the surface. The arbitrary noises kept anyone from completely relaxing. Sleep was impossible, with every pitch and roll they five men ended up tangled together. It was too dark to see the stars; and even if they could, without a starting point to compare, it would be next to impossible to get any type of location. Outside the small sleeping berth, the rain continued to fall in battering torrents. The sound of the wood groaning under the strain of the storm did little to ease their concerns. Jaxx lay on her side looking at the lightning flash in the distance.

She could no longer see the lights of the village, so she knew they were moving away from the island. As far as she could tell, they were moving toward the mainland. But where on the mainland the battered ship would finally make landfall, was up to the Gods.

Chapter 15

An intense burst of sunlight reflecting off the water into his eyes brought Vondal to startled awareness. He looked around, noticing everyone was still sleeping, including Jaxx who was leaning against a coiled sisal rope, snoring away. His first impulse was to dump a bucket of saltwater over her for sleeping while on watch. He grinned. No one would have been able to follow them during the storm anyway. The chance of being located by searchers from the island was little to none. Even if they knew the path the storm was following it would be almost impossible to spot the small fishing boat from a distance. Even if they set sail as soon as the storm eased they had to be several candlemarks behind them. That lead could shorten quickly if they were in the right kind of ship.

It was a beautiful clear day and you could see for leagues if you were high enough. Some of the big full decked ships, a schooner, or a caravel, had three main masks that were thirty feet or higher. They could put a spotter in the crow's nest with a view scope. If one of them located the tiny fifie, they would not stand a chance of avoiding them.

The two triangular lateen sails were furled and tied tightly to the mast. It took at least two able bodies to raise the heavy canvas sails, so someone was about to get a rude awakening if they hoped to make landfall before the second sunset.

Using his hand to shade his eyes, Von scanned the southern horizon, looking for any sign of land. If he remembered correctly from the one time the trader had delivered a load to Hyperion, the island was due north of the city. Even without the sails, the tides should drive the fishing boat ashore somewhere along the coast, but exactly how close they would be to Hyperion was an unknown. The only problem was that if Von noticed the tide patterns after only one trip through the area; the captain of any ship following them would know them, too. It would be foolish to think no one would be smart enough to associate the escaped prisoners with a stolen sloop. They would know exactly what to look for.

Vondal thought about it and decided to wake Brinn. He might not know as much about sailing as Jaxx, but he was a lot easier to deal with when he first woke up. Jaxx needed a few minutes to become human.

Surprisingly, both Brinn and Raffiel were awake when he

crawled back into the sleeping compartment. "Anyone hungry," he asked, then ducked as Brinn tossed a boot his way. He tossed the boot back with a wry grin. "I could use some help raising the sails. Both suns are up. We have to assume they have been looking for us since dawn." He didn't need to go into details. Both men realized they should have been sailing for the safety of the coast much earlier.

Brinn nodded and followed him back outside. His eyes went to Jaxx, asleep on the rope but he did not ask any questions.

Seconds after Brinn came out, Raffi followed, mumbling under his breath about Moth's hair tickling his nose all night. Von bringing up the breakfast no one was going to be eating, only added to his miserable morning.

Von pictured the pale blonde mans' long, curly hair brushing against that prominent aquiline proboscis and had to fight the urge to laugh. " If one of you can handle the halyard; I will attach the shackle to the clew after I make sure the slugs are settled in the sail groove at the luff."

Both men stared at him as if he were speaking an unknown language.

Von sighed and pointed. "Pull this rope when I say pull."

He checked the top of the mainsail canvas to make sure the halyard shackle was tight and moving freely. Then he made sure the shackle was tight in the bottom clews and that the canvas was not torn and both ends were attached. Having a sail tear in a stiff wind could be dangerous. He'd seen a man lose his hand when a line snapped.

"Okay, Now pull." The rope moved easily and the sail was soon up and tight. Jaxx quickly cleated the rope. The wind immediately began filling the canvas.

"So, are we done?" Raffi asked.

"Not quite. Once we get the jib sail up we should make a decent time. Luckily, the old sailor took good care of his boat. The sloop easily rode out the storm and was in much better shape than the passengers.

Jaxx cracked open one eye and winced at the bright sunlight. Resigning herself to waking up, she stretched and rolled off the rope pile onto the deck, then moved to one knee before standing upright. She was surprised to find she had to struggle to get her balance. It seemed like that was another skill she had in one body that she did not have in another. While fighting with a sword she discovered this body was much better than her male form, however, the ax made her feel off balance.

It was also too heavy for her to swing easily.

Von tried to keep a straight face as she wove uneasily across the small deck and sat down on a small wooden box. His lips twitched a time or two, but he managed to keep the grin off his face.

"Any idea where we are," she asked.

"Not really. We must be getting close to the mainland. I saw a couple of gulls flying near the boat and neither landed."

"Good. My stomach is roiling. I think I might be feeling seasick."

Brinn gave a brief nod. "Ocean travel is not Moth's favorite thing to do either. He's lying in the cabin with a pail nearby. Not sure why there can't be much left in his stomach."

Raffi jumped down from the top of the cabin, landing lightly on the deck next to Brinn. " I got good news and bad. Which do you want to hear first?"

"Give me the good news. I have a feeling I'm not going to like the bad."

"There' s land straight ahead. We should be able to reach it before high sun."

"That's great. So, what's the bad news."

"I'm almost certain I saw sails behind us. Only a glimpse

and I doubt they are close enough to spot us. But if they have someone up in the crow's nest, they may have."

"Drasst!" He turned to Von. "What are our chances of making land before they catch us?"

"Assuming it is looking for us and not simply a trade ship heading for Hyperion, it's going to be close. We have a good wind behind us, but so do they. With luck, they will stay far enough from shore to prevent them from being able to spot the boat."

"And if they see us?"

"It all depends on when we find a place to land the boat. This part of the coast is sheered cliffs. Landing spots are few and far between." His expression did not appear hopeful as he scanned the horizon looking for his first glimpse of the approaching ship.

Vondal adjusted the sails to ensure they were catching as much wind as possible. The small sloop danced lightly across the water, its speed steadily increasing as it adjusted to the new wind velocity. Once he finished, he decided to climb up on top of the cabin with Raffiel and take a look for himself.

As Raffi had said, he could make out the tops of the sails. It was a triple mast and by the locations of the mast, it appeared to be one of the newer full decked carracks that had been anchored in the harbor when they stole the boat. Chances are, it would be set up with cannons and a crew of fully armed men. He stared at the sails for a few moments, to assure himself of the approaching ship's progress. She was riding high in the water and probably had an empty hold. It was going to be a race to see if they could reach land before the ship got into range to fire.

He turned to study the land, which was now visible in the distance. For once things were as he remembered, it was a sheer cliff with the sea resting far below the land. There was no easily accessible landings insight.

"Well, how does it look," Brinn asked.

"We should be able to reach the shore before they get near, but once we get there, we may not be able to find a place to land the boat."

He looked at Raffi and Raffi nodded his agreement.

Brinn looked worried. "Any ideas?"

"We need to get close to shore. If Tymora smiles, we can catch the rip an' let it carry us up the coast. Their ships too big, it can't get close enough to catch the rip. But they still have the cannon." Jaxx did not look convinced his idea would work.

Brinn was surprised when Jaxx suggested they head closer to the shore. Then he remembered that she had served on a ship longer than Vondal. "Can you steer us through it?"

Von and Jaxx both laughed. "Ain't gonna be no steerin' while in the rip. You hold on and hope you don't hit anything."

"Hit anything?"

"Yeah, lean out over the rail and look down. We are running atop an atoll. That's razor rock under us. Water is so clear it will fool you. There is no way to know how deep it is. If we hit one of the taller pieces, it could rip a hold in the hull before you know it." He grinned. "Not that it matters now. The rips got us and we have no control over what happens."

Brinn interrupted their conversation. "Better pray to any of the Gods that may hear you." He pointed out to the sea, where it was now easy to see the ship running parallel to the coast. No one could have mistaken the vessel for anything except a slaver. The flag of Caldra flew atop the center mast and several pieces of heavy ordnance pointed their black muzzles from port-holes in her bulwarks. An unusually large crew of sea bronzed, heavily armed men stood near the rails, watching as they closed the distance between the ship and the fishing boat.

"Stay low, maybe they will think they have the wrong ship if they only see Raffiel." Von crouched down by the tiller.

Jaxx and Brinn crawled into the cabin to wake Moth and gather their packs and weapons. It would be difficult to hit the small boat now that it was in the rip, but a lucky shot could sink it the same as a well-placed one.

Jaxx tied the ax to her back and carried her sword and pack. Von's bow and quiver were propped atop Von's pack outside the door. They would stay inside out of sight as long as possible but wanted everything ready to evacuate the ship if they hit a rock.

Brinn was loading anything he thought might save into his pack. There was not any food and the water skins were empty, but he rolled them up and packed them away, knowing they would need them once they reached the shore.

Moth still looked slightly green and woozy as he pulled his boots on. He had never bothered to learn how to swim. There was snow on the ground cycle round in his country. The water was too cold to do more than a quick dunk once every full moon. He knew the chance of finding a safe landing spot was little to none. Without his spellbook he could not teleport, so he faced a choice between going into the water or dying in a fight with the slavers. Neither choice appealed to him.

They were surprised when they heard Raffi coming to the cabin door.

"Tymora loves me! I know where we are. And even better, I know how we can get off this ship." He was grinning as he grabbed for his things. "Look for some short pieces of rope. You will need to tie your weapons so that you have both hands free."

"Are we going to climb the cliff?" Moth was puzzled. Their original plan was to sail down the coast, intending to make a last-minute dash into some small fishing village in hopes of landing with enough time to escape before the larger ship was able to lower boats and come ashore.

"No." He pulled his boots off and slid them into a canvas sack. One by one he removed about a dozen sharp knives, slid them into the same sack, then tied it to his waist. "Be ready when I call," he said before returning to the deck.

Von was already securing his weapons.

No one said anything as they packed the limited supplies they had managed to collect. It was evident from Raffi's unspoken answer they were about to get wet. Packing hardtack and hoecake was a waste of time. He offered the bland food to the others but no one was interested in eating.

Other than the sword, the only thing Jaxx was worried about carrying was the custom boots. She knew that once she changed back, she would need them. None of the others had feet that large. She slid a length of rope through the pull loops and tied it around her waist. Finally satisfied the boots were as secure as possible, she leaned back against the pile of items they were going to leave behind and waited.

Mekiva concentrated as she stared at the bowl of water before her, hoping that she had not made any mistakes. Scrying was considered a simple spell for most second term students. While most of the students preferred using a mirrored surface it was difficult for her to utilize. She had found that water gave her the clearest picture. Nor was she limited by distance, unlike her fellow students. If Von was near water she would see him.

Everything had changed after she returned to school. Master Stolinn had spent considerable time trying to discover why some of her spells failed and others worked too well. After weeks of testing, it was clear to all the instructors. She was not a sorcerer, nor was she much of a mage, even though she could now cast minor cantrips and an assortment of spells. Sometimes they failed; other times they worked too well. She was an Elementalist, able to manipulate the natural elements.

Master Stolinn had explained that the reason it had been so hard to figure out her problem with consistency had to do with her unique ability. Unlike most Elemental Masters, she was able to channel all the elements, not just one. The addition of her training in spell work over the last two cycles had given her an unexpected power, the ability to use both forms of magic. She was an unexpected hybrid, a blend of two distinctly different magics.

Once the Instructors came to this conclusion, her training had changed. She was no longer required to attend magical theory classes. Nor did she need to memorize all the long boring spells. It was doubtful she would ever be strong enough to use them anyway. Instead, her training had shifted to the elements. She had quickly mastered the basic concepts of Earth, Air, Fire, and Water. She was clearly stronger than he was. Within a week he admitted there was nothing more he could teach her. Unless they located someone with the ability to use more than one element, her training was complete.

She blew lightly across the still water and smiled as the Instructors lounge came into focus. She watched them for a few moments before Professor Shalestone realized he was being watched and threw shields around them. Temporarily disappointed, she dropped the scrying and shifted her perception to air, listening in on their conversation.

"about her. She is too powerful to be around the other students. What if she loses her temper and hurts someone?"

Hearing Mistress Weaver complaining about her wasn't unusual. The woman hated her and looked for any excuse to have her expelled.

Professor Stolinn shook his head. "That is exactly why we need her to remain in school. We have no idea of her limits. She has already surpassed the levels necessary to pass her senior trials."

"Yes. Imagine what might happen. She could burn down the entire school. Then where would we be?" Master Wiggins was afraid of his own shadow so his comment didn't surprise her.

"That's ridiculous," Professor Stolinn responded. "She is inclined toward good thou possibly more so toward the chaotic end of the scale, instead of the lawful end. With luck, she will settle into Neutral Good and become a Master one day. I can see her joining the staff in a few cycles."

Master Vitarus leaned forward. "She likes you. Is there any chance you might ask her to let me study that ring she found?" His eyes sparkled as he thought about the ring and what it might be. He was certain from the little Professor Sto-linn had mentioned, the girl had located the lost workroom of Ammaonth. If this ring were one of the mages rings, it could be extremely powerful. Mekiva wore the ring all the time. He was curious if the ring might be magnifying her powers.

Mekiva decided to cut the connection. Master Vitarus's question caught her attention. She had been wearing the ring constantly since she got it. Was it affecting her ability? She carefully removed the ring and set it on a nearby table. Then she began concentrating on the water. She was curious about what was taking Vondal and Jaxx so long to get back home. She blew lightly against the water and waited as the image cleared. Sure enough, it was Vondal. He was lying on his side, sleeping. Then she noticed his arm was raised off the bedding. She expanded the image, then gasped and the image faded, but not before she realized Vondal had his arm thrown across the waist of a blonde-haired woman.

She sat in the room for a few moments trying to get her

breathing under control. Obviously, the ring had nothing to do with her ability to scry. She crossed the room, stopping to re-place the ring on her finger and to grab a cloak, then stomped toward the front of the school. She needed to talk to Gwen. Now!

⚮

The two cannons fired and twin balls of metal flew through the air, landing in the water close to the sloop. Their aim was getting better. It was now a race to see what happened first; he spotted the stone marker, or they scored a direct hit.

Raffi continued to watch the approaching ship as he scanned the cliffside for the white rock. He knew it was close, the stone turtle was in clear sight when standing beside the white rock. And they had passed the turtle. It was time to call the others.

He slipped off the cabin top and told Von it was time to go.

Von looked around, expecting to see some type of beach-head and saw nothing that resembled a way up the cliffs. The ship had turned and was now running parallel to the shore, staying almost in line with the much smaller fishing boat. He was soaking wet from the water being splashed over the railing by the barrage of cannonballs, but only a few had come close to hitting the boat. He used the rope he'd prepared to tie the rudder into place and picked up his sword. Crouching low so that it would be hard for anyone to see him moving on the ship, he made his way to the cliffside of the boat. Raffi was already waiting there with Brinn. Moth and Jaxx were sitting a few feet away inside the mouth of the cabin.

A wave washed over them and the force carried them up against the grey stone wall of the cliff. The tide was coming in. A few more waves like this and the force would break the boat up. He closed his eyes and braced for impact.

Moth winced as the small fishing boat was slammed against the wall of stone. He hoped they were close to the landing Raffi was looking for, he doubted the boat could take many more of this type of damage.

"Don't forget to tie that sword," Raffi said to Von. Then Von saw Raffi climb up on the rail. Before he could do more than open his mouth to call out Raffi dove in.

"Come on Brinn yelled. We have to go now. Dive in and swim toward the rock. When you get close, dive. There's a tunnel to a cave. Hurry."

Von moved directly to the rail without questioning his orders. Jaxx hesitated and then laughed at her fears; she had trusted Von with her life too many times for her to start to doubt him now. If he were going into the water, she would be right behind him. She raced toward the rail. Von was already waiting.

Brinn nodded and they both dove in.

Moth hesitated and Brinn grabbed his hand. " No time to think about it. This boat is breaking up. Go. Dive in." He gave Moth a push then followed him into the swirling water. A large chunk of the boat broke loose, slamming into the stone wall a few feet beyond them.

Brinn could see the wide-eyed panicked expression on the naturally calm mages face.

Moth could barely dog paddle. The bitter cold numbed his muscles and the saltwater burned his eyes and nose. He struggled to swim but his limb s felt heavy and his muscles cramped. Each time a wave crashed over him his fear increased.

Brinn realized he was going to have to make a difficult decision. It was only a question of time before Moth panicked. It was doubtful he could handle what was to come. Now was not the time for him to freeze up or worse grab him and pull him under too. He did the only thing he could, he hit Moth as hard as he could. Then, before the mage fought off the effects of the head blow, he dove deep, pulling the half-conscious man with him.

Chapter 16

The cold water closed over Jaxx's head like a physical blow to her body. She had dived deeper than needed to enter the cave. She felt sand against her feet and pushed upwards struggling upward through the icy water she broke the surface. Without a source of light, the cave was pitch black, so she started swimming toward the sound of voices. Once the water became too shallow to swim she struggled to shore and collapsed. For a moment she lay on the sand coughing and gasping trying to get her breath. Her heart was racing and her chest hurt with every breath. But she was safe.

Brinn gasped as his head broke the surface of the icy cold water. It was dark, he could not see his hand before his face. Nor could he see… "Moth!" He should be able to hear him splashing nearby. He listened but there was no noise at all. "Moth," he called again. He heard a voice calling out from the darkness followed by a splash as someone dove into the water before he submerged. He began a desperate search, realizing that his friend only had seconds before he drowned. Moth had not been able to take a deep breath before Brinn had drug him beneath the surface; he had to be suffering by now.

The cold water and the darkness only added to his fears. His lungs ached, urging him to surface for a breath of air, but he refused, knowing Moth had already passed that point. Then his flailing arms struck something floating in the water. It had to be Moth. He grabbed the outstretched arm and began stroking for the surface. Moth was not moving, not fighting him in any way. Holding his head above the water he began swimming for the shore that had to be nearby.

"Where are you?" he heard Von's voice in the darkness.

"Here," he replied, his voice strained and tight. "I found Moth, but he's not breathing."

"We need to get him on land now! Help! He's not breathing!" He swam toward the voices, towing Moths unresponsive body behind him.

Brinn heard Von's voice then felt someone grabbing Moth's other arm. With both men swimming it only took seconds to pull him onto the dry sand. Von immediately turned Moths head down and began breathing into his mouth and nose. Brinn pumped on his chest. After several deep breaths, Moth seemed to exhale and a large amount of water was expelled. He gasped and began to struggle in their arms.

"Quick, get a healing draught down him. He's gonna fight but he needs it now."

It took all four but Jaxx was able to get the potion in his mouth. Now they had to hope it had been on time.

Moth knew he was dead, but he never remembered anyone mentioning how cold and dark the afterworld would be. He vaguely remembered being dragged below the surface of the water by Brinn, after being tossed off the boat. Then something had struck him in the head. From the amount of pain, he was experiencing, his skull must have been split wide open by the blow. He thrashed about wildly and the movement of his head sent a burst of agony into the hollows behind his eyes. That immediately stopped his movement, but it was still a few minutes before he could think. He was certain his eyes were open, yet he could not see anything. Was he blind too?

He had no memory of coming back to the surface, only a vague belief that his lungs had filled with water, Then nothing. The soft whisper of his name in the nearby darkness startled him. A woman? He tried to take a deep breath and choked.

He fought to clear the fogginess from his mind. The voice sounded familiar, but he could not place it with a face. Then someone grabbed his arms and another held his head while the woman soured a sickly sweet syrup down his throat. He gagged but noticed that his head was no longer hurting. And he was breathing easier. Gradually he began to relax.

"Moth?" This voice he recognized. His mind had no trouble putting a name to this voice…Brinn. Had they both drowned? The afterlife the priests promised was nothing like this. He coughed and spit some more saltwater. That felt better. He could almost take a breath without coughing. Seconds later he found himself on his knees retching up the rest of the seawater along with the small amount of breakfast he had managed to get down.

"Easy. You need to give yourself a few minutes to adjust. Lie here and breathe."

"Raffi?"

"Yes. We are all here."

"I can't see you. I can't see anything!"

"No one can. There is no light," Brinn added. "Maybe in a few minutes you might feel well enough to take care of that little problem."

"Huh? Where?" He had no idea where he was or what Brinn was speaking of. At least he wasn't dead. His muscles were weak and trembling, but the trembling was his body's reaction to what he'd been through.

"In a cave behind the cliff face. Raffiel recognized where we were and led us to the cave. Which was great since the boat was coming apart around us."

"What about the ship?"

"The pursuit was not close enough to see us go over the side. When they find the wreckage, the undertow will have spread it across the shoreline. There will be no way for them to pinpoint exactly where it broke up. There's almost no chance they will know about this cave, Raffi only found it by accident. They will assume we all drowned."

Moth tried to sort out the new information, but this was difficult with the pounding headache he had developed. "Rocks," he muttered.

Rocks? Brinn felt around his body but did not feel any stones.

Moth must have realized what he was doing because he said, "Not under me. I need a couple of small pebbles to use as a focus for the spell."

Everyone began searching. The dry area was covered in sand, setting atop a shelf of solid stone. After a few minutes, it became obvious there was not a rock to be found.

"Does it have to be a rock? I found a couple of seashells." Jaxx slid closer to the sound of the three men's voices. "Someone say something, I need to get my bearings."

"Tyche's tiny tits are bigger than Jaxx's bits."

Jaxx couldn't help smiling at Raffiels' words. She scooted a bit closer and then held out her hand. "Try to reach my arm from where you are."

"Not yet. Move closer."

She slid a bit closer, stopping when her knee struck flesh. "Try now."

She felt a hand slide up her leg, moving a little too close to her groin. "Watch the hands, Raffi," she snarled.

He laughed before moving upward his hand along her torso, skimming lightly across her breasts, to her arm. "Changed my mind, you definitely beat Tyche."

Jaxx knew he was doing it to mess with her mind, so she ignored his taunts and dropped the two shells into his hand without comment.

With a hearty chuckle, Raffi passed them onto Moth.

Ignoring his best friends' antics, Moth began to rub the first shell between his palms, while chanting a quick cantrip. The shell began to glow, gradually increasing in brightness until it lit up an area about a man's length in either direction. He passed the glowing shell to Brinn and repeated the process with the second shell. The two shells did not provide enough light to see the entire cave, but it was enough for them to locate a few more shells. The way out was evident. Even so, everyone insisted on checking the cave before they headed for the surface. Over against one wall was a broken chest, but there was nothing inside it. Other than an assortment of shells, the rest of the cave was empty.

"Wonder if they used it to smuggle supplies during the war? That chest has been rotting for a long time," Raffi said as Von moved to examine the chest. "You think to dig under it?"

Raffi laughed. "I must have dug a score of holes around this place. Nothing. If there was ever anything hidden here it's been removed long before I found the entrance."

"Speaking of entrance…I don't remember you mentioning this cave. Do you Moth?" Brinn's voice was soft but puzzled.

"Found it long before we hooked up. I was being chased

by a pack of wolves. They had already taken my horse. Guess it wasn't enough to feed the entire pack. I literally tripped and fell into the opening." He grinned. "You would have laughed at the expression on that wolf's face when I stepped off the rock and vanished from sight."

Moth sighed. He was bone tired and the idea of walking through the underground cavern and the tunnels linking it to the surface was depressing. But there was nothing to burn in the cave except the remains of the chest and that would barely get a fire started. They needed to get outside where the sun would help dry their wet clothing. Then find something to eat and build a warm fire as soon as possible. And water. You would think after almost drowning he would not be thirsty. Now that his body had recovered and began normal functions, it was clamoring for water. The others had to be suffering, too.

"So, Raffi. Since you are the only one who knows where we are, how far are we from Hyperion?" Moth waited, watching his expression when he spoke. You could learn more from what he didn't say than what he did.??

"Not too far, maybe four nights on foot."

"Well, we won't get there any sooner by standing around here," Brinn said. "I'm ready to see civilization again."

"There is a small village about a half days walk from here. With luck, we can get horses there."

"We are not exactly rich, you know. Those blackguards took everything. All we have is the coin we got off the prison guards." Brinn began walking.

"Then that will have to be enough. I intend to get a horse there, one way or another."

Chapter 17

"We will wait here, while you go on ahead," Von said. He wanted a chance to talk to Jaxx again. There were a few unanswered questions and he wanted answers. But it would have to wait.

About a candlemark before sunset, the small group had gathered about atop a rise to discuss their plans for recovering their lost assets from the owner of the trading post. Now they were sitting on their saddles in a semi-circle debating the best way to take the post without getting anyone killed. The small settled area was located about half a mile west of where they were waiting. They had a clear view of all the buildings and anyone approaching the area, but it would be hard for anyone to spot them. Unfortunately, there was no way to know how many travelers were inside the post. Nor was there any way to know ahead of time, if the people would get involved, or stay out of their 'discussion'.

Jaxx waited impatiently for them to make up their mind. She was ready to go and they kept talking. The horses Raffiel got in the fishing village had been spirited and in excellent shape. No one questioned how he managed to secure five horses or Brinn's decision to travel from the small village directly to the pass through the mountains. Once they were within a mile or so of the trading post, they had turned off the main road, following a narrow game trail that circled west around the populated area. After Moths horse bolted when a snake struck at him they had stumbled upon a shallow creek where they had watered the horses and treated the injured gelding's bite with a few drops of the last healing potion. Now the hungry animals were grazing on the thick green grass that grew along the banks while they scouted the trading post. Scattered copses of trees; twisted bur- oak, cedar, and spindly-pine broke up the drier flatlands, offered cover, and a secluded place to wait for the last sun to set.

Jaxx winced as an unexpected sneeze shot ribbons of pain through her head. She felt lethargic and irritable. Whether it was from riding all day in the sun or stress she didn't know or care. Regardless of the mitigating factors involved, she was not in the mood to listen to everyone chatter like magpies. There was no way they could plan out what was going to happen ahead of time. She was tired of waiting.

She walked back toward where her horse was grazing, snapped his bit back in place, checked and tightened her girth, and swung up on the gelding she'd been riding. She was already on the horse and moving toward the trading post before any of the others realized she was gone.

The sign announcing the trading post offered tasty hot meals and clean rooms. No one seemed to care as long as the beer was good and there was plenty of it. As on the previous visit, there were a few horses tied to the post in front of the main building. Unlike before, there was only one mule in the paddock. Von was going to be happy to see him, a good mule was worth two or three horses. He was stubborn and picky about his food but one of the best pack mules she had ever seen. She allowed herself a brief grin when she saw that one of the horses tied out front, was her dun. She had nothing against the gelding she was riding, but he had short legs and a choppy gait that was not as comfortable as Bards.

No one came out to greet her as she approached. She tied the gelding next to Bard, gave him a pat on the neck, and went inside the trading post. Standing in the doorway allowed her eyes to adjust to the change in lighting. She could see four men sitting at a table playing cards. One was the owner of the post; two she didn't recognize. The final player was Tellar, the friendly old mercenary from the fort who had talked about what a great place the trading post was. All the pieces fell into place. She wondered how many unwary travelers had ended up being conscripted for work in the mines. Did they have families at home waiting for them? She could feel her muscles tightening as her temper rose and hoped she was not showing how irate she was feeling. Taking a deep breath to help settle her emotions, she plastered a fake smile on her face and walked toward the bar. She purposely let her hand rest on the hilt of her sword. It was an old sword, a family heirloom that had belonged to someone's grandfather, with a worn but finely made leather scabbard. Over the cycles, use had polished its hilt so that it shone brightly in the warm glow of the inn's fire. After expecting to make-due with a heavy broadsword made for a much larger man, Jaxx had been pleased to find the antique blade stashed a corner of the equipment room back in the prison. Though too small for most of the men, it was almost perfectly balanced and the right weight for her to use. Her hand would often subconsciously reach to where her ax would normally hang from her larger male body and this sword eased those impulsive movements.

The owner of the trading post lay his cards on the table and stood. Vargas was tall, his head nearly reached the lintel above the door frame. His bristly hair and bushy beard were as dark as night, with a hint of silver along each cheek and side-burn. He made some comment to the other players that made them all laugh and look her way. Then he walked behind the main counter and motioned for her to come over. It was rare she met men that made her feel small, yet she had to raise her eyes to look into his. He could go toe to toe with her normal body.

"Whatcha needin' lass?" Vargas's oily voice hinted that he knew exactly what she needed. "You're a long way from home, to be traveling alone." His eyes traveled to the sword she carried in a sheathe on her hip as if puzzled that a woman would go armed.

"A room for the night. Food for my horse." She tried to act as if she did this all the time and it bored her.

"Aye. We can provide that, easy. We don't get many travel-ers out here, especially women on their own. Rumors are the roads are too dangerous." Vargas reached over and took a key off a board and passed it to her. "Take any room on the right at the top of the stairs. Will you be wanting a tray in your room?"

"That won't be necessary. I will come down." She picked up her pack and went toward the stairs. After she studied the layout of the hall, she chose a room toward the back, went in, and locked the door behind her. The sun was already settling beyond the mountains to the south. Shadows had stretched until it was difficult to separate one from another. It would be full dark within a candle mark. This gave her time to wash up before the others arrived. Whistling a jaunty sea canty under her breath, she opened the window and draped a faded white tunic outside, then headed to the inns' small bathhouse.

Jaxx was still whistling as she entered the main dining room of the trading post a candle mark later. As she hoped, all five men were inside eating when she returned after her bath. She nodded her head to the four men at the main table and took a seat at a table near the back wall. She had a clear view of everyone in the room. Within a few minutes of her sitting down, an older woman appeared with a plate of stew and a basket of warm bread fresh from the oven. She set them on the table and left, returning with a foaming mug of beer, a jar of honey, and a small plate with butter and cheese. There was also a covered bowl that she assumed was some type of dessert. The stew was better than she expected, with plenty of root vegetables, chunks of venison, and a tasty gravy. She dug in, eager to enjoy her meal while she could.

She was finishing up the last spoons full of loganberry cobbler when every light in the Inn went out.

Voices rose in anger as the four men stumbled around the room in the dark. She heard the sound of a chair falling over and muttered curses as the glass broke, then someone managed to strike a light on a lantern that no longer had a glass chimney flue. The lamp was barely strong enough to light the area around the table, but it was enough light for the four men to see that each now had a blade pressed to the back of their necks. None could see the face of the men holding the swords, but the rock hard muscles of their ridged arms were enough to convince them to cooperate.

A dry chuckle came from the rear of the room. Jaxx looked up at the sound. She could see the same man sitting back in the shadows but had no idea if he was armed. Or if he intended to get involved with their forthcoming discussion with the four men. So far he had made no effort to assist any of the other men, however, that could change quickly. None of the others seemed to be concerned by his presence, so she turned her mind back to the man before her.

Brinn used his left hand to remove the sword from Vargas's belt, waiting as the others followed suit. Then he pulled up a chair from a nearby table, turned it around and straddled it, resting his arms and his sword across the back.

While he was making himself comfortable, Moth cast a spell, immediately relighting all the flames he had put out. He looked around, spotting the man in the shadows but did not mention him.

Brinn was concentrating on the men at the table. Vondal joined him, smiling as both men's eyes widened…evidently, they recognized the young man standing before them. The old soldier's eyes darted around the room, searching for Jaxx, but did not associate the tall blonde woman with the muscular dark-haired Duaar.

"Surprised to see me?" Von asked. "Or are you worried you might have to give a refund? Scum like you are only concerned with increasing the size of their purse." Vondal shifted the angle of the curved sword so he could move closer to the table. The longer blade made him uncomfortable. He had been trained to use a rapier and a cutlass, but he always preferred to use a good broadsword like the one he'd hidden in the desert outside the trading post. Before they left the area he intended to retrieve his sword and Jaxx's throwing knives, as well as the two money belts they had buried. That sword had a leather-wrapped handle and was balanced as if it had been custom made for him. He was still unclear on its magical properties, or what the limits of the sword's ability were. Maybe one they were back in Ornatar he could hire a mage to look into it.

The mercenary came up out of his chair long enough for Raffi to jab him with the point of his blade and remind him of the dagger behind his back, before settling back into the chair. Vargas hadn't moved.

"I wouldn't move too quickly. My friend desperately wants an excuse to plunge his dagger into your back. He didn't enjoy the little side trip you provided. The accommodations left a lot to be desired." Brinn chuckled, enjoying watching Vargas and Tellar squirm. He had no intention of hurting the two men he did not recognize, but he also had no intention of letting them leave. Von had not signaled him that they were also involved, so he would have to decide what to do with them before they ended this reunion.

"Speaking of our unexpected ocean voyage, we seem to have left most of our possessions here. We really would like to have our possessions returned…now."

"Of course. If you would allow me to go to my office, I will get them for you." Vargas pasted a fake smile on his face, but the droplet of sweat that trickled down his face betrayed his inner turmoil.

Jaxx could not believe he thought they were that gullible. She looked toward Raffi, who nodded, before walking toward the back of the building. She wasn't sure where the office was, however, she was certain the old woman in the kitchen did. She needed to hurry, she was certain Moth had noticed the man in the corner, but she hated the idea of leaving their backs unprotected.

As she suspected, the old woman was more than happy to show her to the office. It wasn't an exceptionally large room so it shouldn't take long to search it. The first thing she noticed was a leather-bound book sitting open on the desk as if Vargas had been looking through it. She glanced at a few pages, but the glyphs and lettering were in an unknown language. Hopefully, it was Moths' spellbook. Then she noticed a second book with similar writing and decided to take them both. Locating the false floor where Vargas had hidden anything he considered to be of value did not take long. The trade goods they had thought to sell in Hyperion were gone, but she located a sword she was reasonably sure belonged to Brinn and a matched set of daggers. There were also eleven money bags, each holding an assortment of coins and two rings. Her bow and quiver were not in the office, but she was certain she had seen several bows hanging on the wall inside the store. Perhaps one of them was hers.

She gathered everything together and headed back to the public room.

"Looks like we were not the onl, she stopped at the doorway and watched as a swarthy man standing at the base of the staircase raised a small hand crossbow and aimed it at Brinn's back. Before she could open her mouth to call out a warning, the crossbow released the deadly bolt.

Time seemed to slow. She watched as the bolt flew across the room, missing Brinn by inches before lodging in the shoulder of the unknown card player sitting beside Vargas. He fell sideways out of his chair. An inarticulate moan came from his mouth as he struggled to force out words with a tongue that was becoming difficult to move. Poison?

She pulled her sword, turning toward the bowman, but he was already lying on the ground, a black-handled dagger buried deep in his throat. He was still alive but choking on the blood that trailed from the corner of his mouth. He wouldn't last long and no one seemed to be rushing to save his life.

The stranger across the room was no longer sitting in the shadows. Like Moth he had skin so pale, it was almost white. But unlike the good-natured mage, with his waist-length hair the color of moonbeams and those slightly pointed ears, it was clear his blood was not human. She turned and gave Moth a second look, wondering if he kept his ears covered for a similar reason.

"It's about time you decided to get off your arse and joined us," Raffi declared. "Do me a favor and make sure no other snakes are hiding within these walls. They appear to be poisonous."

"I was enjoying the show. Didn't see any reason to interfere with the fun until tall, dark, and deadly slithered down the stairs with his tiny crossbow."

Noticing their attention was diverted by the two dead men and the colorful stranger, the old mercenary snatched a knife from his boot and made a run for the door.

Von had kept his eyes on the three men at the table while Raffi and Brinn talked with their unexpected ally. He saw the former soldier take off and reacted. Breaking into a run he dove for his legs, pulling him to the ground. Tellar sliced at Von with the razor-sharp boot knife, slicing a thin furrow across his chest and right shoulder before Von managed to get a grip on his wrist. He ground his thumb into the raw muscle of his should wound and Von released his wrist. Before Von could get a new hold, he swung, landing a blow that set his reeling. His vision blurred and for a moment he thought he might vomit. His left eye was already swelling, making it difficult to see. Realizing he might not get another opportunity, he slammed his head forward into the older man's face, breaking his nose, before bringing his knee up into his groin. The knife fell from his hand as Tellar whimpered and drew his knees up into a ball, racked by the two bursts of intense pain. Before he could do anything else, the stranger casually kicked him in the head. His eyes rolled up and he didn't move.

Brinn's eyes never left Vargas's face as Von struggled with his partner. Hope, then anger, then fear was reflected in his eyes within a matter of minutes. Then he slumped into his chair and lay his forehead on the table before him.

"Now that the entertainment is over, let's talk about our horses," Brinn spoke sharply, leaving little doubt he was angry.

Vargas shifted uneasily in his chair.

Brinn knew his hesitation wasn't due to reluctance. "So, I take it from the lack of response, our horses are no longer on the premises?"

"I didn't expect you to need them any longer."

Brinn moved five bags of coins to one side, leaving seven more on the table.

"Wait! One of those horses is tied up out front. Tellar was riding it"

Brinn moved one bag back, making it eight. "Then you owe Von and Raffiel for their trade goods. He lifted a bag, weighing it in his palm, then replaced it and picked up a heavier one. From the corner of his eye, he caught Vargas in a brief lift of one corner of his mouth and picked up both bags and transferred them to one of the piles.

The light went out of the innkeeper's eyes.

"Of course, we can't forget the pain and suffering. Since there's no way we can send you to prison, we could always give you fifty lashes and then leave you out in the drylands to fend for yourself." He moved five more bags to the side, leaving one and the rings.

"There's always a third option," Vargas said.

"True. I could slit your throat and leave you in that chair. Much simpler and it might satisfy Moth over the loss of his mare. He raised her from a foal, so I doubt it." Brinn stood up. He placed two bags in his vest and motioned for the others to come and get their share. Moth was fingering his knife as he swept the two bags up. He paused and examined the two rings, then raised his eyebrow.

Brinn nodded and he swept the two rings off the table, gave Vargas a look that could turn a fountain to ice, and started to walk away.

"Wait. I know where the mare is!"

Moth stopped and raised an eyebrow.

Vargas immediately began speaking, "There is a farm south of the fort. He raises hogs. You can't miss it. Said he bought the mare for his daughter, but my guess he intends to breed her. He's been talking about expanding his farm."

Brinn glanced at Moth before pushing the final sack back to Vargas. Both boys were surprised but figured it was best not to ask too many questions. "Everyone satisfied? Ready to ride?"

"I want to take a look at the bows and see if mine is there. Makes hunting a lot easier." She looked at Von. "You go get Hop and I will be there in a moment."

Von had the mule loaded and on a long line when she came out. She switched her pack from the gelding to Bard, happy to feel the big gelding under her again. "Fall back like Hop is giving you problems and pick up our cache. I'll keep everyone moving until you catch back up."

Von nodded and they hurried to catch up with the others. When Von fell behind two candle marks later, she made a joke about him not being able to hold his bowels. When he rejoined them again he managed to suffer through Raffi's snide comments with a wry smile while enjoying the comforting weight of the two money belts.

Chapter 18

"And then Keeyun came riding up on a flashy black stallion with the grey mare on a lunge line." Jaxx grinned and swallowed the last dregs of his beer. He signaled for the barmaid to bring him a refill, took a long draught, and released a satisfied groan, then settled more comfortably in the oversized chair he'd pulled over from beside the fireplace. Moving the chair irritated Addie when he did it, but she knew they were only chairs that fit his lanky body. He was surprised to realize how happy he was to be back home. Home… he had fought against the idea, but that is what it had come to be. He fingered the mithril earring in his ear, happy that the magic was still working. Their first stop after arriving in town was to visit a Mage that Raffiel knew well. Other than a faint difference in coloration, there was no way to tell that his ear had ever been damaged. Then they headed to the Inn and surprised Addie and Tula. Since then they had been talking nonstop about their adventures. They had left a few tiny details out of the story, but Jaxx wanted them to remain a secret.

"So, you're saying he stole the stallion? I'm sure someone will be looking for them." Mekiva wanted to hear everything. Life at school had become routine after the excitement of the road trip. Now that they had figured out she was not only a mage; she was also an Elementalist no one teased her but that didn't make it any easier to be a student. It was lonely. What it meant was she was no longer required to set through all the magical structure classes she hated. Since only one instructor on staff knew anything about training an elemental mage, she got one on one tutoring. However, he readily admitted she had exceeded his meager ability and he had nothing left to teach her. Listening to the boys talk about their adventure made her eager to return to the road.

Von laughed, "I never asked." What Jaxx had failed to mention is that Moth and Keeyun also brought back two other mares, a paint and a black. They had stopped by Brinn's homestead on the way back to leave the stallion and the three mares."

"They sound like a colorful group. When do we get to meet them?"

"You can meet Keeyun and Raffiel in about a candle mark. That is when we promised to meet them. Moth and

Brinn are not in Ornatar. Brinn's wife is due to deliver his third child any day, so he decided to stay home. This will be the first time he will be at home for his child's birth. Moth decided to stay and keep him company. They will catch up with us in a few weeks once Brinn is satisfied everything is alright at home."

Gwen hesitated, unsure how she was going to handle the two newcomers. A devoted novate of Rheaaz, she could not imagine stealing anything, much less several horses. Of course, not everyone thought about it the same way she did. She knew nothing about the beliefs of the enigmatic druid's people and was afraid to ask. Hearing about Raffiel made her uncomfortable. It was going to be strange seeing another Duaar. It had been difficult adjusting to the way people reacted to Jaxx. Two of them were going to be impossible.

"It sounds like you two had quite an adventure. I can't imagine being captured and sold into slavery," Gwen sighed "It sounds so exciting. Life at the temple is so boring. It's nothing like I imagined it would be. Everyone is so old. There is only one other neophyte my age and he is afraid of his own shadow. All he does is eat, sleep, pray and read. "

"You're not having second thoughts are you?" Jaxx asked.

No matter how hard he tried, he could not imagine spending the rest of his life in a temple, especially one that required you to wear draping clothing that covered every inch of your body. Gwen even wore thin leather gloves to cover her hands. Several times in the past he had heard stories about the Shi'i-Lakka being hideously scarred. That their goddess required a sacrifice in exchange for her healing blessings. However, after she almost drowned, he now knew that Gwen was one of the most attractive women he had ever met, even though she was too modest to believe it. She was completely devoted to her goddess and able to perform healings that only a high-level cleric should be able to do. Gwen never answered his question and he let the matter drop.

However, Mekiva raised an eyebrow and Von knew a question was coming. It was her tell, whenever she was about to change a subject that eyebrow quirked.

As he expected, she immediately asked a non-related question. "So, now that the shipping business failed, what are you going to do next?"

Jaxx grinned, then took a handful of coins from a leather pouch and threw them on the table in front of Vondal. "Play cards. Keeyun and Raffi should be here soon. With Tymora's blessing, I might win back some of the coins I lost last night."

Unlike most of the guest houses in the town, Addie's small tavern was more than a gathering spot for old soldiers to sit around and tell stories of their wayward youth. It was not known as a watering hole nor a House of ill repute and games of chance. Instead, the guesthouse was known for clean linen, no bugs, and good home-cooked meals. Rarely did she have a vacancy. That isn't to say could not find a game of cards going on most nights. Tonight, was no different.

Von stacked his coins up beside his mug, grinning from ear to ear. He loved it when he won a bet, possibly because it happened so rarely. "We intend to stay in the same business. We are simply adding a few partners." He glanced up as the door to the public room opened and grinned. "Speaking of partners, here they come now."

Both girls turned to look at the two men approaching the table. They could not have been any different in appearance of they been chosen for that reason. Like Jaxx, Raffi was tall, dark-complexioned, and roguishly handsome. Both men stood well above six feet. There might be a small difference in height, with Jaxx being slightly taller, but he easily a hand taller than any other man she knew. He was about five or so turns older, but they could have been brothers.

The other man shook her to the core. As a child, her father used to tell her stories about the white warriors who came in the cold season and stole away bad children in the night. Dressed simply in soft tanned leathers, with his waist-length silver-grey hair pulled back and braided, Keeyun was her nightmare come to life. Her eyes were locked on his ears. Besides being pointed, they were decorated by multiple ear-rings, many accented with jeweled baubles and small feathers. He appeared arrogant and cold at first glance, but after study-ing him for a moment, she realized it was his high cheekbones and hawk-like nose that made him seem that way. While Moth had eyes so pale in color to be almost silver Keeyun's eyes were a vivid blue, like the sky after a rain. When he smiled his entire demeanor changed, his face warmed, becoming open and welcoming.

Introductions were made and the two men joined them at the table. She noticed that like Jaxx, Raffi moved the other oversized chair over to the table to sit in. Once he made him-self comfortable and the barmaid had delivered his beer, he pulled a pack of dog eared Pakur cards from inside his tunic, shuffled them, and fanned them out atop the table. Both girls watched as they all made their choices and then compared cards. Keeyun pulled the high card and he got to deal the hand.

He was pleased the two young women were interested in the game. The young mage was beautiful. Unlike most unwed women of her age, her hair was not braided tightly; instead, it fell around her shoulders in a fiery halo of color. Her outfit could use some help. The plain robe she was wearing had once been dyed black but now it had faded to a dingy grey. The only thing to help break up the robe's severity was the tight-fitting, black leather belt and an ornate silver dagger strapped to her hip.

The Shi'i girl wore the traditional desert hajib of her people. There was no way to tell what she looked like under that enveloping tent they called clothing, but her honey brown eyes twinkled merrily between her thick black lashes. It would be interesting to see how her mind worked. So many of the desert women were shattered physically and spiritually by the men of their tribe. You were lucky if you received a one-word answer to a question. He grinned. This one was too spirited to be damaged.

"You know how to play?" he asked as he shuffled the deck. Long a favorite of the military during the war, returning soldiers had brought the game home with them and it was now a popular way to enjoy an evening. Like all card games, it required a bit of skill and a whole lot of luck. Not that the game was without issues. The gaming houses had discovered that with the addition of alcohol, Pakur became a steady source of income. It also flowed over into other highly prosperous activities they offered their clientele upstairs.

Addie frowned on gambling, but as long as they kept the pots small, she tolerated them playing after the dining hall closed. The four men never invited anyone else into their game and the same coins passed back and forth amongst them nightly. If one ran out the others tossed him coins to continue playing.

"No," Mekiva said. "It looks interesting."

"Sit and watch for a while. It's not a complicated game, you should pick it up quickly." He dealt out five cards to each player and bets were made. Cards passed back and forth for a moment and the second round of bets was made. Raffi won again. The shrewd Duaar seemed to have an innate knowledge of when his fellow players were bluffing.

The exception was Keeyun. Like many druids, he preferred the solitude of nature and rarely said anything in public areas. He played carefully, betting only when he felt he had a chance to take the pot. It was a given that when he bet more than the minimum he had a solid hand and he usually won on the rounds. Occasionally he bluffed.

Mekiva sat where she could see the cards in Von's hands. By the third round, she was feeling confident enough to join the game. There was one problem, she only had a few coins with her. It didn't take long for her to lose all her money. "Well, it was fun but I'm all out. Thanks for letting me try.

"No problem. We can easily fix that." He pulled out a small pouch and dumped the contents onto the table before her. Gwen moved over so she could watch Mekiva's cards as Jaxx dealt the next hand. The play went back and forth with each player taking cards and placing bets. When it was Mekiva's turn she slid the remainder of her coins into the center of the table.

The others tossed in equal value and play continued, At the end of the hand, Mekiva had won. Grinning broadly, she began pulling the coins toward her side of the table and stacking them before her. Gwen helped stack.

"Who had this coin?" Gwen asked, holding up a silver coin with an unusual design on it.

"Everyone turned to look.

"I think it was one of mine," Keeyun said. He searched through the coins before him, finding two others with the same imprint.

"Look at it Von, it's the same design!"

Von looked at the coin and passed it to Jaxx who nodded, "You are right."

Raffi took the coin from her hand and turned it over. After a minute or so, he passed it back, but still looked puzzled. "Where did you get this?"

Keeyun appeared confused by everyone's sudden interest. He thought for a moment, then said, "You don't want to know."

"I do. I don't care what you were doing when you got it, I need to know where you found it." Raffiel had a gut feeling he knew where Keeyun had found the coins.

"Near the temple."

"Drasst it! You promised not to go alone." Raffi did not look happy.

"You were supposed to be back in three days. After two weeks, I got bored."

Mekiva couldn't see what the problem was. There were at

least five temples in the city and all of them were a short walk from Addie's. She stood up. "I'm ready, let's go take a look."

The others seemed eager to leave at once but Keeyun's next words made them hesitate. "It might be best if we waited until daybreak. They lock the gate in the evening and do not allow anyone in…or out after dark."

Gwen and Mekiva looked at each other. There was only one place in the city that operated under those specific restrictions. But she had never heard of there being a temple inside the cemetery unless he meant in the small altar someone had set up in the noble section of the catacombs. You could wander for weeks inside the maze of tunnels and still not find what you were seeking.

"That does change things," Mekiva said. "I thought you meant a real temple. One of the four in town." She tried to hide her excitement as the anticipation of a possible road trip stole back into her thoughts. Thinking about renewing the search again made her want to rush out and begin gathering supplies. Remain calm and act as if it's another boring day at school.

"It is a real temple, but it's not in town," Raffi said.

"Raffi. I know why the girls are so excited about finding

the coins. What makes you so interested?" Keeyun asked.

"The man on the coin is Raskur Wyvernspur. The treasure hunter."

Jaxx eyes lit up and he leaned forward to pick up one of the coins. He had been weaned on the exploits of his great grandfather. The stories claim he had disappeared long before he was born, but every Duaar knows of his adventures and his missing treasure. The possibility that his family had been tied to Von's family sometime in the past added a fascinating element to their search. He tried to dampen his enthusiasm, but the possibilities were too exciting. "If we are going into the catacombs, we need to go armed and fully prepared for anything that may happen. We could be down there for a while."

Mekiva hid her grin as the men talked about the upcoming trip to the catacombs. She was already making a list of things to pack in her mind. She did not fear she would not be allowed to take time away from her studies. Not only would they be happy to find out she was leaving again, they would probably help her pack.

Von kept quiet. Mekiva and Gwen had that look in their eyes again…

Castillo sat on the paddock fence gazing at the bay mare grazing by the stream. He had returned to the trading post hoping to find some idea of where Vondal was heading. Multiple signs pointed to a small party of men that had ridden away in the direction of Ornatar and had not returned. One of the boot prints matched those worn by Von's Duaar partner but he must have lost a lot of weight in prison. There was a good possibility that one of the other men in the group was Vondal.

He frowned at the idea of following the men with no idea of their final destination. So much for an easy trip out and back home again. He would have to locate them in case one of the men was Vondal. His ring would only take him to a location he was familiar with. Following meant days, possibly weeks, on horseback with no idea when he would be able to return home.

The young mare rolled her eyes at his approach and trotted away. It took him three tries with his rope to catch her, but she settled down as soon as he got the rope around her neck. He pulled the only tack in the storage room that looked like it might fit her, carried it to the paddock, saddled her up,

and swung astride. Seconds later he was flying through the

air. He hit the ground hard and lay back against the grass as

he watched her doing her best to get the offending saddle off

her back. He sighed as she reared up on her back legs and fell

over backward, crushing the leather saddle beneath her. He had

spotted a second horse in the back paddock, an aged gelding

that looked like he was held together by the skin stretched over

his bones. Now he was faced with a choice between riding the

swayback gelding or breaking the young mare. Neither option

appealed to him. From the corner of his eye, he could see

she had finally stopped bucking; the leather saddle was now

scattered around the paddock in pieces. After seeing what re-

mained of the saddle, the old swayback was looking better and

better. Resigned to his fate, he picked up his pack and started

for the back field, hoping that the broken down gelding was

stronger than it looked.

Chapter 19

When Vondal and Jaxx came downstairs the next morning they were unsurprised to see both girls waiting in the dining room, packed and ready to go. The two girls were enjoying morning fest with Raffi, laughing at something he had said. Von was certain his ribald comment had referred to him in some way. Keeyun had finished his food and was heading back upstairs to pack a few last-minute items. From the size of the packs the girls were carrying, no one was taking this excursion lightly. There were too many stories of people going into the catacombs getting lost and dying from thirst or hunger before anyone could locate them. Despite Raffiels claims that he could never get lost in the catacombs, no one was willing to take a chance. There were too many things that could go wrong.

Mekiva was struck by a feeling of anxiety as Raffi talked about the ancient labyrinth deep below the city.

"You make it sound like a terrible place---and we are going there?"

"In some ways it still is," Raffi said. "But anything that

might have harmed us is long dead."

Of course, Jaxx thought, Raffiel might be wrong; how-ever, he was too tired to correct him. "Don't you have classes to attend?"

"I've been excused." Only Professor Tulestone had voiced an opinion on the safety of two young women searching through the underground graveyard. And his concern was for the catacombs not his student.

Von was not surprised. Mekiva had explained every-thing that had happened to her since the girls had returned to Ornatar. After hearing the professor's explanation of why her powers were so volatile he was unsurprised. She scared him at times. He did not understand how a spell worked and what the limitations were but he fairly sure she could do things Moth would not dare to attempt. It became even more confusing when Mekiva said she was a decent magician but her ability to control the elements was much stronger or would be once she gained some control. So far the teachers at the academy had not established the range of her capabilities. She was so power-ful most of them found an excuse to leave the school grounds when she was practicing. At least Gwen was with them. She could usually heal any accidental injuries that they sustained.

He was beginning to feel a bit of excitement himself. He'd awakened at sunrise, choosing his clothes carefully to ensure nothing he was wearing would interfere with his movement in the catacombs. Leather armor didn't squeak or clang while walking. He had to admit the greens and natural leather suited him. It fit well too, unlike Jaxx's new leathers.

Jaxx tugged at his brand-new leather jerkin for the fourth time since he awakened. He needed to take it back to the tailor and have a panel put in to make it a bit bigger. Raffi had taken one look at the black lizard skin pants and vest and rushed out to buy a set for himself. Unfortunately, the tailor had nothing that would fit him in stock. Fillip had promised to make Raffi a set as soon as his supplier brought in a load of tanned skins. Jaxx hoped it was soon since his jerkin could not be adjusted without leather to make the panel.

He missed the colorful red and gold outfit he'd been wearing before being sent to Caldra. The oversized jerkin was the only clothing they had allowed him to keep. After being dunked in the sea and allowed to dry upon his female body the leather was stiff and felt like it was two sizes too small. This irritated him to no end. He had worked the Bosky leather for cycles to get it molded the way he wanted it and now the gilet curved out in the wrong places and was too tight in others. It was packed away in the chest beside his bed in the attic room. He had expected his boots to be in similar shape but whatever Kelvarr had used to cure the leather was waterproof and the boots still fit perfectly. His eyes went to the ax handing above the chest. Carrying the heavy weapon on a hunt through the catacombs would draw amused comments from Raffi but his gut told him to bring it along. He sighed and tied it to his pack then headed downstairs to join the others.

Less than a candle mark later they were standing at the gates waiting as the gatekeeper added their names to a list of visitors. Cycles before the city administration had begun keeping these records to make sure anyone that went in came back out.

The old man looked at the large battle-ax Jaxx said strapped to his back, cocked an eyebrow, and asked, "Are you expecting trouble?"

"Not really, but we have learned to be prepared for anything. Besides, things left inside empty rooms tend to go missing."

The gatekeeper looked carefully at the party noting that everyone except the women was carrying swords. They were carrying bows. Each woman had a full quiver of arrows with them, as well as a heavy pack complete with bedrolls. He thought about asking another question but decided no one would give him a straight answer anyway. He had kept his job by keeping unexpected things he saw to himself. This seemed like one of those times. "The gate closes at dark. If you have not returned by then at least you will be prepared to spend the night inside. Better you than me. I do not like going in there in the daytime. Too many ghosts."

The entrance to the catacombs was an enormous set of metal doors, so large it took four men to open them. Because of this, the doors were rarely closed. Instead, guards were set to ensure no one, living or dead, entered or left the tombs after the sunset.

Unlike traditional cemeteries, the catacombs were a massive maze of interconnecting tunnels and abrupt dead ends. Depending on your social status you could be buried in an exclusive chamber or one of the many mass graves. The elite section was beautiful, with marble floors and ornate arched doorways. They were cared for by the faithful of Mortha, who ensured that no one disturbed the final rest of the noble citizens entombed within the tombs. ornate frescoes described the life and accomplishments mini of the normal born buried within.

After entering the cave, they passed through the public areas of the catacombs, stopping for a short rest in the opulent ossuary, so the girls could examine the way the bones and skulls that made up the walls of the chamber were set together. It had taken hundreds of slaves several cycles to complete the public chapel and ossuary, after which the workers were sacrificed, and their blood used to sanctify the sanctuary. No one was sure exactly how old the catacombs were or how many were buried there. But the estimate was several thousand bodies had been laid to rest over the centuries.

Raffi had heard it all before. He wasted little time passing through the public areas, walking with the unhesitating step of one fully familiar with the way. Hundreds of side passages and scores of places where many paths met, all branching off in different directions, showed Vondal how lost he would be without Raffi. The gruff Duaar held their lives in his hands.

As they move farther in white marble gave way to hand pack mud and clay. The tunnels became narrow and dark making it import it to pay more attention to where they were walking then the walls around them. They continued down the main corridor until at length the passage narrowed, and they came to a series of steps that led into the darkness below. After descending for some time, the steps ended, after which they walked along the level ground, making two rights and a left at hallway junctions before they turned and entered a small vaulted chamber. Raffi continued walking across the room, passing the ornate plinth, before coming to a stop at what seemed to be a blank wall of stones. There he removed a torch from his pack and lit it. "This is the extent of the public areas. During the last war, the Governor thought to utilize the underground chambers to keep the women and children of the city safe. It was a good idea until several members of the invading army followed a cowardly deserter to the entrance of the cavern. Realizing the extent of the catacombs, the commanding officer decided there was no way to know how many men were hiding in the depths below. He ordered his men to set fire to a heap of hay, straw, and greenwood, which they had piled before the mouth of the cave. The smoke penetrated the cavern and in a short time the two thousand wretches it contained—mostly women and children—were suffocated. That was the first time this was used as a burial location, but now it is the end of the official House of Bones."

Mekiva shivered. There was something in the air of a catacomb that was unlike that of any other place she had ever been. It was not the closeness of the cavern walls, or the dampness, or even the sickening smell of freshly turned earth. Caves did not bother her at all. No, it was something different, a certain subtle influence which unites with those things and intensifies them. She could sense the presence of the dead. She looked around and thought she caught a glimpse of someone lurking in the shadows along the edge of her vision. When she tried to see, there was no one there. Knowing that so many people had died inside the cave at one time did little to relieve her discomfort.

Gwen must have noticed it, she was holding onto the icon of her deity and muttering a prayer for the souls residing inside the labyrinth.

"Where do we go from here?" Von asked. Being among the dead did not bother him, he was simply impatient and wondered why Raffi had brought them into a chamber with only one entrance.

"Down," Raffi said. He handed his torch to Keeyun before walking to the left corner, where he knelt and counted seven stones along the base of the wall near the floor, then counted seven up and then four to the right. Once he was satisfied he had the correct stone he stopped, holding his hand lightly on his choice. " This should be it, but if I made a mistake, get ready to run. The gas that escapes will be poisonous."

Before his statement had an opportunity to sink in, he pushed down on the stone. There were a faint click and a grinding sound, then the pedestal holding the casket of someone's long-forgotten ancestor, slid to the side, revealing a flight of stairs going down.

Torch in hand, Raffi led the party into the darkness.

"What do you mean, they never returned to the fort?" Izabal's sour tone could curdle milk. Her eye flashed, revealing her irritation.

Castillo knew he was risking more than his position when he delivered the unwelcome news to Lord Botherton. He had lost two of his men that week to his lordship's temper and did not want to lose another. At least Izabal could be trusted to evaluate his words before she reacted. His eyes drifted to a carafe of wine and he licked his lips. The woman made him uncomfortable and she knew it.

"Exactly what I said. They did not deliver the shipment they were to deliver to Hyperion. No one has seen them. No one has any idea where they are."

Lord Botherton's face colored. He clenched his fists tightly and punched the wall next to the door, cursing when he struck something solid and injured his hand. "Yaaga take his soul! I think I broke my finger. Call for a healer." He walked over to the wine carafe, moved it from the ice, and laid his hand inside the bowl. "And bring me something stronger than wine!"

The door servant ran to take care of his shouted instructions. After repeating the order to bring something to ease his lordships pain to the steward, he grabbed a bottle of the strongest whiskey and ran back to the room.

The house steward decided to fetch a healer himself, using it as an excuse to leave the keep long enough for the enraged lord's temper to fade.

Lord Botherton snatched the bottle from his hand without waiting for a goblet and took a long swig. He glared at the door servant until he backed out of the room, shutting the door behind him." What is taking that healer so long? Izabal, can't you do something about my pain?"

"I can set you on fire, I am sure that will take your mind off the broken bone," she snapped.

"Very funny," he snarled. "What about Vargas. No one goes through the pass without him knowing about it. Have you talked to him?"

"That presents something of a problem." This was the part of the conversation Castillo had been hoping to avoid.

"Don't tell me. He was not home when you arrived."

"Oh, he was home. He was also dead. So is everyone else at the trading post. If he knew anything about Vondal, it died with him."

"Dead? Was it Orrogs?" There had been rumors of tribal raids west of the mountains and Notmyson's tribe was the most likely culprits.

"Not likely. The only arrows I saw were hanging on the wall in the store. Vargas had a lot of enemies. Too many for me to hazard a guess as to which one finally grew tired of his excuses."

"It's not important. We will need to set up a new operation at the trading post before it begins to interfere with production at the mine."

"Speaking of the mines; they were possibly sent to Caldra.

Vargas's books mentioned charging extra for a Duaar. Now that I think about it, there were two recent notations mentioning Duaar, he charged extra for them."

"Then go to Caldra and look for them. If you find Vondal, return him to Ornatar. This may be a simple solution to the Duaar problem. People die in the mines every day." Izabal's eyes gleamed brightly as she imagined the different ways in which that could happen. "Wait. I think I will take a short trip to Caldra. I want to ensure everything is taken care of. You can set up the trading post. Every day it is closed I lose money." She glanced over at the blindfolded woman kneeling in the corner, thought about asking, and then shrugged. Let Castillo have his toys. Instead, she muttered the words to trigger her ring and vanished.

Castillo immediately activated his ring and teleported.

"Wait! Lord Botherton shouted as the pair disappeared. "What about my hand?

Chapter 20

Holding the torch high, Raffi led the group down the stone stairs. No beam of light, no ray of sunshine however weak, would ever enter the hidden passage and relieve the thickness of the oppressive gloom. The sensation of being watched increased as they descended, the darkness so intense that it could be felt around them. The torches light shone out but a few paces and then died away as if something hidden in the darkness was preventing the light from going any farther.

"Do any ever lose their way?" Mekiva asked. The idea of being lost in the labyrinth scared her more than she wanted to admit. And she could not escape the feeling that someone was watching her.

"Often," Raffi said.

"What becomes of them?"

"Sometimes they wander till they find a place they recognize, sometimes they are never heard of again. Every time I decide to explore, I find one or two new skeletons. The first time, I got utterly lost. I was certain I was going to die without food or water. That is when I stumbled across the temple." He stopped talking long enough to take a drink from the waterskin he carried. " From this point on, I am not as familiar with our path. See this?" He pointed to a sigil someone had carved into the stone wall at the bottom of the stairs. "This is my sign. We should be able to follow them. If something happens and we get separated, look for my marks. They should lead you to the temple or back to the stairs."

"Tell us about the Temple?" Gwen's eyes lit up at the idea of seeing a temple without someone hovering over her to ensure she didn't touch the wrong thing.

"No time. Trust me, it's easier to show you." He began walking again. The girls fell in behind him.

Jaxx struck a piece of flint against the edge of his blade and lit the torch that had been hanging on the wall. Then he used the flaming torch to illuminate the passages of the labyrinth below the city. The dust on the floor was thick. Other than theirs and the earlier tracks left by Keeyun the ground was unmarked by footprints. It had been a long time since anyone had been in this part of the catacombs.

Now that they were walking on a flat surface they were able to make better time. The path they followed winded onward with innumerable turnings. Raffiel only stopped once, to point out a pit so deep it was impossible to see the bottom. He looked around as if he had heard something but after a moment he relaxed.

"Deep", Jaxx said, looking at the deep shaft that had been dug into the rock, "and old. Any idea where it goes."

"Below," Keeyun stated. He shifted his pack to his other shoulder but did not add anything to his answer.

"Are there more passages below?" Gwen asked Keeyun but Raffi answered. "Yes. As many as there are here and more still below that again. I have been down three different levels exploring the hidden paths. There are hundreds of branches on each level. Some of the old treasure hunters say that in certain places they go down to a very great depth. Much deeper than I have ever explored."

Mekiva wiped her hands on her tunic. She hated that her hands always got moist when she was anxious. Raffi still had not mentioned if they would need to enter the pit. Of course, he had not said they would not be going that way, either.

Von looked at narrow stairs cut into the side of the opening and wondered if they were safe. He was not afraid but the idea of walking down such narrow steps into the darkness was not something he was looking forward to. Jaxx was not bothered by the possibility of going down them, but Mekiva had paled and he was certain that underneath those robes Gwen was trembling. He wondered about Keeyun but if he was feeling any apprehension, he was not showing it. Other than an occasional grunt and a one-word answer, he rarely showed any response at all.

Before he had a chance to mention the girls' fears to Raffi, he decided it was time to move on and continued down the same tunnel they had been following. No one seemed disappointed over missing the journey deeper into the nether regions below the city.

Von's eyes grew more and more accustomed to the gloom as he walked along. It was easier to make out the sigils Raffi had carved in the stone at each intersection, as well as similar markings others had left in the past. The passageway grew narrower; the roof sank, the sides brushed their shoulders. They had to stoop over and go slow to prevent scrapes. Instead of the smooth walls seen in the newer portions of the tombs, these were rough and crudely chiseled. Subterranean molds and fungous growths overspread them in places, deepening their somber grey color to shades of black and filling the air with a hint of moisture. The smoke of the torches made the atmosphere oppressive. He could not forget the glimpse of white he had caught from the corner of his eye. Despite logic saying they were alone, he was certain someone had been watching them.

At the next crossway, Raffi stopped. "This is where we turn off the main tunnel. From this point on, it will be up to my old memories to guide us. I hope I can remember how to find my way back to the temple."

"Why are we visiting a temple? I thought this had something to do with the Wyvern."

"It does. But keep your voice down. I don't want them to hear us."

"Wait. You don't want who to hear us?" Vondal whispered, but his eyes were constantly scanning the dark tunnels they were about to walk through.

"Ughhhh…I may have forgotten to mention one or two things," Raffi replied. "Keep your sword in hand and we should be fine. We have a cleric of Rheaaz with us."

Von turned to Keeyun. "Did you know about this?"

Keeyun nodded. "Ghouls. They feed on the ones who die while searching."

"We are not dead," Mekiva muttered.

"I'm not a Cleric," Gwen added.

"Unimportant details. That could change if we do not start moving. We need to get to the temple; they won't come inside." Raffiel turned right and began walking. The others hurried to stay close to him. We walked along behind him as he walked an unusual path that seemed to double back on itself twice until the sound of water could be heard in the darkness. By the light of the torches, we could see two things, a small pool of water with a waterfall and several greyish white creatures … ghouls.

"Packs of undead? That's the tiny unimportant detail you left out?" Vondal glanced at Jaxx who was already moving into a position to help protect the girls.

"Run!" Raffi said. "Get into the water, head for the waterfall. Don't let them cut you off." He raised his sword and moved into position to ensure the others were able to reach the waterfall safely. Keeyun ran beside the girls until he reached the edge of the water, there he stopped and raised his sword. As the first undead creature tried to reach one of the running girls, he struck the arm, removing it in one blow. The hungry ghoul slowed but did not stop moving towards them.

Gwen knew they would not reach the waterfall in time.

Then an idea popped into her mind. Pulling off the chain she wore around her neck, she turned and slapped the silver icon against the undead's hand. His flesh began burning and he screamed. The pathetic wails continued as the flames spread across its body. In seconds it was little more than a charred pile of cooling ashes.

Observing how their fellow had burst into flames the other two ghouls moved away from the water, choosing to concentrate their attention on Vondal and Raffi. Jaxx kept his eyes on them and watched as Keeyun helped the two girls reach the waterfall and pause.

"Go on!" Raffi hollered, "Go into the cavern behind the water. We can handle these. But there will be more coming."

"More?" Vondal said as he chopped into the leg of the nearest ghoul. It tumbled sideways to the ground and then began dragging its body along the rock toward the two men.

Raffi was busy swinging his blade and the remaining ghoul. "Watch the arm. Cutting it off only gives them a second way to reach you. We have to set fire to the body parts. They can still infect you." Chopping the ghouls into pieces slowed them down but it did not stop them. Burning them was a time-consuming process since you could not touch the parts, or you risked the infection. Not that he had not tried it. After failing three times and almost getting trapped by several hungry ghouls, he gave up and concentrated on staying away from them until he could reach the safety of the temple.

Keeping one eye on the circling creature and the other on the flesh-eater Von was fighting, Raffi stepped backward, and his boot came down on the still moving arm of the first ghoul. Losing his balance, he fell, throwing one hand out to catch his weight. The snap of the breaking bone echoed throughout the cavern.

Von shouted a warning and he looked up as another ghoul appeared from the shadows heading directly at him. There was no way he could get the sword up in time to prevent it from reaching him. Raffi braced himself as best he could and prepared to fight it off.

Then the ghouls head flew from its body and rolled past him. Seconds later the rest of the body fell to the ground. Jaxx swung his ax again and again, each blow removing another section of the body.

"Thanks. I have no urge to spend the rest of my days eating carrion." He grunted and tried to push up with the hand holding the sword, but that gave the overlooked arm an opportunity. He felt the nails break the skin as the hand clamped on his broken wrist. Drasst! It got me. Raffi struggled to his feet and stumbled toward the water. Once he was waist-deep in the pool he used the side of his sword to scrape the fingers away. He stood in the water, washing as much of the putrid flesh away from his wrist as possible. Only one scratch had broken the surface but that one too many. The infection was in his blood. He was still standing there when Von and Jaxx joined him.

"It get you?" Jaxx asked.

"Yeah. Not good. Too bad she's not a cleric. I don't look forward to fighting my way back to the surface." Raffi realized he was facing a death sentence. The infection spread quickly and changed his body as it spread. The ghouls would not leave the area until another opportunity for a meal appeared. Chances of another treasure hunter entering the hidden section were slim to none.

"Gwen may not be a cleric, but don't give up hope. Rheaaz must like her, she's healed injuries that she should not be able to heal. Let her try."

"Rheaaz might favor her but that doesn't mean she feels anything for me. At this point, it cannot hurt. Let get to the temple." With the men helping, they passed through the waterfall.

Chapter 21

Passing through the waterfall, Mekiva and Gwen stood behind the shimmering stream of water, surprised at how bright it seemed after being inside the dark tunnels for so long. Keeyun signaled for them to stay with him and began walking, following the narrow path along the edge of the underground stream that widened gradually until they reached the opening unto a well-lit cavern. Looking up, they were surprised to see the moon shining brightly through the clouds overhead. Across the narrow gorge was the ruins of a small temple neither girl had dreamed existed two days earlier.

"Well," Mekiva said brightly, "it is definitely off the beaten path." She was surprised to find herself standing outside of a beautiful courtyard, paved with coral colored marble laid in a parquet pattern. Every direction she turned held another surprise, a three-tiered fountain complete with sprays of gently tinkling water, dark mysterious statues, and what could only be described as a temple. Raffi had failed to mention how much light there was within the hidden glen.

Mekiva held her breath, not wanting to disturb the eerie silence that surrounded the white marble building. In spite of the fear that lingered over the unexpected ghouls and the fact that Von and Jaxx were still outside with Raffi, she was overwhelmed by the sense of comfort and security that permeated the chamber.

Gwen appeared enraptured by her surroundings. Her eyes sparkled and beneath the heavy veil, she was smiling. She could feel the love of her Goddess welcoming her home. And that's what it felt like, coming home after being away for a long time. She wanted to take it all in; to embrace whatever was to come wholehearted and with open arms.

"Are you coming?" Mekiva's puzzled voice jolted her back from whatever was holding her mind. She blushed as she realized she had been standing there staring blankly at the temple.

"Yes. I'm enjoying the calm," she replied. At once she began walking.

It was clear that at one time the grounds had held a formal garden and was once cared for and cultivated by loving hands. Here and there flowers still grew in clumps and the remains of rock terraces could be seen alongside the path. There had been a lot of rain in the past few days and the ground was soft and spongy. Shades of green were everywhere. Now, with the weather warming up a heavy mist had formed along the low lying areas near the water. Will -o'-the-wisps danced in the vaporous moonlight; a strangely exotic movement that seemed to caress the weathered stones.

It was a short walk to the temple entrance. Cultivated patches of leftover grass and flowers, long since gone to seed, showed remnants of a loving gardener's care. Gwen picked a bouquet for the shrine as they walked along, mostly daffodils and daisies, with a scattering of azaleas that had somehow survived. By some inner sense, she knew it was okay and that her Goddess would appreciate the gesture. It was a shrine dedicated to Rheaaz; she was certain of that.

Keeyun watched the two girls begin walking toward the temple. His hand fell to his sword as shrill screams rang out, then moving toward them as a shadowed figure leaped from behind a broken pillar, moving directly toward the two young women.

The muscular predator lay atop the cracked plinth and waited patiently as Mekiva and Gwen moved closer. His lithe body quivered at the prospect of the hunt to come. Silently he watched his prey, his sleek body held in perfect stillness. In the tomblike silence of the underground temple, the silent killer could easily hear the footsteps growing closer. He tensed and then sprang…

Both girls shrieked. There was a sudden burst of fire around the area where the young Mir-cat had been hidden. At the last second, he had sensed something was not going as he had planned. With a desperate flap of his wings, the startled kitten somehow managed to get high enough to evade the flames. A faint scent of singed fur floated on the breeze. He yowled angrily and disappeared.

"Drasst it! Twizzle, I could have hurt you. How did you find me?" She quickly dismissed her spell. Mekiva was livid as she scolded the hapless young Mir-cat who had appeared on her shoulder.

Keeyun kept silent. He had learned the hard way not to interrupt an angry woman during a tirade. The fiery young mage was chastising the flying feline as if he understood what she was saying. Mekiva was upset because she had almost killed her pet. Mir-cats were practical jokers, but they were excellent guards Nothing could get close to a camp with him guarding it. Keeyun was curious how the flying feline had gotten into this section of the catacombs. Had he located the hidden grotto from the air, or had he slipped past them in the dark?

Twizzle waited until Mekiva stopped shouting. Then he ran his raspy tongue across her cheek. Sensing her weakening he nuzzled her neck, purring loudly.

She immediately forgave him.

"Should we wait or go inside?" Mekiva was excited to see what was inside.

"Should be safe. Raffi disarmed any traps. Take no chances." Keeyun's eyes kept drifting back to the waterfall. It was clear he wanted to go and help. He waited until the girls began walking toward the main vestibule and then returned to the waterfall.

He returned almost as soon as he left. A pale and shaking Raffi walked beside him. Von and Jaxx carried his pack and weapons as well as their own.

"What happened?" Mekiva asked as they helped Raffi settle down on a marble bench inside the chapel.

"Wrist broke, I think. But that's not the biggest problem. The ghoul managed to scratch him." Jaxx wasn't sure how he felt about Raffi being sick. There were a lot of questions left unanswered. Like how he had known who he was. No one had seen him for seven cycles. He was curious about his homeland

and hoped to have a chance to speak to him alone. So far, that opportunity had not come up. It was almost as if Raffi was avoiding his questions.

He looked at Gwen and she swallowed, doing her best not to show her fears. Rheaaz had granted her the ability to heal but the undead was ruled by her sister Morthea. She had no idea if Rheaaz could remove the infection caused by the putrefied flesh.

"Pass me your knife; it will be easier to cut the material away than trying to remove the tunic. The cloth is shredded anyway." The razor-sharp blade made quick work of the thin material. She thought about saving it for bandages but decided the chance of infection was too great. She examined his wrist, frowning at the broken bone. "It's going to hurt when I set this bone."

"Hurts now. Just do it," Raffi snapped through grated teeth.

She nodded and pulled on his wrist maneuvering the broken bones back into their natural position. The bone easily slipped back into place. The brusk procurer groaned as she pulled but did not complain. She could hear a slight rasp in his breath and that worried her. His skin was clammy but a bead of sweat rolled down his forehead onto her hand. The infection was spreading. The skin around the scratch was already red and inflamed, but the edges of the scrape were a darker purple, almost black color.

She decided that she needed to commune with her goddess before attempting any type of healing. "Try and relax. I need to speak to Rheaaz." His eyes closed but still struggled to breathe. She needed to hurry.

Gwen knelt by the marble altar and ran her fingers along the smooth surface. A sensation of love washed over her. This temple had been dedicated to Rheaaz at one time in the past. She lay the bouquet upon the altar and bowed her head, staying in that position for some time, not saying or doing anything except communing with Rheaaz. Finally, she rose from her knees and walked over to where Raffi.

While she had been praying Keeyun and Jaxx had moved Raffi onto a sleeping pallet on the ground. Mekiva had dipped a cloth in the fountain, using the wet cloth to bathe his forehead and his arm.

"I'm ready. We need to hurry. Rheaaz can only help if he's still human. If the infection has spread too far, he will be subject to her sister's dominion. Once that happens, there is nothing she can do." Gwen checked his pulse, noting that while it was slow, it was also steady. His heartbeat was still strong. Unfortunately, he was now feverish and lethargic. The longer she waited the harder it would be.

This was the first time she had ever attempted to heal an infection of this type. While she was confident in Rheaaz, she was not as certain of her ability to handle what was to come. Making herself as comfortable as possible on the ground beside him, she reached for his damaged wrist and began to pray. A warm yellow glow appeared around the wrist. The same glow flashed momentarily on her wrist before vanishing. As the glow began to spread up his arm, Gwen began to tremble. By the time it reached his chest she was visibly shaking. Sweat began to form on her forehead.

Mekiva dropped down beside her. "Let me help. It's a lot for you to handle on your own. " She held Gwen's hand as the young woman began to pray once more. Keeyun was surprised to see Mekiva begin to tremble along with Gwen. Her eyes darkened and tears ran down her cheeks. But she refused to release Gwen's hand.

Gradually the glow expanded until it covered Raffiel from head to toe. He appeared to be breathing easier and the muscles in his face had relaxed. Gwen was panting and struggling to take a breath. When the final bit of yellow glow had moved from Raffiel to her body she dropped his wrist and Mekiva's hand, then set back on her heels.

Mekiva sighed and rubbed her hand. She looked almost as exhausted as Gwen.

Jaxx had remembered how tired Gwen had been after healing Vondal and moved to help the tired teens to the bed-rolls that they had prepared for them. Soon the two girls were sleeping.

Keeyun bathed Raffi's face and arm; pleased to see there was no sign of the infection remaining. His fever had broken. The discolored skin had disappeared, replaced by a healthy tone and a pinkish scar over the place where the nail had cut into the flesh. He had regained sufficient awareness that he was able to drink some of the water from the fountain. After three or four sips he shook his head and laid back onto his bedroll. Moments later he was asleep.

For a while, the three men sat and watched them sleep. Gradually, the peace of the temple overcame their fears and they joined them.

Chapter 22

The early morning sun streaming down through the open ceiling of the temple woke them at the start of another day

"How are you feeling?"

Raffi grinned. "Much better. I don't know how I will ever thank you enough for what you did."

"Thank Rheaaz, I was the tool in her hands." Gwen appeared to have recovered from her exertions. "Not much for morning fest. Supplies were limited so we need to make the food last."

"I see Twizzle managed to provide his own breakfast." The ever ravenous Mir-cat was finishing off the last few bites of a large white fish he had caught. Raffi had noticed the blind fish swimming in the pool by the waterfall, but no one had thought to bring a fishing line or hooks. Jaxx had mentioned that he could rig one up out of the metal in his boots but hoped he never got that hungry.

Mekiva passed him a mug of hot Kafka. "This might help you get motivated. Everyone is waiting for you to explain how we are getting out. Keeyun and Jaxx are looking around outside. Keeyun says the ghouls are still waiting in the other chamber."

"I'm certain there has to be another way out of the temple. No one would build it in such an awkward location without setting up an alternate exit in case of an emergency. What if the water had risen and they could not cross through the waterfall? The temple was likely abandoned because of the ghouls, however, there are no signs that anyone had died while trapped inside. We need to start looking for a hidden exit."

"As soon as you finish eating we can start the search," she said.

Raffi swallowed the last bit of his kafka. "I ready now. Von, you take the side walls. The girls can help me with the back wall. Chances are that's where the exit is hidden." They began searching for anything out of the ordinary.

Keeyun and Jaxx dedicated their time to locating hidden dangers while the others searched inside. Cautiously they continued the search the ground outside the main sanctuary. The two previous trap falls had been located about the same distance apart. Keeyun was convinced that there should be another dangerous section within a few feet of the doorway.

Twizzles angry hiss and arched back was the only warning they received that they were no longer alone in the temple grounds. At first, no one could see what had the young Mir-cat on edge.

"Get Mekiva. Somethings got Twizzle upset and she's the only one that understands him." Jax left and was back in seconds, the others following.

Mekiva moved to Twizzle's side. She had no idea why he was upset. There was nothing apparent that could prove a danger. The Mir cat's fur was on end. He kept repeating a low rumbled yowl while staring toward the front of the temple.

Then Keeyun said, "Over there, take a look at the fountain. What is it?"

"It's a water weird! Look at it. It's playing in the fountain." Mekiva was fascinated by the unexpected visitor. She had seen one while at school, but the master who had summoned it left it inside the bowl and dismissed it as soon as he was certain everyone had seen it. This one was whirling and dancing in the spray from the fountain.

"Is it dangerous?" Keeyun was not convinced the elemental spirit did not intend anyone any harm.

"They can be. But I do not think this one is. There is no

way it could form inside Rheaaz's temple of it meant harm to anyone here." Gwen was captivated by the creature's antics. It would stretch upward and then drop suddenly down into the water, vanishing from sight, only to reform in the fountain spray seconds later.

Von was surprised by her response. Rheaaz's temple? Well, she did answer Gwen's plea for healing Raffi. "Where did it come from? I thought they lived in another dimension?"

"On another physical plane anyway. It could like it here in the temple. Or someone could have conjured it and lost control. It would be simple for it to follow the stream back to the surface if it wanted to leave. "She set her pack on the ground and laid her bow and quiver beside it. Then she walked towards the waterspout.

"Wait a minute. Where are you going?"

"To talk to the water weird of course." Mekiva rolled her eyes at his reaction.

"You can't go up and start talking to it, it might attack." Von wasn't sure how to protect her from the water spirit if it decided she was a threat.

Mekiva insisted on approaching it. "They are not usually dangerous, and I have an affinity with water." She laughed at his distressed expression. "It should be easy to communicate with it. Aren't you curious why it's here?"

"No, I'm worried about it trying to kill you."

"Water spirits are quite friendly. Well, unless someone sets them up to guard something they do not want anyone to see. But this one does not appear to be guarding anything." She sat down next to the water and waited. Elemental spirits are usually curious and this water weird was no exception. The water formed into a miniature tornado, shooting tiny jets of water into the air when it realized she could understand it.

Vondal watched as Mekiva silently communicated with the creature for several minutes. Then it vanished.

"What happened to it? Where did it go?" he asked.

"Home," she said.

"Home? It went home?"

"Well, I gave it a little push but it's going back to its native plane. It has been here alone for a long time. The wizard that bound it, ordered it to wait and never came back. The binding was weak, it had been fading for cycles. It was simple to break it and release the weird. The water spirit was excited to go home."

"Did it tell you anything?"

"Yes, it did. It said the wizard had passed through a hidden door beneath the altar. But first, it had climbed up on top and pushed on a stone in the wall."

Raffi grinned at her words and immediately climbed atop the marble slab. His eyes swept the rocks that formed the wall before him. It only took him a few moments to locate the rock he was looking for. He was practically beaming as he slid down to a seat on the thick stone that formed the top of the altar.

"So, what gave you that cat who ate the songbird smirk," Von asked.

"I knew this place had something to do with him. And now I have proof."

"Wyvernspur?"

"Yes. Come up here and take a look."

Von and Jaxx joined him on the altar.

"This is what I wanted to show you. Raffi pointed to a small but familiar glyph engraved on a rock set into the stone wall, a wyvern with its wings extended. Exactly like the one they had been following in the burnt-out keep. The symbol of Raskur Wyvernspur.

"False Information! Lies that you hoped to barter for

rotgut whiskey. Better that you use the coin to purchase food. Tell me why I should not drive this dagger through your lying throat and still your tongue forever?" Castillo rolled his eyes as Samsara railed against the miserable thief before him. Blass was a decent pickpocket and a better gaper so Samsara would not hurt him. However, he may wish he were dead by the time the old reprobate got through with him.

"No, my lord. Please! I would not bring the story to you if there was a possibility it was not true. The boy is here in Ornatar; I swear it. He is at the old woman's Inn as we speak. Forget the reward! The information is a gift! A token of my respect for you!" His entire body was trembling. Castillo hoped Samsara finished playing with him before he wet his pants. It took days to remove the foul odor from the carpet the last time it happened.

"I should remove your head and place it on a pole before my door to show all that I do not sanction thieves and liars to come before me. But I may have a way you can keep your worthless head. "

"You, my lord, are a wise and understanding man to forgive this worthless one his indiscretions. Instruct me in what I must do to redeem myself to your good graces."

Castillo shook his head and left the room, eager to leave

before he heard whatever Samsara had in mind. It was easy to verify the information. One of his agents was a regular visitor to the Inn. Tula, the Zarni cook was an artist in the kitchen. He had dropped by a few times to try out the daily special. He wouldn't risk it himself but allowing Norn to enjoy a meal while scoping out the public room was worth a few coins. He was fighting a chuckle as he passed through the door.

Chapter 23

"So, what we do now?" Jaxx was not as excited over Raffi's find as the others. He was certain his fellow countryman knew who he was. Yet he had not asked him anything. This both pleased and perplexed him. He needed to tell Von who he was. It would be really difficult to explain why he had kept it a secret if he found out from anyone but him.

"There has to be a reason it's here." He tried twisting the rock, but nothing happened. Then he tried pushing it. Again, nothing. Finally, in frustration, he leaned against the wall with one palm on the rock to each side of the carving. The rocks moved. Now certain he was onto something, he pushed the two rocks again, applying all his strength. The two rocks slid into the wall. There was a faint click, but nothing happened. "Drasst! I was certain this would open a door."

Jaxx had been watching. "Try pushing the center stone again."

Raffi shrugged and pushed on the etching. The rock felt loose but did not go into a recess as the others had. Then he tried twisting it. There was a slight grinding sound and the altar he was standing on moved a few inches to the left.

"There is something beneath the altar. But the opening is too small." Von tried pushing it but the altar did not move. "There had to be something else. Try turning the rock again."

After attempting to turn the rock again with no luck, Raffi pushed, and the rock slid back into a recess. The altar slid to the left, leaving an open passage, with stairs going down. "We need to hurry. The egress may be on a timer. And there is no way to know it will open again." Raffi jumped down and grabbed his pack. "Drasst. The fire is out. We need to light our torches."

"Hold it away from your body. I know a little cantrip." Mekiva spoke a few words in a melodic language and pointed a finger. Flames short outward, barely missing Raffi who jumped back. Luckily, the tip of the torch stayed within the fire's path. "You call that a little cantrip? We could have used you during the fight with the ghouls." He turned to Von. "A word of advice—do not ever make her mad."

Keeyun actually smiled.

"It might be a good idea to stay quiet until we are certain there are no more little surprises waiting on us," Raffi said as he stepped through the narrow opening.

Everyone quickly lit their torches and followed close behind him doing their best to walk carefully and as silently as possible. Occasionally the silence was broken by a faint groan or a mumbled curse, but no one was speaking out loud.

Unlike the tunnels of the catacombs, the passageway they were walking through was dry and well-constructed. The floor had been leveled and sealed and there were stone supports along the wall at regular intervals. Not only was the finish as good as any seen in major cities; the builders had also decorated various sections with carvings depicting historic battles and other memorable scenes. Other reliefs portrayed animals, religious deities, and forest landscapes.

"If I didn't feel like a deer with hounds baying at my heels, I'd be enjoying this," Jaxx whispered, breaking the silence.

The wearied group pressed on, past the point of exhaustion. Their initial burst of adrenaline-induced walking had long since shifted to a wearisome shuffle that barely kept them moving through the crystalline fantasy world they had discovered.

Jaxx was puzzled. The unusual writing nagged at him. The carvings were familiar; as if he had somehow walked these halls before. But that did not excite him as much what Raffi was pointing to.

A short distance down the hall, carved into the lintel over the doorway, was a sigil in a language he was remarkably familiar with. A few steps beyond, the hall opened upon an elaborately carved balcony, big enough for all of them to stand comfortably beside one another. Overhead… way… way…way up overhead, the rocky surfaced ceiling of the cavernous structure could be dimly made out. A wide staircase sculpted from natural stone coiled downward following the natural curves of the wall, occasionally widening into balconies before ending in a sloping floor that merged into a broad avenue.

Keeyun was examining a stone obelisk that stood in the center of the balcony. Carved into the stone in raised relief was the same wyvern, down to the tiniest detail, like the one inscribed on the front of the medallion. He tapped Jaxx on the shoulder and pointed at the carving.

"Still think we made a mistake to come this way?" Jaxx crowed. He stared around the cavern, amazed at the architecture that surrounded the doorway. Not since leaving his family home seven cycles earlier had he seen such detailed carving. It was clearly Duaar handiwork, no other race worked stone in so proficient a manner, although Jaxx was unfamiliar with the style of carving used to produce the beautiful sculptures in stone that surrounded them. Multiple impressions passed through his mind as he struggled to remember more from his childhood. *I was so young when I was sent to live with my uncle. I know I didn't see anything like it in the castle. Stoneshield is a newer holding, built only a few hundred turns ago. Uncle Jasper is not much of a talker, especially when it came to discussing my mother and my father. But he often spoke of his father-my grandfather. All I remember of my life before my mother died are tiny bits and pieces, memories long hidden by time, bursting forth when I least expected them. But now this---it was unbelievable! Maybe it was time for me to reconnect with my family. But am I ready to give up my freedom?*

Mekiva was experiencing an entirely different emotion, -despair. She was tired. The idea of another staircase going down to another level was more than she could handle. She slowly slid down until she lay prostrate at the feet of her worried friends.

"Drasst," Von cursed under his breath, berating himself for overlooking the young woman's condition, concern showing on his face. She was too stubborn to admit how tired she was. He vaguely remembered her saying how exhausted she always felt after casting a spell. He dropped to his knees beside her, raised her head to his chest listening for her breath, then relaxed noticeably as she moaned a soft sigh and snuggled deeper into his arms. Mekiva's breathing was shallow but steady and there was already a warm color returning to her cheeks. Lazily she opened her eyes and smiled up at Von, a look so innocent and pure that he felt immoral holding her.

"Don't hover over her like that," Gwen snapped crossly, "give her some room to breathe."

"What happened?" Mekiva asked drowsily, burrowing deeper into Von's arms.

"You fainted." He maneuvered her body into a sitting position without releasing her, fearing loss of even that small concession. Gwen shot him an exasperated look and then smiled after she realized Mekiva was holding him just as tightly.

Raffi muttered something about moonstruck calves to Keeyun who choose to remain silent.

Until now, Jaxx had not truly accepted how fragile the two young girls were. Other than the ghouls, they had calmly faced any of the myriad obstacles that they had encountered along the way. It appeared the girls were better at masking their condition than he had realized. Both were exhausted, somehow, he needed to find a way for them to get some rest soon. But in the meanwhile, …he picked up the small bags Mekiva and Gwen had been carrying and added them to his already heavy pack. "We'd better keep moving," he said. We have no way of knowing if there are undead in this area. We can make up ground after we get off the stairs."

"I wish Twizzle would show back up," Mekiva said. "I've been trying to reach him. All I get is a general feeling of safety and curiosity. I know he's all right but that's about it."

"The passage is open, there's nothing to prevent him from tracking us. He's probably stalking something to eat." Descending the stairs proved to be much faster than anyone expected, the stonemasons had crafted the steps to a universal height and smoothness that allowed them to practically run down them. Once they reached the bottom they were faced with a new decision. The cavern was far larger than it had seemed from above. Even Jaxx, who had spent most of his youth exploring caves with his friends, was humbled by the enormous space. Many of the jutting stone formations were so ancient they had grown together into natural columns that reached from floor to ceiling.

Seen from above the floor of the cavern had appeared to be nothing more than another room. Now, by the lantern's light, they could see that it was, in fact, an ancient road, stretching off in two directions… neither going toward home.

Struck by another of those déjà vu moments in which his mind flashed on something that until that moment he had no idea he knew, Jaxx uttered the word "levasst".

"Levask? Von asked, what's that?"

"Not levask, a levasst, a passage linking the surface to the underground. That's what the secret tunnel is. I'm sure of it now. And that would make this," he said, pointing his hand at the strange underground paving, "an Ungdrrin Ankorr, a sort of ancient underground roadway. That would explain the obelisk and the carvings. I have never heard of one located this far to the east. I'm familiar with a smaller version near Balcom's Breach in the far western mountains, but it doesn't compare with this place."

"Are you sure? If you are mistaken, we may be heading into bigger problems."

"I know, I know, caves this size could hold a virtual labyrinth of sinkholes and underground rivers," Jaxx replied. "I'm positive it's a levasst."

"You must have seen the word written somewhere, maybe back in Craven holding?" Raffi asked, hoping to get some type of validation.

"It's possible. But I left Craven holding over fifty turns

ago. I'm certain no one at Stoneshield holding ever mentioned it."

Raffi kept his expression neutral even though Jaxx had confirmed his identity… and made him a rich man. There was a large reward offered for the whereabouts of the Craven Heir. Of course, now he had to make sure nothing happened to him, a dead heir was worthless. He glanced up, noticing an odd expression on Keeyun's face but it was gone in an instant, replaced by his usual blank stare.

"Wonderful. It's a road. But can it get us out of here?" Gwen asked. "I need to feel the sun again."

Jaxx enjoyed how Gwen's hopeful expression brightened up her dirt-streaked face in such a charming way. Even though the veil covered the bottom half of her face, her eyes and eyebrows were extremely expressive. She reminded him of Twizzle at times, all soft and cuddly except when threatened, then you had better beware of his sharp claws. He failed to notice the glare the druid scout gave him when Gwen smiled.

Keeyun's mouth tightened and his eyes narrowed, displeasure evident in every movement. "It should be easy to locate an exit. They're all clearly marked if you know what to look for."

"Then we need to start looking," she replied.

Keeyun seemed to be considering a reply, but instead, he

turned and began walking down the right side of the tunnel. Raffi shrugged and followed him.

The Duaar builders must have poured thousands of manual work candlemarks into the completion of the vast underground roadway. Jaxx was humbled by the vast monument to a mason's creative ingenuity that had been built by men like him. Striding down the ancient road he imagined he could hear the pounding of the hammers and picks of the artisans that had labored to build it. He admired the expert cutting of the stones, pointing out the sharp corners and delicate grout lines. He smugly drew the girl's attention to the carved blocks uniform size and to the precision in which they were joined to complete the perfectly level walkway. It was almost as if he had done the work himself.

Tyche and Tycho – the twin Duaarien Gods of Luck, had not been with them so far. Not long after they started their march along the abandoned Ungdrrin Ankorr, Jaxx had found two delicately carved glyphs signaling a door or exit. The first was blocked by fallen stone and dirt, way beyond the efforts of the small group. They traveled the second until the runoff from an underground river made it too hazardous to risk. Mekiva volunteered to tie a rope to her waist and swim down into the murky water in hopes of finding a way out, but no one was willing to risk her life unnecessarily. The two marked exits were about the same distance apart, leading Jaxx to believe that there should be another opportunity soon. Tired and discouraged they backtracked to the main tunnel.

He was wrong.

First one candlemark had passed, then two, then five and now they were nearing the end of the sixth candlemark underground. The beauty of the Duaarien architecture had faded, replaced by a tedious ennui, an ever-present weariness that sapped everyone's energy regardless of how often they rested. It was not the cavern itself, the temperature remained at an unvarying level that was comfortable without being cold. There were sufficient food and water to keep them all satisfied, even though the prospect of another meal of trail rations added to their depression. The hope of finally leaving the dark tunnel was the only thing keeping the group from being torn apart by despair.

Gwen surprised them all. The young girl's cycles of caving experience oftentimes alerted her to possible dangers that even Jaxx missed.

Twizzle had rejoined the group after his 'grand exploration adventure', dropping his bloody gift at Mekiva's feet. She praised him for his offering, while inwardly shuddering at the mangled remains of a blind ivory-skinned reptile. Buoyed by her praise, the Mir-cat had taken to entertaining himself by weaving in and out among the natural pillars, effortlessly maneuvering between the monolithic stalagmites and stalactites in an unusual display of aerial beauty and grace rarely displayed by the shy and elusive creatures. Occasionally the Mir would break away from his flight, darting out from behind the towering stones in a playful attempt to startle whichever victim he decided needed chastisement--- or a good laugh.

Von smiled at his antics. The winged cat made a valiant attempt to rouse Mekiva from her depression. He blamed himself for the girl's misery. Instead of jumping at the chance to spend time with Mekiva, he should have put his foot down and forced the girls to remain in town. Now, look where his impulse had got them…lost underground; with no idea where they would end up.

Keeyun had taken to ranging ahead of the group in hopes of locating an exit. His cynical expression upon his return did not bode well. "We may have to make another detour off the main tunnel. The roadway is blocked ahead. There is no way we can get through it, even with the proper digging tools. I found a side passage about a league ahead. The floor of the bypass slopes upward away from the main tunnel."

"Do you think it's a way out," Mekiva asked.

"I do not know. Should I go on ahead, or wait so we can check it out together?"

"Wait," Von said after a quick consultation with Raffi and Jaxx. "It's time to take a break anyway. The girls need to rest."

Mekiva had to fight back the urge to snap at Jaxx's insensitive remarks. She sighed; her mouth had gotten her into enough trouble without taking her frustrations out on the others. Everybody was tired and on edge. Any excuse to take a break was welcome. She was thirsty and she felt the start of a killer headache coming on. "Water would be great. Food too."

Gwen smiled tentatively at Von and Jaxx. "Maybe some sleep?"

Jaxx stopped, held the water bottle up to the light to check the level, and then shook it once before passing the bottle on to Mekiva. "Not much left, so go easy. Better pass it to Gwen, she must be thirsty, too. We will find a spot to make camp soon." He glanced at Raffi, who nodded. When everyone started walking again, he fell back to walk beside Von.

"This offshoot may be our last chance."

"We have enough rations to last a few more days. But unless we find freshwater soon, it will not matter. Castillo would be amused if we escaped his men only to die of thirst down here."

"Well, keep that to yourself. The girls seem to have lost their sense of humor." They both laughed.

"Did I miss something?" Mekiva asked as she waited for the two men to catch up.

"--- how hungry I am for a hot meal," Von answered quickly. "I never thought about how hard it would be to locate firewood underground. You can bet I'll carry something burnable along with me next time I decide to travel an Ungar-Orkin."

"Ungdrrin Ankorr," Jaxx snapped, "if you're going to use it in a joke, at least get the name right."

"At least I can joke about things.'

"Being lost underground is not funny," Mekiva added. She immediately regretted her comment when Von shifted his irritation to her.

"Yet you think it's all right to whine and pout. And complain, let's not forget the complaints."

"What if I do complain sometimes? Give me one good reason I should stay quiet? No answer? I thought not." She placed her hands on her hips, her eyes flashing a silent warning.

"Slitch," Von's muttered.

She froze. He would not dare! She glanced sideways at Gwen, but the Shi'i-Lakka woman only rolled her eyes. Traitor, she thought viciously as she stomped away without telling Von where he could go.

Gwen shrugged, mouthed a silent warning about moon sickness to Von, and then followed her.

"Let it go, Von," Jaxx said with a laugh at the dazed expression on his friend's face. "Some battles you cannot win."

Jaxx was right, it might be better to give Mekiva a little space. But he could feel her glaring at them both until they found a place to camp for the night.

Chapter 24

Step by step, Jaxx slowly backed away from the quiescent Naga, cringing from the crackle as his foot landed on a dried-out section of recently molted skin. His fingers gripped his ax handle tightly, holding it close to his body in fear of it accidentally hitting something and making a noise that could rouse the somber reptile. He crept backward, meter by meter, careful to keep any sounds to a minimum. The uneven floor of the tunnel slowed his retreat to a crawl. At the first sign of movement, he froze, waiting, holding his breath then letting it out through teeth clenched tight together....then slowly began backing again.

Even though he had been the last to enter, he chose to be the last to back out of the small grotto, allowing the others the best opportunity to retreat without disturbing the massive creature. Naga were meat-eaters and some could cast spells, making them a serious threat. This one was sleeping but it was doubtful he was alone. His mate would be nearby. Possibly an entire nest of them.

It had been one of those days. After three cycles in the tunnels, everyone was sick of walking in the dark. All talk centered on how to find an exit and the need to see the sun again. Unfortunately, things were getting worse. The Duaar worked tunnel had deteriorated to the point of being little more than a series of carved out passages between natural caverns. The upward slope had increased slightly, allowing them some hope that an exit to the surface could be close by. But no one had seen anything to signal they would find a way out anytime soon.

Then they stumbled on the sleeping snake.

"Do you think it saw us?" Von mouthed anxiously, "are we safe?"

"Safe? No. But it did not see us. Naga's are almost blind. They hunt by smell or by feeling the sound in waves, like a bat. It has sensitive ears; our voices would have awakened it. Stone magnifies vibrations," Jaxx replied. It was unlikely the Naga had entered its dormant stage; the dry skin had been shed some time ago. And a hungry Naga would not give up its prey until it has fed.

"What should we do?" Von whispered. "Do you think we

can outrun it?

"No, it's way too fast, the sound of our footsteps would guide it right to us. By now it has found our scent and will not stop hunting us until it makes its kill. Running is not an option. At least one of us would be dinner long before we made it to the next chamber. Our only chance is to outsmart it."

Keeyun huffed. "Cave snakes are highly intelligent. I doubt we will be able to fool it."

Jaxx agreed but he didn't want to scare the others. "I have a plan that might work. Here's my idea…"

Von and Raffi listened as Jaxx outlines his plan. His idea was dangerous, but the only other option was fighting. He glanced at Keeyun, but he was not paying any attention to the three men. Instead, he was trying to rearrange the girl's packs to make it easier for them to run.

Von listened to Raffiel 's plan, occasionally asking a question when something he said did not make sense. He had never fought a Naga. In fact, until now, he had never heard of a giant snake with a humanoid head and arms. But the plan was solid if a bit unorthodox. Jaxx had pointed out they Naga only laired near water. Water they urgently needed.

"It's risky, but what have we done since we started this trip that wasn't?

"Take this," Keeyun said to Von as he passed him a length of rope with a grapple attached. "There's a rock sticking out above that mushroom. It should hold your weight. Get the girls up first." He pointed to a group of giant mushrooms. The trio of smoky black mother-n-laws tongues rose majestically toward the roof of the cavern to the height of six tall men before spreading out into a fluted cap. "You'll need to get everyone up on top as soon as you can. Then dig into the top as much as possible and stay quiet. Rub the pulp all over your body. It won't be easy to deal with the odor, but the stench should keep it from tracking you."

"What are you going to be doing?" Gwen asked.

"Watching for the Naga. I want Jaxx to get a head start, they are fast."

Raffi looked unhappy about Jaxx's plan. "Maybe I should be the one that it follows. You need to stay with your friends."

"Have you ever been a miner?"

"No. But…" The idea of his reward becoming part of a Naga's meal didn't sit well.

"End of discussion. I have."

"If you stay still and remain quiet, I can get it to follow me. Once it passes into the tunnel, it will not be able to turn around until it gets to the large chamber where we camped."

"You're going to run several leagues with a Naga on your trail?" Mekiva was convinced Jaxx was losing his mind.

"No. There's a natural crevice in the rocks we passed a short walk beyond the entrance to this chamber. It extends back a short way before turning and ending. I can fit into it, but the Naga is too big. I'm going to be bait."

"How about letting me be the bait," Von asked. "I can slip into anything you can fit your body into. And I'm much faster."

"True, you can get into the hole, but how are you going to get out? That Naga is hungry---it's going to be mad over losing his meal…and probably vindictive. It may decide to simply block the crevice's exit out of spite. I intend to take my hammer and ax with me and dig my way out the opposite side."

"I can dig," Von muttered.

"I realize that, but its solid rock. I know how to follow the natural crystallization. And another thing, Naga's make vitriol. I have felt it before, it burns like nothing you've ever felt. I figure I dig myself a hole before he strikes, most of the acid will stick to the rock walls and not come near me."

"He's going to get himself killed," Gwen murmured, "but he's our best chance."

Von nodded but wisely held his tongue. He envied Jaxx, but not enough to endanger everyone else to feed his vanity.

"Well, I'm not waiting around to see if the Jaxx can outrun it," Mekiva said. She clambered up onto a nearby rock formation and then leaped from it to a slightly taller mushroom. Working her way from one giant group of fungi to another one, she gradually made her way higher until she reached a perch on a slightly shorter, but much larger mushroom near the gigantic black toadstool. She waited while the others joined her. It took seconds for Von to hook the grapple and line to the rock over the biggest mushroom. He had tied knots every few feet along its length making it simple to climb. Once he reached the crown of the smelly fungi he signaled for the others to come ahead. He was satisfied with the height, but the foul odor made it difficult to breathe. The surface of the spongy mushroom cap was uneven with rough patches that allowed the group easy footholds as they clambered across it. Finally, only Raffi and Jaxx was left on the ground.

Glancing down at the Mir cat atop the other mushroom, Vondal wondered what was going through his mind. First, the flying feline scratched out a deep nest in which to hide, then he rolled in the pulped fungus. The kitten's ability to snatch some enjoyment out of such a dangerous situation was a bright moment to be treasured. But the danger was real and moving closer every second. He sighed as he rubbed the putrid juice into his skin. It could be a long time before he found a chance to bathe and wash his clothing. At least they would all stink together.

Despite his earlier show of confidence Jaxx was worried. What if there were more than one? Raffi had mentioned that Naga were often magic users. He did not understand magic. When people used magic, it made him nervous. Sometimes it scared him. Mekiva scared him more than he wanted to admit. He had no idea what he would do if the Naga began casting spells. Doubts began to set in as anxiety overcame his con-fidence. It had seemed like a good idea when he was talking about the plan but now reality was taking all the fun out of it. The idea of snatching a bit of pleasure out of such a dan-gerous situation was something the girls would never under-stand… or condone. His heart was pounding in his chest. His hands shook as adrenaline coursed through his body. Earlier he had made a slight modification to the original plan; one he knew the others would not like. He traveled up the tunnel until he could no longer see the soft glow of the insects that lived off the yeast and spores scattered along the floor of the cavern. Then he backtracked to the narrow opening. The dirt inside was hard-packed, with little sand, similar to clay that had been exposed to the sun. It wasn't quite as hard as stone, but it would still be difficult to cut his way through it. No, he would have to trick the snake, get it far enough into the tunnel that it had no other choice but to continue. Leaving his ax and tools inside the crack in the wall he turned and trotted back down the passage to where he could easily see Raffi.

Except Raffi was not there. The Naga was!

"I think I can see it, it's entering the cavern," Gwen whispered to the others. "It's big. Much bigger than I thought it would be."

"The face is creepy. It's almost human…except for those teeth." Mekiva crossed her arms as a shiver went down her spine.

Vondal slid closer to Gwen and peered in the direction she was pointing. Like the Shi'i girl, his vision was greatly affected by the limited light. He strained to get a good look as the Naga slid its great body into the room. Though larger than any snake he had ever seen, it was visibly a reptile, its muscles contracting and expanding as it writhed closer. He could see at least two limbs, but they appeared to be atrophied. Unlike a snake, it had a head shaped like one of the big spiny swamp lizards down near the river mouth, but the features on its face were human. Oversized yellow eyes with black slit pupils were glazed over with a milky film. As it moved it opened and closed its mouth showing several rows of sharp teeth and a long thin tongue. It used its tongue for guidance, touching the tip to various objects as it wended its way around the rocks and fungus on the floor of the cave.

"Do you think it suspects we're here?" Mekiva whispered. The two girls crouched farther down into the pith of the mushroom.

"Jaxx said it was following our scent, so I'm sure it knows we came this way. He claims most are not particularly intelligent, about like a dog. But they are diligent hunters and rarely leave a trail once they start a pursuit."

"You said most. What about the others?"

Keeyun grunted. "Magic users. Sadistic mages that enjoy

torturing their prey."

"How will we know if this one is a mage?" Mekiva knew there were innate mages, the ones who could cast high-level spells without learning the process of magic.

"Trust me. You will know."

"I hope Jaxx has made some progress in his digging. If the Naga blocks the exit, he's going to have to cut a passage back into the main tunnel thru the back of the fissure. The cleft in the rock is too narrow for it to follow him."

"What will stop it from digging him out? It does have two legs, even though they look like it hasn't used them in a long time." Gwen had wiggled closer to the edge to get a better look.

"It may try to dig, but the crack extends back farther than its legs can reach."

"How does Jaxx expect to lure it into the tunnel?" Mekiva asked quietly.

"He claims the Naga will chase him. The crevice is about twenty body lengths in. Once the snake moves most of its body into the narrow tunnel, it will not be able to turn around until it reaches a section large enough for it to maneuver. The nearest place is where we camped. That should give us more than enough time to get away. Of course, it may decide to simply lie outside the crevice until he dies. Jaxx says they can be spiteful. That might even work in our favor since it will give him more time to dig. He's got to get out, get back to us, and give us time to escape before the Naga figures out it's a trick."

"Well, I hope he's ready because Raffi just started climbing the rope."

"Shhhhhhhhhh," Gwen whispered. "It might be close enough to hear us. Better not take any chances."

They a good view of the Naga as it drew near to their hiding spot. They were close enough to count the long slender spines that encircled the neck and continued down the spine of the behemoth. It may not be tall enough to reach the cap of the mushrooms, but that would not prevent it from pushing them over it suspected they were there.

Whenever the gigantic serpent stopped and looked around, seeking the freshest scents to follow, the spires would flare out. Possibly the snake used them to detect vibrations or sounds.

Vondal slid backward until he was lying next to Mekiva. She had a tight grip on Twizzle, who fought to escape. The Mir-cat was fascinated by the cave snake and was most likely planning his next prank.

The Naga grew excited as it neared the spot where they had climbed to their hiding spot. It was searching the ground, clearly surprised to lose track of so many scents at once. It patiently nosed around the nearby rocks, using its tongue to check for traces of its prey. Not finding any recent scents to follow, it settled down onto the back half of its body, raising the front half nearly fifty feet into the air and slowly rotating its head. Occasionally it would pause, and the spikes would flare again. Everyone froze, no one breathed, and no one moved a muscle.

"Yah, Yah! Hey stupid. Look over here! Yah, Yah!"

Beating his belt knife against a nearby rock, Jaxx launched into a rollicking ditty about a sea captain caught with too many wives. Vondal winced at the ribald chorus, certain Mekiva would be offended by the risqué lyrics. Instead, he was startled to see her mouthing the words, silently singing along with his loud brusque friend. Even Gwen's eyes were twinkling above her veil.

Jaxx's detraction worked, the question of the vanishing scents forgotten, the Naga lowered itself back to the ground and immediately began undulating in his direction The steady clang of his knife against a rock rose in volume, stopped after a minute---doubtless as Jaxx checked the Naga's progress---then started up once again, accompanied by more of the Duaars off-key singing. Either the Naga had the Duaars' scent, or it was tone-deaf, for it eagerly sought the source of the ungodly noise. Spines waving madly, the cave snake wove its way through the pillars and rocks, moving directly toward the entrance of the main tunnel.

The sight of the beast as it crossed the threshold brought an unusual combination of relief and trepidation. Vondal had to force himself to remain hidden as he watched impending death slithering straight to his friend's hiding spot.

"I can't see it anymore," Vondal said as he made his way over to the rope in preparation of climbing back down to the cavern's floor. *Drasst! I wish I could tell how far the wyrm has traveled into the tunnel. It was moving fast. If it's past the crevice, we need to grab Jaxx and make a run for it. Too bad he didn't get to hear Mekiva singing, guess they have more in common than I thought.*

"Here wormy, wormy, wormy… Yah! Yah! Yah!"

Jaxx shook his ax at the Narp, egging it on into the tunnel. Once he was certain it was on his trail, he turned and started running toward the narrow crack in the wall of the tunnel. Every so often he turned his head, watching over his shoulder as the giant cave snake slithered his way. *Drasst. I think I may have misjudged its speed. I don't know if I will reach the opening before it reaches me.* The tunnel floor was smooth, every paver fit perfectly to the next. Unfortunately, while making it easier for Jaxx to run, it also provided nothing to slow the Naga's approach. His heart was pounding as adrenaline flowed through his system. It would be close, but he was going to make it. Then his foot landed the one paver that wasn't level with the others. He tripped and went rolling across the floor of the tunnel. As he scrambled back to his feet he could see the entrance to his bolt-hole, only six or seven strides away. The Naga was twenty strides back and closing fast. He got to his feet and ran. He refused to look back, knowing even that slight delay could make the difference between his reaching safety and becoming the snakes' next meal. Diving for the crack as the Naga released a stream of vitriol he felt a momentary feeling of triumph. Then he screamed.

Chapter 25

Jaxx awoke to a circle of worried faces.

"How long have I been out? And where are my clothes?" He looked around, surprised to find he lay on the ground in a small cavern that looked nothing like the mushroom chamber. All he was wearing was his small clothes and his boots, but someone had draped a cape over him to preserve his modesty.

"Not too long. Gwen took care of the burns. But there's no saving your clothes." Now that there was no chance Jaxx would die from his injuries, Von thought it hilarious that once again he was reduced to underclothing and his custom footwear.

"Drasst it all. That was my best shirt. All I've got left is the patched one I tore pulling Gwen from the stream."

"Wait till you look at your feet," Von said. "At least you can use what's left of your shirt for patches."

Jaxx frowned as he examined his boots, noting one now had a string of irregular holes where the worm's acid had eaten through the tough hide sole and up the side of the boot. He needed a new pair, but he doubted there was a cobbler within a fortnight's march that could come close to duplicating the intricate work done by Kelvar. He carried a piece of leather in his pack for minor repairs. He could make a temp patch for the soles. The acid damaged sides and upper leather was not going to last much longer. With no options available to repair the damage, he settled with putting on two pairs of socks and then he tied the boot together with laces made from a strip of boar hide Keeyun had removed from inside his pack. He could walk but he was not going to walk fast. He looked around, wondering where they were.

Von answered his unspoken question. "Raffi and I carried you. Keeyun carried the packs. We had to stop and rest. Now that you are awake you can walk. We should keep moving, the Naga has to be on our trail by now."

Everyone decided additional distance between them, and the Naga was more important than Jaxx's comfort. Rest stops became almost non-existent. The oil in their one lantern ran out and they were rationing the last two torches, leaving the group walking in near-total darkness. The makeshift torch barely cut through the preternatural black gloom. Only the smooth perfection of the Duaarien paving tiles and the faint glow from the carrion worms allowed them to make any progress at all. The tunnel had narrowed until they were forced to walk one by one which slowed them, but everyone felt it was too narrow for the Naga to navigate. There had been several side passages they had passed by, many large enough for the Naga to traverse. The idea that he could have taken a short cut and be waiting for them at the end of the narrow passage was at the forefront of everyone's mind.

Strangely, Mekiva wasn't affected by the loss of their primary light source. Several candlemarks after the light went out she realized that she could see, albeit not always what she was looking at. It was as if she was somehow seeing through Twizzle's eyes. *Another benefit of our bonding,* she decided. This thought remained until he caught and ate a skinny white lizard with an exceptionally large amount of blood. She could see the bright red spurts and hear the crunch of the creature's bones every time the Mir cat took a bite.

Gwen, who' been dragging her fingers along the tunnel's sidewall as she followed Raffi, stopped walking. "There's got to be water nearby," she said excitedly, "the walls of this passage are wet and covered with moss and slime. Look, see how they glow." She held up her fingers. The spotty growth gave off a soft phosphorescent radiance; a faint greenish light that made it much easier to navigate through the tunnel.

Finding freshwater was the incentive everyone needed. Hunger wasn't an immediate problem; however, the last few meals had been eaten dry, with only a swallow of tepid water to wash them down. Freshwater meant no more rationing, at least for a while. With Raffi in the lead to guide them and the soft glow of the moss lighting the way, they moved swiftly. The eager Duaar rounded several bends and then stopped, signaling for silence… In the distance, they could hear the welcome sounds of rushing water!

"Why are we stopping?"

"Stay here and let me check it out." Raffi slipped along the last of the tunnel in darkness. Gradually his eyes adjusted to the dim glow of the moss allowing him to see throughout the open cavern. The hollowed-out area was as large as the mushroom cave and could easily be home to several Nagas. The shadows were too thick, he couldn't make out any openings along the walls that could be used at a den or the entrance to a shortcut. There was no sign of cracked or broken bones scattered around the cave, such as he'd seen near the Naga's nest. He took a chance and walked toward the sound of water.

The underground chasm was ragged, cutting into the

floor of the cavern as though someone had taken a giant ax and let it fall randomly across the path of the road. In the distant past, someone had linked both sides of the divide with a bridge made of ropes and wood planks. Jaxx pulled at the ancient bearing braces holding the main support ropes, but they were rusted solid and stiff with age. He tugged heartily at the ropes causing a puff of dust to fly from the tops of the anchoring posts. Even though the hemp squealed in protest, they seemed to hold solidly.

"Seems safe. Come on," he called out.

Everyone moved closer to have a better look at the water they desperately needed, flowing so far below. As the men's bodies drew together to discuss their options, Gwen noticed Mekiva glance over her shoulder, peering back in the direction they had traveled. The strange girls' pensive look and furrowed brow was an expression Gwendolyn had quickly learned to recognize. She was talking to Twizzle again. The diminutive maiden shifted impatiently, hoping to draw the attention of one of the men. No one noticed because everyone was too busy arguing their points. The men had been debating for several minutes and seemed no closer to a decision than when they started.

"Perhaps if we tied all the ropes together, it would be long enough to reach the water," Jaxx suggested hopefully. His eyes kept moving from one section of rope to another, mentally measuring and combining each part. No matter how he combined them, there was not enough length.

Vondal shook his head. "Waste of time if you ask me. If there was a practical way to reach the water, it would've already been done." He stared forlornly at the underground river, freshwater so near he could taste it---so close--- and yet so far. Von stifled a groan. Their only option was to continue walking…and rationing.

Keeyun pointed out something to Raffi and he nodded his agreement. "I don't know about crossing this, these ropes look pretty old to me. They may not support my weight, much less yours. If it breaks, it's a long way down to the bottom."

"Well, what do you suggest," Vondal asked. "Our choices are cross the bridge or go back."

"We just lost one option," Gwen shouted as she came running toward the foot of the bridge, with Mekiva right behind her. "Someone's coming. And they don't sound happy."

"Probably ran into a hungry Naga along the way." Jaxx quipped while rubbing his stomach playfully. Von tried not to crack up at Jaxx's comic behavior but failed, bursting into a hearty fit of laughter, followed by Raffiel and Keeyun.

"You men need to get a life," Mekiva said with a sideways cut of her eyes.

Gwen failed to see the humor of the situation. "They're about half a league back and coming fast. We either cross the bridge or fight and I don't like the odds."

"Like we have any choice," Mekiva muttered. "Okay, no more than one of us on the bridge at a time. Jaxx you go first. If it holds you, we'll all be fine."

"We don't have time to test it out," Gwen interrupted before Jaxx had a chance to argue. "Just go. Von will be right behind you."

Everyone held their breath as he took his first steps across the ancient bridge, the old ropes creaking and straining from his weight but showing no signs of breakage. Von walked quickly across and motioned for the next one to follow. Keeyun grinned and trotted across. Impatient as always, Gwen decided the faster she crossed, the better. She practically ran across, each step causing the bridge to swing wildly.

"The distance is deceptive. It's farther than it seemed," she shouted back, "but if you don't look down, it's not so bad."

The old bridge was still moving as Mekiva started across. About halfway across she made the mistake of looking down and panicked. Despite Gwen's desperate urging, she could not force her body to take another step.

Raffiel cursed. She needed to get all the way across before he could cross. There was no way to know if the ancient ropes could support his added weight. But she looked so scared. Just do it. Step by step he approached the panic-stricken girl, his weight causing the bridge to groan and sway with each step. Reaching the terrified healer, he swung her body around so that she could see the approaching danger. The bouncing torches in the tunnel announced the group's imminent arrival. "Kiva, we don't have time for this", he pleaded, but it was as if her muscles were locked in place.

"Gwen, can't you do something to make her move? A blessing or something!" Von was torn as the first scout of the group tracking them passed through the tunnel mouth into the river cavern. Jaxx and Keeyun had their bows out but it was a long shot, especially in the dim light. For anything

Gwen's mind went blank. She racked her memory for anything that might work. Could she ask the Goddess to make Gwen start walking? No, but a protection from fear spell, that might work--- and she was certain Rheaaz would honor it!

Murmuring a silent prayer to Rheaaz, imploring her assistance,

she began chanting as she made her way back to the center

of the bridge. A warm glow enveloped her followed by a faint

scent of newly mowed grass and sweet-smelling flowers. One

touch and Mekiva immediately started walking, Gwen con-

tinued humming aloud as though on a pleasant summer stroll

across a grassy meadow. As she walked backward step by step,

she kept her eye on the darkness. She could hear the raucous

group that drew closer to the end of the tunnel.

"Raffi! Start running. The bridge will hold you all," Von

shouted.

"I'll wait a little longer and give the girls a chance. If they

catch up with me, cut the ropes behind you. It will be better to

lose one of us, than all of us."

"Cut the bull, I'm not going to cut the ropes and leave

you on the other side. Either you start walking this way, or I

am coming back. I am sure the rest will be right behind me. We

don't have time for you to play martyr!"

Raffi looked at the girls walking slowly toward the end

of the rope bridge and then gauged the distance the unknown

group had to travel before reaching them. He had to slow

them down. Not exactly what I had in mind when I bought it, but what the heck, he thought as pulled a small flask from his vest. I can always buy more. As he ran, he dripped a bit of the content of the flask onto the planks of the old bridge. The Tincture of Rose was as oily as it was expensive, greasy to the touch but clear in color, it was almost invisible on the shadowy bridge. Anyone accidentally stepping in the mixture would likely slide, at the least, it would slow them down. He also sliced his knife through the twisted hemp line, hoping that whoever was following, would be moving too quickly to think of spacing themselves out. Their combined weight should cause the strands to separate, making the already unstable bridge even more treacherous.

As the first pair of heavily armed men made their way into the dim light he sighed. Gynark mercenaries. It would be Gynarks.

They were all tall, all over 6 foot and well-muscled. From a distance, they appeared to be more animalistic than humans, like large cats that walked on their hind legs. Their movements were graceful and like most felines, so light they did not disturb the ground as they walked. Up close they looked more human with long fur on their heads that merged into the shorter body molding hair that covered most of their body. Thick black lashes framed almond-shaped eyes. The golden color and elliptical pupils reminded Raffi of the Mir cat. They had claws like a cat, too. He wondered if he had wasted the expensive oil. Not that it would matter if he didn't get across this bridge before they caught up to him.

Castillo was not in the mood for further mishaps. He had lost three men to the Naga and several more were injured. Now, the overconfident fools he was stuck with were yelling as they rushed the bridge, confident their quarry was finally trapped with no chance of escape. His disgusted expression did not change as the bridge started swinging wildly beneath the excited mercs. Not a brain amongst them. At least they were well trained, even if a bit pig-headed when it came to following orders.

He groaned as one of the leaders slipped and fell, missing his grab for the rope. Seconds later there was a splash in the water below. It was too bad Gynarks did not swim. Several of the men following him were having trouble walking on the slick boards. Even with their claws, the oil made it difficult to stay upright. They were moving much slower than when they first started across the rope bridge. He saw the first section of a rope snap. That's when the first screams began.

Raffiel felt the strands start to give way behind him and immediately gripped the old rope tightly with both hands, bracing his legs as best he could. With a strangled groan and a high-pitched twang, the partially sliced strands of rope sepa-rated-- first one, then another and finally all at once. Caught unprepared, most of the Gynark raiders lost their balance and fell screaming into the depths below. One or two managed to grab onto the ropes that still dangled overhead and by the sides of the walkway, but they were now more concerned with stay-ing alive than pursuing the small band. That was good since he was hanging above the rushing water and needed time to climb up. Then the first arrow struck the plank above his head.

The survivors now on firm ground regrouped, shouting empty threats while peppering the area around Raffiel with arrows. He was still dangling from the ropes near the far end of the old bridge. Von began shooting back as Mekiva rushed to string her bow to help. Twizzle added to the noisy confusion, strafing the bowmen with his claws, hissing, and yowling loudly, generally making a nuisance of himself.

Raffi used the broken section of the dangling bridge like a ladder, pulling his body upward to rejoin his friends. The cocky Duaar wasn't even winded from his efforts. He perched upon the stanchion beside the now impassable bridge, symbolically thumbing his nose at the remaining mercenaries.

Mekiva reached up and jerked an arrow from his backpack, "Don't push your luck."

Raffi flinched. It had been so close…the thought brought a shiver to his spine.

"I hate to spoil your triumphant display of cocky valor, but we need to get moving. Let it go. please." Von decided humility had to be a forgotten trait among Duaar men.

"Not that it matters," Jaxx added, "but between the Naga trick and dropping most of his men into the gorge, I think we've made Castillo mad. A lesser man would give up and go back, but I somehow doubt it will even cross his mind. He'll figure out a way across the river gorge, even if he kills every man in his command doing it" He glanced back at the man standing at the edge of the crevasse with a sardonic smile on his face...."and next time he won't be so considerate."

Chapter 26

Keeyun had good news when he returned from scouting the path ahead. They had located a tiny trickle of water that flowed into a natural basin in the next cavern. It would take more time than they could spare to fill the empty waterskins, but it allowed everyone to drink their fill and rest.

"There's an exit glyph ahead, maybe half a candle mark along the tunnel. I managed to get the door open, but I could tell it's been a long time since it's been used. The passage inside gradually slopes toward the surface and it's partially blocked by stone and dirt. It must not be a large blockage, I could feel the air moving through it, but I didn't want to spend too long trying to dig my way through."

"Why do you sound so worried? Is something else bothering you?" Gwen asked. She had been spending a lot of time talking to Raffi and Keeyun over the last few days. Jaxx was surprised by how much that bothered him.

"The Wyvern was different from the others… something about its expression… I don't know…it was weird, almost macabre. My flesh was crawling as if someone was standing next to me and waiting. It shook me. Perhaps we should continue onward past that door. I could scout ahead again."

"We don't have a choice," Vondal stated flatly. "We need time to collect more water and there's only enough food for one or two meals. Even if we assume Castillo can't find a way across the ravine and take time to fill the water skins, we may not have enough food to make it to another exit. If there is any way we can clear the blockage, we are leaving this place now. "

Mekiva agreed. "I agree. Everyone digs, even Twizzle. It's about time that freeloader earned all the food he's been scarfing down."

"We will wait a while before we try it, give everyone a chance to get some sleep. We all could use the extra rest."

Raffi looked uncomfortable with the decision but relaxed after Keeyun offered to scout back along the tunnel to see if anyone had figured out a way to repair the broken bridge.

Von covered Mekiva with the blanket from her bedroll and then joined Jaxx by the fire.

Raffi helped Gwen to her feet, and they walked back to where Mekiva was sleeping. "You should get some sleep. I'm probably overreacting to the wyvern. I'm certain it is a way out." He walked away before she had a chance to reply. Gwendolyn still didn't fully trust him, but he knew he'd win the tiny Shi'i over eventually. Too bad Jaxx had his eye on her. He felt as if he was betraying his country by spending time with her. But he had no intention of stepping aside, even for the heir.

Mekiva wasn't making it any easier. She somehow managed to find an excuse to join them any time he tried to get Gwen alone. Raffi's eyes darkened as he thought of the fiery chestnut-haired mage. Vondal was crazy about her, he was certain everyone could see it--- Gwen certainly could---everyone but Mekiva. But she was so young, not even sixteen and a student at Rosemont. That meant money, her family would never allow her to bond with a penniless adventurer.

Gwendolyn was different. Her parents were hard-working tradesmen and far from wealthy. The idea of her developing feelings for him was both wonderful and short-lived. Any type of intimacy with an unfledged novitiate was forbidden. Despite the attraction, Gwen probably considered him little more than a friend. She would never give up her Goddess for a wandering thief …or a prince in exile.

Life isn't fair. Jaxx scratched a bit harder as the winged kitten shifted position, snuggling deeper into the blanket beside him. Von and Mekiva are head over heels about each other, even though she hasn't realized it yet. But Von isn't naïve enough to think Mekiva would give up magic, even for love. It'll be cycles before she learns how to control her powers. To act on it now would risk endangering anyone she cared for. She would never risk hurting Von with magic fueled by runaway passions. I would love to have that kind of relationship one day. At least you love me … Jaxx yawned as the soft rumbling purr of the contented Mir lulled him asleep.

Chapter 27

The marked doorway was open and passable as Raffi had described it. Inscribed over the door was a rune identical to the one Mekiva had copied from the wall in the secret room. Even the detail on the wyvern was the same. So why did he feel so wary? Jaxx refused to accept it was all paranoia.

"Maybe it's because it's gloomy." Gwen pulled out a candle stub from her pack, but Jaxx slapped the flint from her hand as she started to strike a spark.

"Wait--- can't you smell that odor? That is what was bugging me its gas, methane. There's got to be a natural pocket in the rocks. It's leaking. Put out the torches now."

Raffi had already extinguished his torch. "He's right. No open flames or we risk an explosion, we'll have to clear it in the dark."

"How can we move the rocks without making any kind of a spark?" Von asked.

"You can't, you're not strong enough. Raffi and I can dig out the rocks and Twizzle can clear away the dirt. It will take a while to open this passage enough to squeeze through. Stay out of the way so we can work."

The girls knew that Jaxx was only being careful, but it still didn't make them feel any better about not helping. Muttering between themselves they moved back down the passage until they could no longer smell the odor. Keeyun simply shrugged and found a place to stretch out and take a nap a bit farther down the tunnel.

Long ago miners had opened-up a nine-foot-wide vertical channel to reach into the hidden highway but had soon abandoned it after no valuable minerals had been found. At some time in the past, an explosion had caught several delvers off guard and they had died in the blast. The remains of several miners, bones long devoid of flesh and brittle with age were scatted among the rock and dirt blocking the pass. Jaxx stopped digging long enough to say a quick prayer for the dead before pushing on with their task. Wonder if one of them was Raskur? Naw, there are too many stories floating around. Too many places he was seen. Slowly but surely, the pair worked to clear the rubble from the blocked tunnel.

Mekiva watched for a while but staring into the dark was giving her a headache, …she was feeling sleepy. I'm not tired, so why is it so hard to keep my eyes open. I should have paid more attention to Master Stolinn's lesson on inert gasses. Maybe it would be better if I took a nap. She slipped to the ground and was promptly joined by Gwen.

"Did you feel that?" Jaxx asked. He stopped digging and listened. In the distance he caught a faint rumble, a sound he recognized and dreaded.

"What? The breeze? I've been feeling air moving for a while now."

"Not air! There! Feel that shake? We need to move now! Get the others, Hurry!"

Looking in the direction of the sound, Raffi frowned. Then the floor of the tunnel began to vibrate. That was never a good sign. They needed to get everyone out now. "We need to get out of this section of the tunnel. There are no braces. Run. Do not look back, run as fast as you can."

The shaking was followed by a low moaning roar that built into a growing rumble. Jaxx was swinging wildly at the last two or three rocks blocking the way, no longer concerned by the possibility of an explosion. Either he cut a path now or the gas exploding would be the least of their problems.

"Follow Keeyun. He knows what to look for." Raffi motioned for everyone to move quickly; almost shoving Gwendolyn behind Mekiva in his hurry to get her past the blockage in time to avoid anyone being crushed.

Von practically shoved the drowsy girls along the narrow passage in his rush to reach the exit. The strange vibration was building until the ground began to shake. The shaking was followed by a low moaning roar that built into a rumble. Rocks started falling as the ceiling began to give way. One of the larger pieces hit Von's leg throwing him to the floor of the tunnel. He struggled to push the heavy rock off and stand back up.

Mekiva gasped and tried to turn back.

"Keep running, I will help Von. Go!" Raffi moved to help get the rock off Von's leg. The others were out of sight. He knew Keeyun would keep them moving until the trembling stopped. There was no way they could outrun the danger with Von limping on one leg. Their only option was to go back and hope they could find an area reinforced by support beams. The two men began stumbling back along the tunnel. Suddenly there was a horrific crack and a cloud of choking dust billowed out of the tunnel behind them. Then tons of rock and dirt filled the area where Twizzle had been sleeping.

Keeyun sighed when he spotted the heavy support beams and signaled to the others it was safe to stop and rest. Everyone collapsed onto the ground, eager for any opportunity to catch their breath but their eyes remained on the tunnel behind them. He could see Jaxx stumbling closer. What was taking Raffi and Von so long? They were not that far behind them.

The vibration increased to a growing rumble and dirt trickled down along the walls. The noise increased and then there was a horrific crack, followed by a cloud of choking dust that billowed out of the tunnel behind them. They all stared at the crumbled ceiling that continued falling long after the initial cascade of rubble. The tunnel behind them was gone. Raffi and Von were still inside.

The girls were unharmed but Keeyun had not escaped unscathed. He wiped at the stream of blood trickling down his forehead and shook his head sadly, thinking about the kitten who had been sleeping on his bedroll. There was only a slight possibility the Mir-cat had escaped the collapse.

Jaxx immediately began digging at the slide, using his hands and the ax to move the rubble. The others rushed to join him.

"Do you think they might have survived?" Mekiva asked,

her voice loud in the sudden silence.

"Call out!" Jaxx listened but he could not hear anyone answer his calls. He refused to believe they were not alive. They were simply trapped on the other side of the slide. If the debris from the fall was too thick for sound to travel through; it was probably too thick for anyone to dig their way out. Von and Raffi would have to find another way around the blockage. Ironically, several tons of stone and dirt also blocked their only known return route. The only option was to find another exit.

Earthquakes were common in this area. There were always safety tunnels built, cross halls that might add a little time to their walk but connected each section for this exact reason. Von might not know how to navigate but Raffi should be able to find a way around the cave in. In the meanwhile, they needed to continue walking until they spotted one of the safety tunnels. Once he located the nearest one, he would leave Keeyun with the girls and go back and search for Von and Raffi…or their bodies.

The blade on the hunting knife broke but he managed to lever the final rock off his leg. It was scraped up and swollen but he didn't think it was broken. Sweat rolled down Vondal's forehead, the wet moisture making tiny channels in the dirt and dust caked on his face. Weak, bleeding, and slowly sliding into shock, he struggled to maintain consciousness long enough to reach some kind of safety.

"Jaxx?" he called out. "Raffi? Anyone?" There was no answer. He had no idea if anyone had survived. For now, he had air. That took care of his fear of slowly suffocating, alone in a dark tunnel. Not that air would help if he could not find water.

There was no light at all, no chance that he could see so he used his sense of touch as a guide. He began crawling, carefully working his way along the floor of the tunnel, his arms stretched out before him as he used the uneven feel of the rocks and dirt to guide him along in the darkness. He struggled along the uneven surface until his knees were raw and bleeding. The silence of the tunnels was made even more ominous by the eternal darkness around him. There was no way he could know how damaged the tunnel system had become after the tremor. Never had he felt so alone. He called out once more, but his calls met with silence.

At last, there was no longer any rocks or dirt to be felt, only the smooth even texture of well-worn stone. There was still no light, no sign of any type of opening that would help his get out of the subterranean prison. Then his hand came down on a hobnailed boot. "Raffi!"

The surly Duaars voice came out of the darkness, "Took you long enough. I was beginning to think you were not coming."

"Took me a while to get the hang of maneuvering around the rubble in the dark. I must have lost my torch in the quake."

"Same with me. It's easier if you crawl."

"Found that out the hard way," Von replied. " I expected to find you back along the tunnel closer to the slide."

"There's only one way you could come. I knew you would show up if you could."

Von did not respond to his comment.

"I don't suppose you are wearing boots like Jaxx?"

"No, But I intend to get a pair made as soon as I get back to town." Von covered his head as dirt and rock began showering down on them again.

"Aftershock," Raffi said. "We need to keep moving."

"Shouldn't we be going back to the slide? Maybe we can dig through it."

"We would be dead long before we made a dent in the

rubble. No, the only way out is through a burakin."

"Burakin?" Von was puzzled. Jaxx had been teaching him the Duaar language but he had never mentioned that word.

"It's a mining term, kind of an emergency exit. The opening to one is right beside me. But first, we have to move this rock." He didn't mention that he had already tried to move it. Several times. He had been ready to try again when Von grabbed his ankle.

Von crawled closer to the rock, noticing how it almost blocked the small opening. There would be no walking through the burakin. That didn't bother him, even though he wasn't looking forward to inflicting further damage to his knees. The possibility of an aftershock hitting while they were deep into the connecting shaft worried him. If the tiny tunnel became blocked they would have to back their way back out of the shaft.

Turning his back to the rock, he used his legs to push as Raffi shoved it in the direction he wanted it moved. Beside him, Raffi grunted as he pushed against the rock the two men needed to shift away from the burakin. The aftershocks added to the rubble and made moving the rock harder, but they were determined to clear the exit. Then something licked his nose.

Jaxx did his best to hide his apprehension. Several tons of stone and dirt now blocked their return route. Von and Raffi were still missing. They had been sitting next to the burakin for several candle marks hoping to hear some sign of life.

Then they heard Twizzle meowing.

"How did he get in front of us?" Gwen asked. "Did you notice him?"

Jaxx shook his head and Keeyun appeared puzzled. Neither man had noticed the Mir while they were digging. But they were pleased to see him. If the flying kitten made it through the burakin, there was a distinct possibility Von and Raffi were still alive.

"Jaxx? Raffi? Can you hear me?"

His eyes welled when he heard, " Keep talking, we are almost there."

Chapter 28

Someone had previously opened up a nine-foot wide vertical channel to reach into the interior but had abandoned it cycles ago after the ore played out.

The Mir cat was perched on a ledge about halfway up a narrow shaft that had supplied air to the abandoned mine.

There was a light source somewhere above them, however, there was no way to judge the distance by the soft glow. But there was enough light to see the slick sides that offered little or no hand or footholds for a climber.

Jaxx rifled through his pack. Once he found the rope and grapple he was looking for, he took a second length of rope from Keeyun and tied it together, braced his shoulders against the wall, then shimmied up the first rope using his legs to brace against. His eyes moved from side to side as he dropped toward the ground, studying the walls of the tunnel. This tunnel seemed to be in good shape, much better than the one they had entered through. But there was no way he could climb it. To get outside, someone would have to free climb up the narrow shaft, then secure a line. It wasn't going to be him.

"I'll climb it," Von offered. He dropped his weapons near the wall, braced his back against the other wall, and began inching up. He made it about halfway before he slipped and started sliding back down the rope.

Keeyun shook his head when Raffi raised an eyebrow. Climbing was never something he had been good at. Raffi and Keeyun were willing to try however, both men failed well short of where Von had begun sliding.

"Maybe you should try again," Jaxx said to Von.

The two women had been watching the men try and fail without comment. Jaxx was astonished when Mekiva began helping Gwen remove her burka and robes. Her face was as beautiful as he remembered, however ….

"Stop staring and help me brace the rope," Mekiva snapped. "Gwen, are you ready?"

Gwen nodded. Then she jumped up bracing one foot on each wall. Once she was satisfied that her grip was stable, she adjusted the rope tied around her waist and began moving up the air tube. Instead of trying to use her arms to pull herself up, she used her legs to brace against one side and slid her back up the opposite wall a little at a time. Moving one foot at a time, she worked her way upward in a steady motion.

"What in the nine hells are you, woman?" Von demanded indignantly. "You are supposed to be some kind of holy cleric, not a spider!"

Gwen gave him a wink but did not answer as she continued to ascend the rope until she could reach out and grab hold of the lip of the rough opening. She rested for a minute on Twizzles ledge, then disappeared, only to reappear a few seconds later at the top of the air shaft.

"Now for the tricky part," she joked, smiling down at Von. "I'm going to try to hold the rope tight as you climb," she called out to Von after she tied off the end of the rope to a nearby tree. "Its secured so don't worry about it not holding your weight. Wrap the rope around your arm and brace your feet against the wall. It will take the strain off your arms."

Raffi stood impatiently below, holding tightly to the end of the rope, ready to catch him if he fell. His hands were already blistered and sore from his slide down the rope, scraping his body against a sharp rock on the way up was something he could do without. This tunnel seems to be in good shape, much better than the one we'd crawled through. Perhaps the connecting passage was an afterthought?

With minutes Von was hanging directly beneath her on

the rock face, with both feet braced atop the narrow ledge.

Twizzle immediately began chewing on his foot. Once he realized Von was not interested in playing, he gave it one final swat and disappeared into the side drain.

"How did you fit inside the drainpipe," he asked after realizing Gwen must have climbed it to get to the top.

She laughed but did not answer.

After securing the line, she tied the end of the second rope Von had carried with him into a loop, passing it around a rocky protrusion and then through a second loop she had fashioned into the length. With a twist of her wrist, she produced a sliding knot, using the techniques her brothers had taught her while rock climbing as a child. After she had tied the second safety line to an outcropping, she lowered the slip harness back to Raffi.

The reserved Shi'i girl seemed to be enjoying herself. Raffi was having trouble keeping his mind on the climb and off her half-naked body.

Gwen ignored his stares and called out to Jaxx instead. "Once Keeyun is in the sling, you and Raffi can both help us pull him up. Once he's on top, he can help us pull Mekiva to the top. Maybe between the four of us, we can lift you and

Raffi."

Keeyun kept his eyes moving from side to side as he was being raised, mentally measuring how close his body came to be scraping the walls of the tunnel. Sooner than he expected he joined Gwen up on top and Mekiva was climbing into the harness down below. "Who taught you how to climb that way?" he inquired. "I've never seen anyone do it like that before."

"I grew up in the mountains. I've been climbing through caves for cycles. Back home, we did it for fun. The knot I used is for rappelling and climbing. It enables you to lift more weight than you normally could, which is a great help since its gonna take all of us to lift those two."

"Then let them climb the rope. If one slips the other can break his fall. It's not that far to the bottom."

"True. It just seems high."

"The question is do we want to listen to them harangue us about it?"

Keeyun looked thoughtful. Then he shook his head.

"You ready down there," Von called to his reluctant partner. "You've got to get it over with sooner or later."

Jaxx delivered an unmistakable rude gesture before he

stepped into the harness.

Jaxx moved slowly along the new passage, listening for any sounds that might signal that the small group was not alone. The shaft appeared to have been unused for ages. Dust covered the surfaces as it had in the tunnel that collapsed. This section had once been an operating mine, the tunnel was raw dirt and rock, not carved and finished stone. The walls were lined with bracing posts and stacks of rough-cut timber were scattered along the sides as if the workers had stepped out for a break and would be back at any time. As grateful as Jaxx was for the wood stacked around, it was the feel of the cool breeze against his face that brought the biggest grin to the young Duaars face The smell of the crisp clean air was intoxicating after breathing in the stale underground air for so long. He in-creased his pace; almost running toward the opening he knew was ahead. Finally, a small glimmer of light broke through the darkness.

Jaxx forced himself to slow down as he walked through the darkness toward the distant glow. His gut said it was a way out, but he refused to believe it could be that easy.

Von, walking close behind, increased his pace, racing Jaxx toward the beacon of hope where there had been none for so long.

Jaxx scurried up the slope, pulling himself hand over hand and then paused listening … nothing. With the light from the sun shining fully on his face, he reached out for the lip of rock that would take them out of this hateful pit forever.

Mekiva hugged Gwen, mumbling something about a hot bath. And soap, scented with lavender and camellia. She could go back to Rosemont! Master Stolinn was never going to believe what they had been through. Basic spellcraft will be a breeze after fighting Gynarks, avoiding the undead and out-smarting a giant cave snake while traveling an ancient levasst. But it hadn't been all bad. Dangerous or not, she had to admit this had been one of the best adventures of her young life. It was almost over! Jaxx was standing at the mouth of the tun-nel about five hundred feet away and she could see sunlight streaming around him. She could even make out a range of mountains in the far distance. They were safe, so why did he look so disappointed?

"Tyche hates me," Jaxx groaned as they joined him, look-ing down at the desolate landscape far below. "Where else would we be after escaping from the Moraga's depths but the middle of Azaar's Bane."

353

Drop by and visit me at

www.bellbookandclaw.com

On Facebook at @vcsanford

or Victoria Sanford

and on Instagram at

@vcsanfordbooks

I would love to hear from you!